The Scarecrows' Wedding

Julia Donaldson

ALISON GREEN BOOKS

Axel Scheffler

Betty O'Barley and Harry O'Hay
Were scarecrows. (They scared
  lots of crows every day.)
Harry loved Betty, and Betty loved Harry,
So Harry said, "Betty, my beauty, let's marry!
Let's have a wedding, the best wedding yet,
A wedding that no one will ever forget."

Betty agreed, so they hugged
   and they kissed.
Then Betty said, "Harry, dear,
   let's make a list."

"Just as you say," answered Harry O'Hay,
So they wrote down the
    Things they would Need on the Day:

A dress of
white feathers

a necklace
of shells

Lots of
pink flowers

two rings

and some
bells

Then Harry gave Betty O'Barley his arm
And the scarecrows set off on a
    hunt round the farm.

They hadn't gone far when
   they spotted some geese.
"Oh, geese, if you'll give us a feather a-piece,
You can come to our wedding,
   the best wedding yet,
The wedding that no one will ever forget."

"We will," honked the geese, and they each gave a feather.

(A spider friend offered to sew them together.)

"Hooray!" cried the scarecrows.
    They hugged and they kissed,
And they hurried back home
        and crossed "dress" off their list.

Then Harry gave Betty O'Barley his arm,
And they set off once more
        on their hunt round the farm.

They hadn't gone far when some cows gathered round,
And the bells round their necks made a wonderful sound.
Ring-a-ding ding! Ring-a-ding ding!
"Oh, cows, will you please come and make your bells ring
For our wonderful wedding, the best wedding yet,
The wedding that no one will ever forget?"

A dress of
white feathers

a necklace
of shells

Lots of
pink flowers

two rings

and some
bells

"Yes," mooed the cows. "We can tinkle our bells."

Then a crab scuttled up
with a necklace of shells!

Some mice found two rings
in a bin. (They were certain
The rings had belonged
to an old farmhouse curtain.)

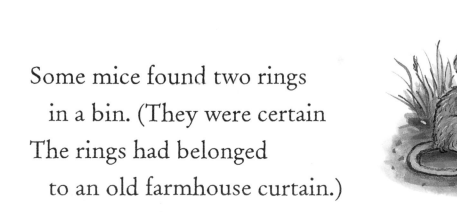

"Hooray!" cried the scarecrows.
   They hugged and they kissed.
"Pink flowers are the only things left on our list."
Then Harry said, "Betty, dear, I can find those.
Why don't I pick some while you have a doze?"

"Pink flowerzzz? Pink flowerzzz?"
   buzzed a big stripy bee.
"I can find you a field of pink flowerzzz!
   Follow me."

So the bee led the way, and they travelled for hours
Till they came to a field full of pretty pink flowers.
Harry stood thinking. "I won't pick them yet.
I'll need to find water, to keep their stalks wet."

"Just follow me,"
   croaked a lumpy old toad.
"There's a lovely wet pool
   at the top of this road."

They climbed up the road.

It was terribly steep.

"I'm tired," said the toad,
so they stopped for a sleep.

Early next morning they came to the pool.
"This water," said Harry, "is beautifully cool,
But now I need something to carry it in –
A jug or a vase or a cup or a tin."

"I think I can help," said a small squirly snail.
"I can show you the way to a very fine pail."

So the snail and the scarecrow
set off on their way,

But the snail was so slow . . .

. . . it took more than a day.

Betty was worried.

"What's happened to Harry?
Where is the scarecrow
I'm planning to marry?"

The farmer came by with a frown on his face,
And he made a new scarecrow to take Harry's place.

"Good day," said the scarecrow. "I'm Reginald Rake."
He took Betty's hand and he gave it a shake.

"Together," he told her, "we make a fine pair.
You're really quite pretty, apart from your hair."
Then he jumped in the tractor and told her, "Hop in.
I'm a really fast driver. Let's go for a spin."

But Betty said, "No – I must wait here for Harry.
He is the scarecrow I'm going to marry.
We're planning our wedding, the best wedding yet,
The wedding that no one will ever forget."

Reginald laughed. "You'll be waiting for ever.
Forget about Harry! I bet he's not clever.

"I must be the cleverest scarecrow alive.
I can sing lots of songs. I can dance, I can drive!
I'm dashing! I'm daring! I'm cool as can be!
I can even blow smoke rings
 – just watch me and see!"

And he took out a big fat cigar from a packet
The farmer had foolishly left in his jacket.
"But smoking is *bad* for you!" Betty exclaimed.
"Really you ought to be feeling ashamed."

"Don't be a fusspot," said Reginald Rake.
"My smoke rings are staggering, make no mistake."
He struck up a light and he tried hard to smoke . . .
But straight away started to splutter and choke.

What happened next was completely unplanned:
The lighted cigar tumbled out of his hand.

It fell to the ground – and it started a fire.
Betty screamed, "Help!"
as the flames flickered higher.

But Reginald Rake said, "I'd better be off,"
And he bounded away with a terrible cough.

Then suddenly,
  who should appear on the farm
But Harry O'Hay,
  with a pail on his arm.

"Betty!" cried Harry. "My own future wife!"
He poured on the water – and saved Betty's life.

Then they picked up the flowers, they hugged and they kissed,

And they said, "Now that's
everything crossed off the list."

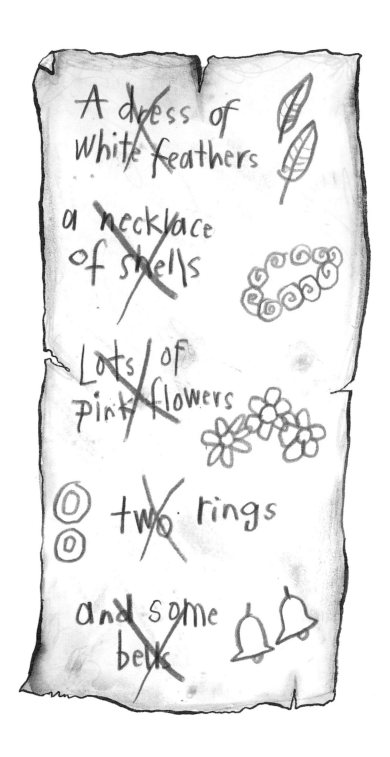

A dress of white feathers

a necklace of shells

Lots of pink flowers

two rings

and some bells

So Betty O'Barley and Harry O'Hay
Wed one another the very next day,
And everyone (even the snail, who was late)
Said, "Don't they look happy?" and, "Don't they look great?"

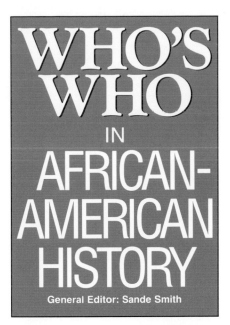

WHO'S WHO
IN
AFRICAN-AMERICAN HISTORY

General Editor: Sande Smith

WHO'S WHO
IN
AFRICAN-
AMERICAN
HISTORY

General Editor: Sande Smith

SMITHMARK

This edition published in 1994
by SMITHMARK Publishers Inc.,
16 East 32nd Street,
New York, New York 10016

SMITHMARK books are available for
bulk purchase for sales promotion and
premium use. For details write or
telephone the Manager of Special Sales,
SMITHMARK Publishers Inc.,
16 East 32nd Street, New York,
NY 10016. (212) 532-6600.

Produced by Brompton Books Corp.,
15 Sherwood Place,
Greenwich, CT 06830

ISBN 0-8317-9190-X

Printed in Hong Kong

10 9 8 7 6 5 4 3 2 1

PAGE 1: Ralph Bunche.
PREVIOUS PAGES: Jesse Jackson.
ABOVE RIGHT: W.E.B. DuBois.
RIGHT: (left to right) Lena Horne, Rosa
Parks, Carol Moseley Braun.
OPPOSITE TOP: Martin Luther King, Jr.
OPPOSITE BOTTOM LEFT: Count Basie.
OPPOSITE BOTTOM RIGHT: Alex Haley.

AARON, Hank (Henry Louis)
1935-

On April 8, 1974, in Atlanta Stadium, he hit his second home run of the season – the 715th home run of his major league career – and surpassed Babe Ruth's long-standing record as the homerun king of American baseball. Born in Mobile, Alabama, Aaron played sandlot baseball as a boy and then played professional ball with several Negro League teams, including the Black Bears and the Indianapolis Clowns. In 1954 his hitting caught the eye of the Braves – then in Milwaukee, later in Atlanta – for whom he played from 1954 to 1974. In 1974 Atlanta traded him to the Milwaukee Brewers, and he finished his major league career in the city where he

Kareem Abdul-Jabbar in 1988, admiring a presentation plaque showing the jerseys he wore during his playing career.

had begun. After he retired in 1976 Aaron became an executive vice-president for the Atlanta Braves. His many career highlights include leading the National League in 1956 with a batting average of .328 and leading the league both in home runs (44) and runs batted in (132) in 1957, his best season. He led the Braves to their World Series victory over the New York Yankees that year and was voted the National League's Most Valuable Player. By the time of his retirement in 1976 his lifetime batting average was .305, with a total of 755 home runs and 2,297 runs batted in. During his career he was named to 20 consecutive all-star teams, and in 1982 he was elected to the Baseball Hall of Fame, with 406 out of 415 votes. After retirement, in addition to working in the Atlanta Braves "front office," he has worked for better opportunities for African-American baseball players and young people. In 1990 he published his autobiography, *I Had a Hammer*. The title reflects his nickname, "Hammerin' Henry".

ABDUL-JABBAR, Kareem
(b. Ferdinand Lewis Alcindor)
1947-

Now universally acknowledged to be one of the two or three all-time greatest basketball players, as Lew Alcindor he guided his New York high school basketball team to record highs. He then went on to lead the University of California at Los Angeles to three consecutive National Collegiate Athletic Association titles (1967-1969) and won the Most Valuable Player award for all three of those tourna-

ments. Several NCAA rule changes were introduced in response to his 7-ft. 2-in. height and skills, but even the pros could not contain his trademark "skyhook" shot. He was drafted by the Milwaukee Bucks as the first pick, and he led the Bucks to a World Championship in his second year, 1971. That same year he also legally adopted the Muslim name, Kareem Abdul-Jabbar, that he had been using since 1968. Traded to the Los Angeles Lakers in 1972, he led the Lakers to five World Championships before retiring in 1989. He holds many National Basketball Association records, including total points (38,387), games played (1,560), and field goals made (15,837). On retiring he devoted himself to various business interests and community benefactions.

Rev. Ralph Abernathy.

ABERNATHY, Ralph David
1926-1990

A civil-rights leader famous for his joint endeavors and close friendship with Dr. Martin Luther King, Jr., Rev. Abernathy was born in Linden, Alabama. Pastor of the Montgomery First Baptist Church, when the Montgomery Bus Boycott took place he became one of its key organizers. Co-founder of the Southern Christian Leadership Conference, he took over after Dr. King's assassination in 1968. In May of that same year he led the Poor People's Campaign on Washington, D.C. His autobiography, *And the Walls Came Tumbling Down*, was published in 1989.

ADDERLEY, Cannonball (Julian)
1928-1975

One of the most popular alto saxophonists of the early 1960s, Adderley led quintets (1959-1975) that epitomized the earthy, soulful, bluesy, hard bop style of modern jazz. Born into a musical family in Tampa,

Florida, he was graduated from Florida A&M University and taught and performed in the Tampa and Washington, D.C., areas before breaking into the Manhattan jazz scene in 1955. He played and recorded with Miles Davis (1958-1959) before launching his own immediately successful quintet with his brother, cornettist Nat Adderley. The quintet's hits included "This Here" (1960), "Mercy, Mercy, Mercy," (1967), and Nat Adderley's compositions "Work Song" and "Sermonette".

AILEY, Alvin
1931-1990

Ailey was widely regarded as the most respected African-American choreographer of his generation, attaining international fame after founding the African-American City Center Dance Company (eventually known as the Alvin Ailey American Dance Theater) in 1958. Born in Rogers, Texas, he was a star athlete in high school and briefly attended college after graduation. He then moved to New York City to concentrate on his life-long love: dance and choreography. His work combined classical ballet with Afro-Caribbean and modern dance, drawing on many aspects of the African-American experience. Almost immediately he

LEFT: Cannonball Adderley.
BELOW: Alvin Ailey teaching blind and partially-sighted students in 1986.

achieved success, founding his own dance company and taking it on a State Department-sponsored tour of Australia in 1961. In Australia his troop's stark style won it both brickbats and plaudits. In 1971 he founded a dance school to which he added a junior level the next year. Between 1971 and 1973 he choreographed nine entirely new works, an astonishing achievement. Among his greatest accomplishments were the dances he created for Samuel Barber's opera *Antony and Cleopatra*, which opened the new Metropolitan Opera House in Lincoln Center in 1966, and his choreography for Leonard Bernstein's *Mass*, which opened the John F. Kennedy Center for the Performing Arts in Washington, D.C., in 1972. Ailey's dance troupe toured throughout Europe and visited six continents, winning many honors.

Ira Aldridge in *Titus Andronicus*.

ALDRIDGE, Ira (Frederick)
c. 1805-1867

An international sensation as a Shakespearean actor, Aldridge's famous *Othello* was never seen on stage in the United States. It is not known where – perhaps in Africa or New York City or Maryland – or when – sometime between 1804 and 1807 – he was born. What *is* known is that he attended the African Free School in New York City until he was 16 before joining the African Grove Theater troop there in 1821. Soon thereafter he worked his way to Great Britain as a ship's steward. He studied acting in Glasgow, Scotland; and in 1825 made his first known appearance on the London stage in *Turinam or A Slave's Revenge*. In the following years he played throughout the English provinces, as well as in London and in Europe. He was married twice, first to an English woman and then to a Swedish opera singer, and had three children. His first appearance as Othello came when he replaced the famous Shakespearean actor Edmond Kean at the Theater Royal when Kean was too ill to perform. In the following years he gave command performances for many of the crowned heads of Europe, including the monarchs of Sweden, Prussia, Austria, and Russia. In 1867, while performing the Lodz, Poland, and planning a triumphant return tour of the United States, he was suddenly taken ill and died. His career is commemorated by a tablet at the new Memorial Theater in Stratford-upon-Avon, England.

ALI, Muhammad
(b. Cassius Marcellus Clay, Jr.)
1942-

Beyond being one of the greatest boxers of all time, he made himself an inspiration to people of color throughout the world. Born in Louisville, Kentucky, Ali's promise as a fighter was clear when he was still a boy. From 1956 to 1960 he fought as an amateur under his birth name, Cassius Clay, winning 100 out of 108 matches. His triumphs included the Golden Gloves and Amateur Athletic Union titles as well as the light heavyweight gold medal in the 1960 Olympics. After the Olympics, financed by a consortium of Louisville businessmen, he turned professional and won his first 19 fights (1960-1963). Despite his impressive record, his 1964 defeat of Sonny Liston for the world heavyweight championship took boxing fans by surprise. By this time he had already announced that he had joined the Nation of Islam (1957), and in 1964 he changed his name to Muhammad Ali. By the mid-1960s it seemed that nothing could stop Ali: he successfully defended his championship nine times between 1964 and 1966. But in 1967, when Ali refused his draft induction notice on religious grounds, he was stripped of his title. Stating that "I ain't got nothing against them Viet Cong," Ali held firm but was out of the ring for three critical years. In 1971 he attempted a come-back against Joe Frazier but lost. Shortly thereafter, the Supreme Court overturned his conviction, and he journeyed to Zaire, Africa, to attempt to win back his title from George Foreman. A 4-1 underdog in the fight, Ali won with a knockout. Between 1974 and 1978 Ali successfully defended his title 10 times, finally losing to Leon Spinks. Once

OPPOSITE: Muhammad Ali at the time of his 1964 victory over Sonny Liston.

ABOVE: Muhammad Ali in 1991.
RIGHT: Debbie Allen.

again it seemed that it was all over for Ali, but once again he came back, regaining his title from Spinks later that year. His last professional fight was in 1981, when he lost on points to Canadian heavyweight Trevor Berbick. By then even Ali's most devoted fans could see that his best boxing days were behind him and that he was no longer capable of the famous Ali shuffle and the quick punch that allowed him, in his own words, to "float like a butterfly, sting like a bee." Retiring with 56 wins, 37 knockouts, and five losses, he took to the talk-show circuit and traveled abroad for international causes. Fans were saddened to notice Ali's awkwardness of motion and uncharacterisic hesitancy of speech, which led to speculation that he had suffered permanent damage in the ring. Whatever the cause, it was announced that Ali was suffering from Parkinsons's Disease. He will long be remembered for his grace in motion, his outbursts of poetry, and his willingness to set his career aside for his principles.

ALLEN, Debbie
? 1950-

A dynamic, all-round theatrical talent – dancer, singer, actress, choreographer, director, and producer – she was born in Houston, Texas, and received her A.B. from Howard University. Her first Broadway roles were as a dancer and singer in such productions as *Purlie* (1973) and *Raisin* (1973). She gained national exposure in the TV series, "3 Girls 3" (1977) but had her greatest success as the demanding dance teacher in the TV series *Fame* (1982), for which she directed, choreographed, and produced some of the later episodes. She gained new respect for directing the TV series *A Different World* (1988-1991). She continued to appear in Broadway musicals, including revivals of *West Side Story, Guys and Dolls*, and *Sweet Charity*. Nominated for a variety of awards, she has received several Emmys for choreography; since 1990 she has also choreographed several of the Academy awards ceremonies. She has increasingly devoted herself to directing television shows. Her sister is Phylicia (Ayers-Allen) Rashad, best known as Bill Cosby's wife on TV's *The Cosby Show*.

ALLEN, Richard
1760-1831

Born a slave in Philadelphia, and sold to a farmer in Delaware, Allen was converted to Methodism and then converted his owner, who allowed Allen to buy his freedom. Allen became a Methodist Church preacher (1784). In 1787, a year after joining Philadelphia's predominantly-white St. George's Methodist Episcopal Church, he and his friends were told that they could not worship in the main-floor pews and would have to sit in the gallery: they all walked out. He formed the Free African Society (1787) and established a separate Methodist church for blacks only. In 1816 several independent black Methodist churches came together to form the African Methodist Episcopal Church; Allen was ordained (April 11, 1816) as the first bishop. A patriot, he supported the War of 1812. He strongly opposed ideas of sending African-Americans to colonize in Africa.

ANDERSON, Marian
1902-1993

Marian Anderson, who has often been called "the world's greatest contralto," was born in Philadelphia, where she sang

made her long-overdue debut at the Metropolitan Opera in Verdi's *Masked Ball*: she was the first African-American ever to appear at the Met. In 1957 Anderson toured the world for the State Department, and in 1958, she was appointed to the U.S. delegation to the United Nations. After receiving the Presidential Medal of Freedom in 1963, Anderson embarked on a worldwide farewell tour that lasted two years. In 1982, on her 80th birthday, she was honored with a Tribute at Carnegie Hall. Grace Bumbry and Shirley Verrett (both former recipients of Marian Anderson scholarships) were among the cast.

ANGELOU, Maya
(b. Marguerite Angelou Johnson)
1928-

A prolific and inspiring poet, writer, performer, and educator, Angelou was born in St. Louis, Missouri, and studied dance with Paul Primus in New York City. She later taught modern dance at The Rome

ABOVE: Marian Anderson.
RIGHT: Maya Angelou.

in her church choir as a girl. Her talent and versatility were immediately obvious, for, though untrained, she was able to sing soprano, alto, tenor – even bass parts. When she was 19 she began to study voice with Giuseppe Boghetti, and by the time she was 23 she had won a major vocal competition in New York and become a soloist with the New York Philharmonic. This would have been an impressive achievement for any young singer, but it was doubly so for an African-American who had had to contend with considerable prejudice. After returning to her hometown and working with the Philadelphia Symphony Orchestra, she traveled to Europe and studied there on a scholarship from the National Association of Negro Musicians. The best-known moment in Anderson's career came in 1939 when the Daughters of the American Revolution refused to allow her to sing at Constitution Hall in Washington, D.C. Appalled by this apparently blatant racial discrimination, Eleanor Roosevelt intervened, and Anderson gave her concert on Easter Sunday at the Lincoln Memorial before an audience of 75,000. The same year she received the Spingarn Award, the highest annual award given by the National Association for Colored People. Yet racism continued to limit Anderson's opportunities, and it was not until 1955 that she

Opera House and at the Hambina Theatre in Tel Aviv. Active in the civil rights movement, she is best known for her poetry and for her serial autobiography, which began with *I Know Why the Caged Birds Sings* (1970). The four companion volumes, spanning 35 years of her life, are remarkable for their depiction both of a black woman's discovery of her identity and of the community that helped to shape her. In 1993 she read "On the Pulse of Morning: The Inaugural Poem" at the inauguration of President Clinton. She has received several honorary degrees and has taught at many colleges.

ARMSTRONG, Louis (Daniel)
"Satchmo" "Pops"
1901-1971

Famous in his later career for versions of show tunes such as "Hello Dolly" performed in his inimitable gravelly singing voice, master cornettist Armstrong's fame as an entertainer was preceded by his

Louis Armstrong (fourth from left) when he was in King Oliver's band in 1922.

career as one of jazz's most innovative pioneers. Born into extreme poverty in New Orleans, "Satchmo" began to play the cornet at the age of 12 while serving a term for delinquency at the Colored Waifs Home. By 1919 he was playing with Kid Ory's bands in New Orleans and with Fate Marable on Mississippi riverboats. He joined King Oliver's trailblazing Creole Jazz Band in Chicago in 1922 and spent 1924 with Fletcher Henderson's equally pioneering band in New York City, where he also performed as a soloist on recordings with Bessie Smith and leading blues artists. His classic "Hot Five" and "Hot Seven" recordings (1925-1929) established the role of the soloist, shaping the course of jazz for the next two decades. Armstrong scored his first show-business hit in 1930 with "Ain't Misbehavin'," and for the next 17 years he was featured in big bands in increasingly commercial settings. In 1947 Armstrong formed his Dixieland-style sextet the "All Stars," with which he toured internationally, often under State Department auspices as America's Goodwill Ambassador, until his death. He appeared in over 50 movies.

ASHE, Arthur
1943-1993

Ashe initially won respect as the first African-American to break into the world of international tennis; but by the time he died of AIDS in 1993 he was equally admired for his humanitarian work. Born in Richmond, Virginia, Ashe learned to play tennis at the Richmond Racket Club, which had been founded by Dr. R.W. Johnson. Johnson, who had sponsored Althea Gibson's early career, also sponsored Ashe, who won the Junior Indoor Tennis singles title in 1960 and 1961 and was ranked 28th in the U.S. while still in high school. In 1961 he entered UCLA on a tennis scholarship and was ranked as the number one amateur U.S. tennis player throughout most of the 1960s. In 1975 he defeated Jimmy Connors at Wimbledon (6-1, 6-1, 5-7, 6-4), becoming the first African-American male to win there. In 1981, after quadruple bypass heart surgery the previous year had ended his tennis career, he was the first African-American to captain the U.S. Davis Cup Team. Thereafter he worked to open tennis to

Arthur Ashe in 1968, when he won the U.S. Men's Singles Tennis Championship.

young African-American players and was the co-founder of the National Junior Tennis League. In 1992, after it became known that he had contracted the AIDS virus from a blood transfusion, he worked tirelessly for AIDS education. His books include *A Hard Road to Glory, Portrait in Motion, Off the Court, The Illustrated History of African-Americans in Sports,* and *Advantage Ashe*. His last book, *Days of Grace: A Memoir* (with Arnold Rampersand), was published shortly after his death in 1993.

ATTUCKS, Crispus
?1723-1770

Little is known about the early life of this legendary figure of the American Revolution. He is believed to have been of mixed Native American and African descent, and he is thought to have been either an escaped or freed slave. About 1750 he appeared in Boston, Massachusetts, as a seaman and dockworker and had assumed the name "Michael Johnson." On March 5, 1770, he was apparently eating in a tavern near the Boston docks when he heard of a disturbance involving some Bostonians protesting the British soldiers guarding the Custom House. By contemporary accounts, he picked up a cordwood club and with a group of sailors went to the scene. In the ensuing melee some soldiers fired their rifles. The 6-ft. 2-in. Attucks was killed on the spot, four others also died, and seven were wounded. This was instantly called "the Boston Massacre," and Attucks was regarded as a martyr by the more revolutionary patriots. In 1880 a statue of him was dedicated on Boston Common.

AUGUSTE, Donna
1958-

As an African-American woman in the highest echelons of the computer world, Donna Auguste has become accustomed to being introduced as the "first and only." Born in Beaumont, Texas, and of partial Native American descent, she earned her undergraduate degree at the University of California at Berkeley and then was the first black woman to enter Carnegie Mellon's Ph.D. program in computer science. After working summers at Xerox's Palo Alto, California, research center, in 1983 she joined Intellicorp, a California firm working to employ artificial intelligence programs in computers She left Intellicorp in 1990, and, after bicycling around Japan (and learning some Japanese), she joined Apple Computer as a software engineering manager and soon was managing the team that produced the Newton, launched in 1993 as the first computer capable of operating directly from an individual's handwriting. In 1993 she joined U.S. West as a researcher developing multimedia technology for interactive cable television. A skilled musician, she plays the guitar, piano, and percussion and is working on developing a notation system that captures the dynamics of oral musical traditions, such as African-American gospel and various forms of Native American music.

The death of Crispus Attucks in 1770.

B

BAILEY, Pearl
1918-1988

A multi-talented, highly-visible show business personality, the irrepressible Bailey was born in Newport News, Virginia, and began touring as a dancer after winning a contest in Philadelphia in 1933. She sang with the big bands of Noble Sissle, Edgar Hayes, Cab Calloway, Cootie Williams, and, after 1952, with her husband, drummer-bandleader Louis Bellson. She starred in the Broadway musical *St. Louis Woman* (1946). Her success in the movie *Carmen Jones* (1954) led to numerous film, TV, and stage roles, including the African-American production of *Hello Dolly!* (1967-1969). She hosted a TV variety show (1970-1971) and published her autobiography in 1968.

BAKER, Ella Josephine
1903-1986

Best-known for her work in the civil rights movement during the 1950s as interim director of the Southern Christian Leadership Conference, Baker first became a social activist in Harlem during the 1930s depression. Her commitment to women's rights led her to work with the Women's Day Workers and Industrial League and to write a book on the exploitation of domestic workers (*Crisis*, 1935). In 1958 she organized a voter registration campaign for the Southern Christian Leadership Conference. Impatient with SCLC's slow pace of progress and top-down leadership, she supported the foundation of the more militant Student Nonviolent Coordinating Committee in 1958 and the Mississippi Freedom Democratic Party in 1964, thus serving as a bridge to the black power movement of later decades.

RIGHT: Pearl Bailey.

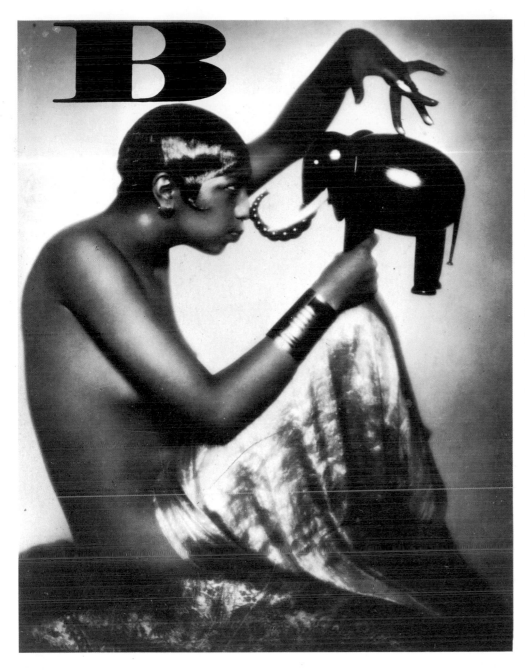

Josephine Baker.

BAKER, Josephine
(b. Freda Josephine McDonald)
1906-1975

Josephine Baker's international celebrity, outspoken opposition to discrimination, participation in the French Resistance, and post-war activities on behalf of orphaned and deprived children made her a major African-American figure of the twentieth century. Born in St. Louis, Missouri, she had an unhappy family life and ran away from home at an early age. She began touring as a dancer in vaudeville (and was first married) when she was 13. In 1921 she remarried, acquiring the surname Baker. She made her Broadway debut in the chorus line of *Shuffle Along* in 1923 and began singing in Harlem's Plantation Club. In 1924 she appeared in *Chocolate Dandies*. In 1925, stranded in Paris with the failed *La Revue Negre*, she appeared in an all-black act at the Folies Bergère and rose to instantaneous stardom on the wave of French enthusiasm for jazz and everything associated with it. Performing topless on a mirror wearing only a g-string of fake bananas or walking a leashed leopard on the Champs Élysées, Baker cultivated a partly comedic, uninhibited, yet increasingly sophisticated image built on her lively dancing, scat singing, and infectiously energetic manner. She remained the toast of France, of which she became a citizen in 1937, for five decades. After her 1928 tour of Europe and South America and first film appearances, she returned to the U.S. to star in the *Ziegfeld Follies* (1936) but failed to impress the critics. Professionally frustrated and disgusted with second-class citizenship, she returned to Paris, where she married her third husband, Jean Lion, a French Jew (1937). Targeted by the Nazis in 1939, she served with distinction in the French Resistance and entertained Allied troops. Following her fourth marriage, while on an American tour she insisted on playing only to integrated audiences and became the center of a famous media event when columnist Walter Winchell called her a communist and a Nazi collaborator (1951). On a Far Eastern tour in 1953 she adopted the first two of 12 orphans of various nationalities – her "Rainbow Tribe" – whom she housed in her French estate in what she termed an "experiment in brotherhood." Baker returned to the States to address the crowds at the 1963 Civil Rights March on Washington and to make fund-raising appearances at Carnegie Hall. She performed at Carnegie Hall to benefit UNICEF a decade later. She died in 1975, following the gala opening of a new show celebrating the fiftieth anniversary of her Paris debut.

James Baldwin.

BALDWIN, James
1927-1987

A novelist, essayist, and playwright whose influence went far beyond his printed words, Baldwin was born in Harlem, New York. His father was a preacher, and during high school young James preached at a Harlem pentecostal church. After graduation he began writing essays for a number of journals; from the beginning, his writing was grounded in his experience as an African-American, and he wrote strongly against racism. In 1948 he went to Paris and began to write fiction with the financial support of various fellowships. His first novel, *Go Tell It On the Mountain* (1953) was clearly an autobiographical work. His second novel, *Giovanni's Room* (1956), dealt openly with a young man's coming to terms with his homosexuality. His essays collected in *Notes of a Native Son* (1955) gained him a wider public, and he returned to the U.S. in 1957 and became involved with the civil rights struggle as both an activist and a writer. Both his fiction and non-fiction work explored the psychological effects of racism, and in further essays, collected in such volumes as *The Fire Next Time* (1963), he came to be regarded as one of the most eloquent voices raised against racism. Among his novels are *Another Country* (1962), *Tell Me How Long the Train's Been Gone* (1968), and *Just Above My Head* (1979). He also had four plays produced, including *Blues for Mr. Charlie* (1964) and *The Amen* (1965). He spent his last years in France but returned occasionally to the U.S. to teach.

BANNEKER, Benjamin
1731-1806

Although he spent nearly his entire life on one farm, Banneker had an important influence on how African-Americans were viewed during the Federalist and Jeffersonian periods of American history. Born in Baltimore County, Maryland (present-day Oella, Maryland), Banneker was the child of a free black father. He had little formal education, but he became literate

Benjamin Banneker (here misspelled).

and read widely. At the age of 21 he built a clock with every part made of wood – it operated for over 40 years. After the death of his father, he lived on his father's 100-acre farm, largely secluded from the outside world, his sisters doing housekeeping for him. Self-taught in the fields of astronomy and surveying, he assisted in the survey of the Federal Territory of 1791 and calculated ephemerides and made eclipse projections for a book called *Benjamin Bannaker's* (sic) *Pennsylvania, Delaware, Maryland and Virginia Almanack and Epheremis*, published during the years 1792-1797. He retired from tobacco farming to concentrate wholly upon his studies. He corresponded with Thomas Jefferson and urged Jefferson to work for the abolition of slavery.

Imamu Amiri Baraka.

BARAKA, Imamu Amiri
(b. LeRoi Jones)
1934-

As LeRoi Jones, Baraka was one of the leading poets of Greenwich Village's "Beat Generation" in the 1950s. In the 1960s he was one of the founders of the American Theater for Poets and saw his plays *Dutchman*, *The Toilet*, and *The Slave* produced off Broadway. In 1966 he returned to Newark – where he had been born and had received his education at the local Rutgers campus – and took the name Imamu Amiri Baraka as a sign of his Muslim faith and commitment to Afro-Islamic culture and black nationalism. He has continued to publish both prose and poetry, including *Reggae or Not!* (1982), and his plays have been produced both in the United States and overseas, especially in Africa.

BASIE, Count (William)
1904-1984

One of the great swing band leaders, Basie, born in Red Bank, New Jersey, began playing piano at the age of six. He performed in vaudeville until he was stranded in Kansas City in 1927, where he found work as a sideman. By 1935 he had formed his own band, and with it he made nationwide tours throughout the 1940s. He established a new and enduring 16-piece prototype for big bands in 1952 and began touring Europe in 1954. During the 1960s his band accompanied and recorded with many major vocalists, including Frank Sinatra and Sarah Vaughan. He performed with all-star groups during the 1970s and continued touring with his band.

BATTLE, Kathleen
1948-

From the moment of her 1977 Metropolitan Opera debut she was one of the most admired and popular operatic sopranos of her generation. A graduate of the University of Cincinnati Conservatory of Music, she has won kudos both in the United States and abroad for her performance of Elivira in the *Italian Girl in Algiers*, for her widely acclaimed Rosina in the *Barber of Seville* and for her Adina in *L'Elisir d'Amore*. In 1987-1988 she appeared as Zerbinetta in the Metropolitan Opera's star-studded production of *Ariadne auf Naxos*, also starring Jessye

Count Basie (at piano) and his band.

Norman as Ariadne. Her many recordings of both opera and lighter music are widely popular, and for a number of years Battle was a regular on the Met's gala New Year's Eve concerts. In 1994, however, the temperamental singer and the Met's management had a falling out, and she was dropped from the Met's roster. Her other U.S. and international engagements, however, continued as before, and her career was not seriously affected.

BEARDEN, Romare
1912-1988

Bearden was born in Charlotte, North Carolina, but grew up in Pittsburgh, Pennsylvania, and New York City. He studied art at both Pittsburgh University and

Columbia University. In 1950-1951 he also studied art at the Sorbonne in Paris and while there met the artists Joan Miro and Henri Matisse. Before his stay in Paris, Bearden's work had been heavily influenced by Social Realism; he returned to the United States influenced both by Cubism and his own African heritage. Thereafter, he was eager to experiment with techniques of photomontage and collage and to depict the life of African-Americans. His work appeared on the covers of *Time, Fortune*, and *The New Yorker*. His many shows included exhibitions at the Carnegie Museum in Pittsburgh (1937), the Institute of Modern Art in Boston (1943), the Corcoran Gallery in Washington, D.C., (1965), and the Boston Museum of Fine Arts (1970).

Bearden's work is in the permanent collections of a number of major museums. Several of Bearden's best-known works are "Street Corner" and "He is Arisen". Once when asked what he hoped to do in his work, Bearden replied that he wanted to "redefine the image of man in terms of the black experience." In addition to his artistic work, he founded the Cinque Gallery in New York to give young black artists a venue and published several books, including *The Painter's Mind* (1969) and *Six Black Masters of American Art* (1972).

BECHET, Sidney
1897-1959

One of the great originals of American music, Bechet pioneered soloing, as opposed to the ensemble playing of traditional New Orleans-style jazz, and with Coleman Hawkins established the saxophone as a jazz instrument. Born into a musical New Orleans family, he mastered the clarinet early and became one of the first jazz players to receive critical attention. After switching to soprano sax in 1920 he played with Duke Ellington, profoundly influencing his style, and toured Europe into Russia. He was one of the centerpieces of the mid-1940s Dixieland revival. He settled in France in 1951 and stayed there for the reminder of his life, exchanging his second-class U.S. citizenship for veneration.

Sidney Bechet (right) at the International Jazz Festival in Paris in 1949.

James Beckwourth.

BECKWOURTH, James P.
1798-c. 1867

One of the pioneers who opened the Far West, Beckwourth was born in Virginia. He moved to St. Louis, and, after being associated with the Ashley brothers' fur trading company, he became a "mountain man" in his own right. He married several different Indian woman and lived among the Crow Indians from 1825 to 1833. He served in the U.S. Army during the Mexican War and in 1850 discovered a pass through the Sierra Mountains that still bears his name. He moved to Missouri, then to Colorado, fought in the Cheyenne War in 1864, and settled near Denver. His life story was recounted by T.D. Bonner in *Life and Adventures of James P. Beckwourth, Mountaineer, Scout, and Pioneer and Chief of the Crow Nation of Indians* (1856, 1892).

BELAFONTE, Harry (Harold George)
1927-

Prominent in recent years for his work with UNICEF and his efforts on behalf of third-world minorities, the former "King of Calypso" enjoys star status as an actor and singer who helped give mass appeal to folk music during the 1950s. Born in New York City and raised partly in the West Indies, his many film and TV credits include the male lead in *Carmen Jones* (1954). After a false start as a jazz singer, he concentrated on folk singing and scored major hits with "Jamaica Farewell" and "Banana Boat Song". His *Calypso* (1956) was the very first million-selling album, and his records continued to be bestsellers into the 1960s. A civil rights advocate, he marched with Dr. Martin Luther King, Jr., raised thousands of dollars for the movement, and enlisted the support of his fellow entertainers. He produced the first integrated TV music shows (for which he won Emmy Awards and was fired by his sponsors). Belafonte records, acts, and performs sporadically, using his energy and enormous prestige primarily to help relieve racial and economic suffering.

BELL, "Cool Papa" (James Thomas)
1903-1990

Combining speed, daring and batting skill, Bell ranked in the top echelon of baseball players in the Negro Leagues. Twice he reached double figures in home runs and led the league in stolen bases in his Hall of Fame (1974) career. Later a switch-hitting outfielder, he had broken in with the St. Louis Stars as a pitcher. He often regretted that he had not continued as a pitcher, for his knuckleball was almost unhittable, but he had to admit that it was also almost uncatchable.

OPPOSITE: Harry Belafonte (center) at the 1963 March on Washington.

ABOVE: Derrick Bell.

BELL, Derrick Albert, Jr,
1930-

A lawyer and educator, he began his career at the U.S. Department of Justice (1957-1959), then worked with the Legal Defense & Education Fund of the National Association for the Advancement of Colored People from 1960 to 1966. Returning to academe, he held appointments at Harvard Law School (1969-1980, 1986-1992), was dean of the University of Oregon Law School (1981-1985), and served as visiting law professor at New York University (1992-). He left Harvard in 1992 to protest the absence of African-American women on the law school faculty. His books include *The Elusive Quest for Racial Justice* (1987) and *Faces at the Bottom of the Well* (1992).

BERRY, Chuck (Charles Edward Anderson)
1926-

Singer, guitarist, and songwriter Chuck Berry was the biggest pre-Beatles influence on rock music. Born in St. Louis, Missouri, and trained as hairdresser, he launched his solo career with Chess Records in Chicago in 1955. His classic hit songs "School Days," "Rock and Roll Music," and "Johnny B. Goode" became favorites with teenagers of all races. Although prison sentences for violation of the Mann Act dampened his popularity, his "My Ding A Ling" (1972) was his most successful record, and Berry became an inaugural member of the Rock 'n Roll Hall of Fame in 1986.

OPPOSITE: Chuck Berry.

BETHUNE, Mary McLeod
1875-1955

One of the most influential American women of her generation, and clearly its most famous African-American woman educator and public official, she was born the 15th of 17 children to former slaves on a cotton farm in Mayesville, South Carolina. Her life took a critical turn away from the drudgery of farm labor and poverty when her mother recognized her potential and enrolled her at the age of ten in the nearby Trinity Presbyterian Mission School. Her performance there led teacher Emma Jane Wilson to encourage her to enroll in the Presbyterian Scotia Seminary in Concord, North Carolina, in 1888. After her graduation in 1894 she enrolled as the only African-American student at evangelist Dwight Moody's Institute for Home and Foreign Missions (the Moody Bible Institute) in Chicago, hoping to be sent as a missionary to Africa. The Moody Institute, however, discouraged African-Americans from missionary fieldwork in Africa. Deeply frustrated, she returned to the South to teach at the Haines Institute in Augusta, Georgia (1896-1897). In 1898 she married Albertus Bethune, but the marriage was not a happy one and ended in a permanent separation in 1908. By 1904 Bethune had moved to Daytona, Florida, and had founded a school for African-American women modeled on her alma mater, Scotia Seminary. She later said that the school began with "five little girls, a dollar and fifty cents, and faith in God." During the first years in the rented schoolhouse the pupils used homemade elderberry juice for ink and wrote with quills they fashioned themselves. Bethune's mission was to train young woman in home economics, which they could use either with their own families or in domestic service, and to train teachers for future generations of African-Americans. In 1912 Bethune's school won the supreme accolade: a visit from Booker T. Washington, whose interest led to welcome contributions from his white benefactors. In addition, Bethune zeroed in on the "snowbirds": wealthy northern whites who

Mary McLeod Bethune, the first black woman to head a major federal office.

wintered in Daytona. Bethune's choirs raised money by giving frequent perform-ances of spirituals at local hotels. In 1923 the college became coeducational and was renamed Bethune-Cookman College (the second name honoring a white missionary who had fought for rights for blacks). During the Great Depression the little col-lege almost went bankrupt, but Bethune kept her dream alive by austere measures. In 1935 the National Association for the Advancement of Colored People gave Bethune its highest prize, the Spingarn Award, given annually for the "highest or noblest achievement by an African-American." If Bethune had died in 1935, her career would have been a distin-guished one, but she went on to serve under President Franklin D. Roosevelt in the National Youth Administration, becoming the Director of the Division of Negro Affairs – the first African-American woman to head a federal office. She was the only woman among Roose-velt's African-American advisors, often called the "Black Cabinet." Throughout her life she held countless important posi-

Eubie Blake (right) with Noble Sissle.

tions in the African-American com-munity, most notably as president of the National Association of Colored Women from 1924 to 1928. In 1952 she represented President Harry S Truman at the innaug-uration of William Tubman as President of Liberia. Her life-long achievements were recognized by the nation in 1974 when the Mary McLeod Bethune Memorial was dedicated in Washington, D.C. This bronze monument was the first statue of of a woman and of an African-American to be erected on national park ground in the nation's capital.

BLAKE, Eubie (James Hubert)
1883-1983

A master of classic piano styles and the composer of some of America's best-known standards, Eubie Blake was born in Baltimore, Maryland, and began study-ing piano as a child. While still a teenager he played in bordellos, traveling minstrel shows, and at grand hotels in Baltimore and Atlantic City. In 1916 he began his long collaboration with lyricist Noble Sissle, with whom he also performed as "The Dixie Duo." Together, they created

many classic ragtime hits. Their first Broadway show, the famous all-black musical *Shuffle Along* (1921), included the hit song "I'm Just Wild About Harry". In the ensuing decades Blake led orchestras and composed numerous songs and musicals with Sissle and other lyricists (Andy Razaf supplied the lyrics to his 1930 signature song "Memories of You"). Blake entertained the troops during World War II and helped found the Negro Actors Guild. After slipping into retire-ment, he was rediscovered in the late 1960s and honored as a great American original. The musical *Eubie* (1978) cele-brated his songs. He continued perform-ing until shortly before his death.

BLAKEY, Art (Arthur)
1919-1990

Famous for his powerful, emotional drumming, Blakey spearheaded his Jazz Messengers, a kind of "finishing School" for outstanding young players, from 1954 to 1990. Born in Pittsburgh, Pennsylvania, he began performing as a pianist, switched to drums, and joined Fletcher Hender-son's band in 1939. Playing with Billy Eck-

Art Blakey.

Arna Bontemps.

stine's band (1944-1947), he worked with Charlie Parker, Dizzy Gillespie, and other jazz innovators. After an extended trip to Africa (1948) he became house drummer at Blue Note Records, where he recorded classic tracks with Thelonious Monk. His Messenger bands were later among the leading exponents of the bluesy, lyrical, hard bop style.

BOLDEN, Buddy (Charles Joseph)
1877-1931

Although he lives in legend as the originator of jazz and as the "first jazz trumpeter," all that is certain of Bolden's musical career is that he played the cornet, led successful bands, and was immensely popular in turn-of-the-century New Orleans. Born there in 1877, Bolden took up the cornet at the age of 17, and by 1900 he enjoyed city-wide fame. A charismatic crowd-pleaser whose rise coincided with the emergence of Black Storyville, he may well have contributed to the standardizing of the New Orleans jazz ensemble and repertory. But because the musical career of "Buddy the King" predated the recording of jazz, we can only guess at how he influenced the form. He was institutionalized for schizophrenia from 1907 until the end of his life.

BOND, Julian
1940-

This well-known civil rights activist and legislator was born in Nashville, Tennessee; his father, Horace Mann Bond, would become president of Lincoln University. He attended Morehouse College and in 1960 was arrested at a sit-in protesting segregation at an Atlanta cafeteria. He was one of the founders of the Student Nonviolent Coordinating Committee (SNCC) and served as its communciations director. In 1965 he was elected to the Georgia House of Representatives but was originally denied his seat due to his opposition to the Vietnam War. The U.S. Supreme Court ruled in his favor, granting him his seat in 1966. He went on to the Georgia Senate (1975-1987) and since 1988 he has served as a visiting professor at a number of schools. He was one of the co-founders of the Southern Poverty Law Center (1971).

BONTEMPS, Arna Wendell
1902-1973

This leading figure in the Harlem Renaissance, a novelist and close friend of Langston Hughes, was born in Louisiana and raised in California. From 1943 until 1963 he was the librarian at Fisk University in Nashville, Tennessee, a secure position that allowed him time to write. His novels include *God Sends Sunday* (1931), which went on to Broadway as the musical *Saint Louis Woman* (1946) and *Story of the Negro* (1948), which won the Jane Addams Children's Book Award in 1956. With Langston Hughes, he edited *The Poetry of the Negro 1746-1949* (1949) and *The Book of Negro Folklore* (1958), both influential works in raising awareness of African-American literature. Bontemps's correspondence with Langston Hughes was published in 1980.

BRADLEY, Ed (Edward)
1941-

One of the most prominent African-American TV news commentators and anchormen, Bradley began his career as a freelance reporter covering the 1965 Philadelphia race riots at $1.25 an hour. He joined WCBS radio in New York in 1967. In 1971 CBS sent him first to its Paris bureau and then to Vietnam, where he spent 18 months, leaving when he was wounded by mortar fire, but returning to cover the fall of Saigon. During the 1976 election he covered the Jimmy Carter campaign and became one of the three CBS White House correspondents after Carter's election. In rapid succession, he became anchorman on the CBS Sunday Night News, the first African-American to hold that post, and a panelist on the popular Sunday night program "Sixty Minutes." His many awards include three Emmys.

L.A. Mayor Tom Bradley (left), standing beside Governor Pete Wilson, in 1992.

BRADLEY, Tom (Thomas)
1917-

After retiring from the Los Angeles Police Department as a lieutenant in 1962, Bradley practiced law briefly, but he soon entered politics. He was elected to the city council in 1963 and reelected in 1967 and 1971. In 1973 he was elected mayor of Los Angeles, becoming the city's first African-American mayor. He was re-elected for four more four-year terms. Bradley successfully won increased federal grant money for Los Angeles, maintained a balanced budget throughout most of his term in office, and was widely credited with calming the city's racial tensions. In 1993 he announced his decision not to run for another term.

BRAUN, Carol Moseley
1947-

In 1992 Braun was elected Senator (D.) from Illinois, becoming the first African-American woman to sit in the U.S. Senate and only the second African-American since Reconstruction to be a Senator. The daughter of a Chicago police officer, Braun received a law degree from the University of Chicago and worked in the U.S. Attorney's Office, where she won the Special Achievement Award. In 1978 she was elected to the Illinois House of Representatives, where she was voted Best Legislator each of the ten years she served. In 1988 she became the first African-American to hold high office in Cook County when she was elected Cook County Recorder of Deeds, an important stepping-stone to her Senate race.

BROOKE, Edward W. (William)
1919-

Born in Washington, D.C., Brooke was graduated from Howard University in 1940. He was a captain of infantry in Italy in World War II, and he won the Bronze Star for bravery. After the war he was graduated from Boston University Law

Senator Carol Moseley Braun in 1992, with Bill Clinton and Al Gore.

School and served as the attorney general for Massachusetts from 1963 to 1966. As a Republican, he won election to the U.S. Senate from Massachusetts in 1966; he was the first African-American to be elected to the Senate since the period of Reconstruction. He served in the Senate from 1967 to 1979 and then became the chairman of the National Low-Income Housing Coalition in 1979.

BROOKS, Gwendolyn
1917-

The first African-American woman to win a Pulitzer Prize, Brooks was born in Topeka, Kansas. She received her A.B. from Wilson Junior College in Chicago in 1936 and went on to teach in many colleges around the Chicago area. A prolific poet and writer, in 1950 she won the Pulitzer Prize for her verse narrative *Annie Allen*. In 1968 she was named the poet laureate of Illinois, and in 1990 Chicago State University established the Gwendolyn Brooks Chair in Black Literature and Creative writing in her honor.

BELOW: Gwendolyn Brooks.

ABOVE: H. Rap Brown (right) with Stokely Carmichael in 1968.

BROWN, H. Rap
1943-

This civil rights activist was born in Baton Rouge, Louisiana. He took part in voter registration drives in Mississippi in 1964 and became the chairman of the Student Nonviolent Coordinating Committee in 1967. He was an advocate of black power and violent confrontation with white racists. In 1968 he was charged with inciting a riot in Maryland and was then convicted of carrying a gun between states. In 1971 he was convicted and sentenced for armed robbery and assault. He was released from prison in 1976.

BROWN, James
1928-

"Soul Brother No. 1," born in Barnwell, South Carolina, began his career as a gospel singer in Macon, Georgia. By 1962 his precision high-energy performances established him as a leading star of rhythm-and-blues. In 1968 his "Say It Loud, I'm Black and I'm Proud," became an anthem of the Black Power movement. He was one of the first African-American performers to take complete control over his career. Still one of the seminal influences and most significant figures in African-American pop, Brown is an inaugural member of the Rock 'n Roll Hall of Fame and a Grammy recipient for "Living in America" (1987).

BROWN, Jim (James N.)
1936-

A football Hall of Famer (1971), Brown rushed for 12,312 yards for the Cleveland Browns in only nine years, while averaging a National-Football-League-record 5.2 yards per carry. The muscular fullback weighed 233 pounds but had speed and balance. The only African-American on the football squad during his freshman year at Syracuse University, Brown attained the All-American rank in football, track, and lacrosse. After his football career Brown acted in films, including the *Dirty Dozen*. He established the Black Economic Union and remains active as a fundraiser.

Cleveland Browns fullback Jim Brown.

BROWN, Lee Patrick
1937-

A longtime law enforcement official, he was already a patrolman while an undergraduate at Fresno State University (B.S., 1961). He earned a doctorate in criminology at the University of California at Berkeley (1970) and taught at Portland State (1968-1972) and Howard University (1972-1975) before returning to law enforcement. He served Portland, Oregon, as sheriff (1975-1976); Houston, Texas, as police chief (1982-1990); and New York City as police commissioner (1990-1992). Author of many articles, recipient of many awards, he was named Cabinet-level director of the Office of Drug Control Policy – "drug czar" – in 1993.

BROWN, Ron (Ronald Harmon)
1941-

Secretary of the U.S. Department of Commerce (1993-), he is known for "firsts." He was the first African-American member of a fraternity at

Ron Brown in 1992.

Middlebury College (1958-1962), the first African-American partner in the 140-member Washington law firm of Patton, Boggs & Blow (1981-1993), and the first African-American chairman of a major political party (the Democratic National Committee, 1989-1993). He had been an army captain in Germany and Korea, and he then served the National Urban League in various roles (1968-1979), culminating in vice president of Washington operations. Considered a unifying influence, he helped direct the presidential campaigns of Edward Kennedy and Jesse Jackson.

BROWN, Sterling
1901-1989

An influential figure in the Harlem Renaissance, Brown was a poet and teacher (Howard University, 1929-1969) who encouraged numerous young African-American writers, as well as focusing serious critical attention on previously neglected folk artists such as Ma Rainey and Blind Lemon Jefferson. His *Negro Poetry and Drama* (1937) and *The Negro in American Fiction* (1931) were among the first work in what came to be known as African-American studies. Beginning in 1941, he edited *The Negro Caravan*, a reference work on African-American

literature. Although his own poetry is not widely read today, he was once called the "dean of American Negro poets".

BROWN, Tony (William Anthony)
1933-

A TV producer, educator, and filmmaker, he earned an M.S.W. from Wayne State University (1961) and was a columnist and city editor for *The Detroit Courier*. From magazine work and hosting various TV shows, he became executive producer of National Educational Television's "Black Journal" (1970) and founder and first dean of Howard University's School of Communications (1971-1972). As producer and host of TV's "Tony Brown's Journal" (1978-), he is the creator of the first and longest-running black public affairs series. His awards include an LL.D. from the University of Michigan (1975) and the Public Service Award of the National Urban League (1977).

BELOW: Tony Brown (left), interviewing actor James Earl Jones in 1979.

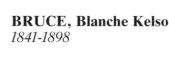

ABOVE: Blanche Kelso Bruce.

BRUCE, Blanche Kelso
1841-1898

The first African-American to serve a full term in the U.S. Senate and one of the most prominent African-American public officials of the nineteenth century, he was born a slave in Prince Edward County, Virginia. He was tutored by his master's son, worked as a printer's apprentice, and escaped from slavery when the Civil War began. He briefly attended Oberlin College and in 1864 organized the first school for African-Americans in Missouri. In 1869 he moved to Mississippi, where, under Reconstruction policies, he prospered as a landowner and became active in local politics. After serving as sheriff and superintendent of schools he was elected to represent Mississippi in the U.S. Senate, where he served from 1875 to 1881. He fought hard for African-Americans, was a full participant in the Senate's activities, and gained great respect: at the 1880 Republican convention he got eight votes as the candidate for vice president, and 11 votes at the 1888 convention. After his Senate service, he was registrar of the U.S. Treasury from 1881 to 1885 and again from 1897 to 1898. During the same period, from 1889 to 1893, he also served as the recorder of deeds for the District of Columbia.

BULLINS, Ed
1935-

Bullins was an influential figure in the black theater movement of the 1960s. He was a co-founder of Black Arts West in San Francisco, a member of the Black Arts Alliance, the resident playwright at Harlem's New Lafayette Theater, and the editor of *Black Theater* magazine. His first play to be produced was *Clara's Old Man* (1965); in the 1970s, he won three Obie awards. Although his plays have been less frequently produced in the 1980s and 1990s, he has continued to hold influential posts at the American Place Theater (1973-) and The Surviving Theater (1974-).

BUMBRY, Grace Ann
1937-

The daughter of a railroad worker and a schoolteacher, surrounded by a musical family, she became a star of twentieth-century opera. In high school she became known to contralto Marian Anderson and

Grace Bumbry in *Carmen*.

appeared on Arthur Godfrey's "Talent Scouts" show. At Northwestern University she became the protégé of Lotte Lehmann. She debuted with the Paris Opera (1960) and at the Bayreuth Festival (1961), receiving many curtain calls for her portrayal of Venus. Her distinguished international career has included mezzo and soprano roles. She has made a number of recordings and has appeared in a performance at the White House.

BUNCHE, Ralph Johnson
1904-1971

Bunche was both the first African-American to be a division head in the State Department (1945) and the first African-American to win the Nobel Peace Prize. Born into poverty in Detroit, orphaned when he was only 11, he was raised by his grandmother, a former slave. He attended the University of California on an athletic scholarship (A.B., 1927) and earned his M.A. (1928) and Ph.D. at Harvard (1934). Throughout the 1930s Bunche taught at Howard University in Washington, D.C., where he became chairman of the political science depart-

ment. Bunche's long career in government began at the Office of Strategic Services (1941-1944) and continued at the State Department (1944-1947). While at State, Bunche served on the committee that drew up that portion of the United Nations charter that dealt with trusteeships and territories. The work was a useful preliminary to Bunche's long and distinguished career at the United Nations (1946-1971), where he served first as head of the Trusteeship Division and later as director of the Department of Trusteeship and Non-Self-Governing Territories (1948-1954). During these same years he served as the Acting Mediator for the U.N. Palestine Commission (1948, 1949) and won the Nobel Peace Prize for his efforts to mediate the Arab-Israeli truce of 1948. If this was his most notable achievement, it was by no means his only one: he later directed U.N. peacekeeping efforts during the Suez crisis (1956), in the Congo (1964), and in Cyprus (1964). Ill-health hastened his retirement, and when he died he was the most highly honored African-American of his generation.

Ralph Bunche, signing autographs in 1950.

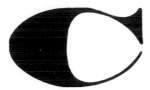

CALLOWAY, Cab (Cabell)
1907-

Famous for his extroverted manner, flamboyant zoot-suited appearance, and scat-singing – his "Hi-De-Hi" became part of the language – Calloway led one of the most successful bands of the 1930s and 1940s, making a major contribution to jazz through the quality of musicians he hired and allowed room to solo. Born in Rochester, New York, and raised in Baltimore, as a versatile song-and-dance man he began fronting bands in Chicago (1928) and rose to prominence when his own band replaced that of Duke Ellington as the house band at Harlem's Cotton Club (1931). After 1948 Calloway performed solo mainly in musical theater, notably in *Porgy and Bess* (1952-1954) as Sportin' Life (a role Gershwin modeled after him) and *Hello Dolly*. He appeared in the film *The Blues Brothers* (1980) and in the show *His Royal Highness of Hi-de-ho: the Legendary Cab Calloway* (1987).

Cab Calloway (right), with Bill Robinson.

CAMPANELLA, Roy
1921-1993

An automobile accident put "Campy" in a wheelchair, but nothing ever put a damper on his spirit. He started his baseball career in the Negro League at the age of 15. The Hall of Fame (1969) catcher was the natural leader of the Brooklyn Dodgers from 1948 to 1957, taking them to five pennants. He hit a total of 242 home runs, was an All-Star eight times, and was named

Stokely Carmichael (foreground) in 1966.

Most Valuable Player three times (1951, 1953, 1955). In retirement, he continued to personify baseball's greatness, touring the country and providing inspiration for fans of all ages.

CARMICHAEL, Stokely
(later Kwame Toure)
1941-

A carpenter's son born in Trinidad, he emigrated to the U.S. in 1952 and by the mid-1960s became the activist who popularized the phrase "black power." While attending Howard University (1960-1964) he became leader of the Student Nonviolent Coordinating Committee, changing its focus from integration to "black liberation" and "black power," stressed the need for black-run organizations and self-defence. Gifted and articulate, he was prime minister of the Black Panthers in Oakland, California (1967-1969) and for many symbolized black violence. He and his South African wife, the singer Miriam Makeba, lived in Guinea awhile, and he wrote *Stokely Speaks* (1971), a book that dealt largely with his new interest in Pan-Africanism.

Diahann Carroll in 1968.

Vinnette Carroll in 1979.

CARROLL, Diahann
1935-

Born in New York City, versatile show business personality Carroll began her career as a nightclub singer and a model. She began working in films in the 1950s and first appeared on Broadway in *The House of Flowers* (1954). She starred in *No Strings* (1962) and was featured in the movie *I Know Why the Caged Bird Sings* in 1979. Her appearance in *Julia* made her the first African-American woman to star in her own TV series.

CARROLL, Vinnette
1922-

At 25, Carroll was on the verge of completing a Ph.D. in psychology at New York University when she decided to pursue her dream of becoming an actress. In time she would also become Broadway's first African-American woman director. She made her professional debut in 1948 in *The Little Foxes*, and has won an Obie for her performance in *Moon on the Rainbow Shawl* and an Emmy for *Beyond the Blues*. For many years she served as artistic director of the Urban Arts Center, and she shepherded the musicals *Don't Bother Me, I Can't Cope* (1972), *Your Arm's Too Short to Box with God* (1976) and *I'm Laughin' but I Ain't Tickled* (1976) to Broadway.

CARSON, Benjamin Solomon
1951-

Born in Detroit, Michigan, and raised by his mother, Carson was called the "class dummy" in the fifth grade, but his mother, though illiterate, pushed him to read and excel. He went to Yale University on a scholarship, earned his M.D. at the Uni-versity of Michigan (1977) and in 1985 he became the director of pediatric neuro-surgery at Johns Hopkins Hospital (one of only three African-Americans to head pediatric neurosurgery departments). In 1987 he led a 22-member team that suc-cessfully separated Siamese twins, one of the most difficult operations known to medicine. A Seventh-day Adventist, he has always made a point of lecturing to youth groups.

CARTER, Benny (Bennett Lester)
1907-

One of the three most influential alto sax-ophonists of the premodern era, Carter also pioneered composing and arranging in the entertainment industry for African-Americans and jazz musicians. Born in New York City, he worked with Duke Ellington and other major bands of the 1920s and led his own units in the 1930s, at the same time supplying arrangements for Ellington, Goodman, Calloway and others. After settling in Hollywood (1944), for the next 40 years he supplied compositions and arrangements for motion pictures and TV, performed as a soloist, and appeared as artist-in-resi-dence at Princeton and other universities. During the 1970s he recorded with Dizzy Gillespie, Count Basie, and Milt Jackson. He has continued recording and perform-ing into the 1990s.

Benny Carter and daughter in 1935.

CARVER, George Washington
c. 1860-1943

One of the best known agricultural scientists of his generation, Carver was born into slavery near Diamond Grove, Missouri. Slave raiders kidnapped Carver and his mother when he was a six-week old infant. Carver's mother was never recovered, but his owner allegedly ransomed back the infant with a $300 prize race horse. Although Carver had to work and live on his own while still a boy, he managed to finish high school and became the first African-American student to enroll at Simpson College in Indianola, Iowa. He then put himself through the Iowa Agricultural College (now Iowa State University) by working as a janitor, earning a B.S. (1894) and M.S. (1896) in agricultural science. Carver taught briefly at his alma mater – the first African-American to do so – but left in 1896 to join Booker T. Washington at the Tuskegee Institute in George. He directed Tuskegee's agricultural research department continuously until his death in 1943. At Tuskegee, Carver concentrated on persuading Southern farmers to end their virtually exclusive reliance on the cotton farming that had leached the soil of nutrients, producing increasingly poor crops: Carver encouraged farmers to diversify and plant sweet potatoes and peas. In order to make these crops more profitable, Carver did extensive research, producing more than 300 derivative products from the peanut and 118 from the sweet potato. He never patented his discoveries, once remarking that "God gave them to me, how can I sell them to someone else?" In 1923 Carver won the Spingarn award, the highest annual prize given by the National Association for Colored People. In 1938 he took $30,000 – virtually his entire life's savings – and founded the George Washington Carver foundation to continue his work after his death. When he died in 1943 the rest of his estate went to the foundation. He was buried beside his great friend and mentor, Booker T., Washington, on the Tuskegee campus. Carver's epitaph sums up his humanitarianism: "He could have added fortune to fame, but caring for neither, he found happiness and honor in being helpful to the world." The Carver National Monument in Diamond, Missouri, where he spent his boyhood, commemorates his life and accomplishments.

George Washington Carver, with some of his students at Tuskegee Institute.

CHAMBERLAIN, Wilt (Wilton Norman)
1936-

Universally hailed as one of basketball's greatest players, Chamberlain grew up in Philadelphia. When he entered high school he was already 6-ft. 11-in; by the time he left he had attained full growth, 7-ft. 1-in. Well before his graduation from high school his skill at basketball and his great speed had attracted scholarship offers from 77 major colleges and some 125 smaller schools. Chamberlain chose the University of Kansas, where he was an All-American and led the team to the NCAA finals in 1957, but after two years there he left to play professional basketball with the Harlem Globetrotters (1958-1959). He then (1959) was drafted by the Philadelphia Warriors, for whom he played center (1959-1965), and was promptly named rookie-of-the-year. In 1960 he made the first of his 13 appearances in National Basketball Association All-Star games. He played with the Warriors until 1968, then finished his career with the Los Angeles Lakers (1968-1973). A complete list of Chamberlain's statistics – he holds or shares 43 NBA records – would require a volume of their own. Until displaced by Kareem Abdul-Jabbar, he was the leading scorer in NBA history (31,419 points); he has the second highest career scoring average – 30.1 points a game; he has the most career rebounds (23,924) and the most rebounds in a game (55). In his greatest season he averaged 50.4 points a game, scored a record total of 4,029 points, and in his single most memorable game he scored 100 points, with the most field goals (36) and the most free throws (28) in any game. He was named the NBA's most valuable player in 1960, 1966, 1967, and 1968. In 1978 Chamberlain was elected to the Basketball Hall of Fame. After retiring, he became the coach of the short-lived San Diego Conquistadors, but then concentrated on managing his own business interests.

CHARLES, Ray
(b. Ray Charles Robinson)
1930-

Singer, pianist, and composer Ray Charles – "The Genius" – was born in Albany, Georgia. He lost his sight when he was six and learned to play piano and compose in braille at a school for the

Wilt "The Stilt" Chamberlain, when he was with the Philadelphia Warriors.

Ray Charles in 1985.

blind. Orphaned at the age of 15, he began performing and moved to Seattle in 1947. After scoring some hits on Swing Time Records, he switched to Atlantic Records in 1952, and there he began to develop the rougher blues-and-gospel style that became a major influence on black popular music and white rock 'n' roll. In 1955 Charles recorded his landmark hit "I've Got a Woman" with a passionate arrangement of horns, gospel-style piano, and vocals that presaged the soul music of the 1960s, epitomized in his timeless hit "What'd I Say" (1959). The multifaceted Charles has recorded with jazz greats and sold millions of records in genres as diverse as country-and-western and Broadway standards. A cultural icon of the first magnitude, Charles became a major promotional image for Pepsi-Cola and is much in demand for appearances at national patriotic and political events.

CHAVIS, Benjamin Franklin, Jr.
1948-

Clergyman and civil rights activist, he majored in chemistry at the University of North Carolina, then became a minister for United Church of Christ and the Director of its Commission for Racial Justice. In 1971, after a white-owned grocery store was burned down following a racial disturbance in Wilmington, North Carolina, he and nine others (they would soon be known as the Wilmington Ten) were convicted on arson and conspiracy charges. In 1980 the conviction was over-

turned. By that time Chavis had earned a divinity degree from Duke University; later, he earned a Ph.D. in theology from Howard. In 1993 he was named executive director of the National Association for the Advancement of Colored People, but in 1944 he was forced to resign amid controversy.

CHESNUTT, Charles Waddell
1854-1932

After working as a legal stenographer for Dow Jones, Inc., on New York's Wall Street, Chesnutt returned to his native Cleveland, Ohio, in 1887, where he was

Charles Chesnutt.

admitted to the Ohio bar. Until his law practice began to prosper he continued to work as a stenographer and began to write fiction in his spare time. In 1887 the prestigous *Atlantic Monthly* published his short story "The Gophered Grapevine". In 1889 *The Conjure Woman*, a collection of short stories, was published, followed the next year by his first novel, *The House Behind the Cedars*. Although his publications in journals such as the *Atlantic Monthly* helped to eradicate the "color line" in publishing, Chesnutt came in for some criticism from members of the Harlem Renaissance, who found his viewpoint too much limited to that of the educated black middle class.

Shirley Chisholm in 1972.

CHISHOLM, Shirley
(b. Shirley Anita St. Hill)
1924-

The first African-American woman elected to the Congress, Chisholm was born in Brooklyn, New York, but spent her early childhood with her grandparents in Barbados. She received her A.B. degree from Brooklyn College in 1946 and her M.A. from Columbia University in 1952. She taught in Brooklyn and served as an education consultant to New York's Division of Day Care before her election to the state assembly in 1964. In 1968 she was elected, as a Democrat, to the U.S. House of Representatives, where she served until 1982. She was an aggressive advocate of progressive legislation throughout her term, and in 1972 she even campaigned for the Democratic presidential nomination, the first woman and the first African-American to do so. In 1993 President Clinton appointed her ambassador to Jamaica.

CHRISTIAN, Charlie
1916-1942

A major influence on the development of modern jazz and a pioneering guitarist whose rhythmic and harmonic innovations influenced nearly every jazz guitarist who followed him, Christian was born in Dallas, Texas, and raised in Oklahoma City. Exposed to the blues-oriented Kansas City-style jazz, he began playing guitar at the age of 12 and was performing professionally at 15. After joining Benny Goodman's sextet (1939-1941) he liberated the guitar from its strictly rhythmic role by using an electric guitar to play saxophone-like single-note solos. His altered chords and long improvisatory lines greatly influenced Dizzy Gillespie, Charlie Parker, Thelonious Monk, Kenny Clarke, and others involved in the development of bebop at Minton's Playhouse in Harlem.

ABOVE: Eldridge Cleaver in 1968.
LEFT: Kenneth Clark in 1986.

CLARK, Kenneth Bancroft
1914-

A psychologist, he is known for research that revealed the damaging psychological effects of racial segregation on black children in schools. His 1950 report underlay the landmark Supreme Court decision outlawing segregation (*Brown v. Board of Education*, 1954). Educated at Columbia University (Ph.D., 1940), he worked on Gunnar Myrdal's study of racism, *An American Dilemma* (1944), and introduced Americans to "behavioralist" thinking. He was the first African-American member of the New York State Board of Regents (1966). In 1986 he founded a firm to consult on racial issues. His many scholarly writings include *Dark Ghetto* (1965).

CLEAVER, Eldridge
1935-

A social activist and writer, Cleaver was born in Wabbeseka, Arkansas. While serving a 12-year sentence in jail he received his high school diploma. He was also converted to the Black Muslim faith in prison and wrote and lectured after his release. In 1969 he was sentenced to prison after an alleged shoot-out with Oakland police, and he fled the country to avoid the term. He had more legal troubles in Algeria, where he was connected with a skyjacking incident. Returning to the U.S. in 1975 to face charges, he was eventually paroled. In 1984 he ran unsuccessfully for Congress as a conservative independent. His writings include *Soul on Ice* (1968).

COLE, Johnetta
1936-

In 1987 Cole became the first African-American woman to head Spelman College in Atlanta, Georgia. Entertainer Bill Cosby and his wife Camille (a Spelman alumna) honored Cole's appointment with a $20-million gift. Born in Florida, Cole received her A.B. at Oberlin College and her Ph.D. from Northwestern (1967). She has taught at many institutions, including the City College of New York (where she directed the Latin American and Caribbean Studies Program) and Washington State University (where she headed the Black Studies program). She is the author/editor of *All American Women* (1986), *Anthropology for the Nineties* (1988) and *Conversations* (1993).

COLE, Nat "King"
(b. Nathaniel Adams Coles)
1917-1965

A highly influential jazz pianist, Cole was the first African-American male to attain mainstream acceptance as a popular singer and the first African-American to host his own network TV show. Born in Birmingham, Alabama, and raised in Chicago, he began recording with his brother in 1936. The piano-bass-guitar instrumentation of his King Cole Trio was widely emulated in the 1940s and 1950s. Following his national hits "Straighten Up and Fly Right" (1943) and "The Christmas Song" (1946) he de-emphasized his piano playing. Cole appeared in several movies and portrayed W.C. Handy in *St. Louis Blues* (1958). Among his other memorable international hit songs were "It's Only a Paper Moon," "Too Young," "Nature Boy," "Walking My Baby Back Home," and "Unforgettable".

COLEMAN, Bessie
1893-1926

The first African-Americn woman to earn a pilot's license, Coleman was born in Atlanta, Texas. She did manicuring and managed a chili restaurant in Chicago before she turned to aviation. Unable to gain pilot training in the United States, she went to Europe to earn first a local pilot's license (1921) and then an inter-

Nat "King" Cole.

Bessie Coleman in 1923.

national pilot's license (1922). She returned to the United States, where she barnstormed, did stunts, and lectured on aviation. She intended to establish an aviation school for young African-Americans, but she died in a crash in Jacksonville, Florida, when her plane controls jammed. Many people were inspired by her, and numerous Bessie Coleman Aero Clubs were formed.

COLEMAN, Ornette
1930-

Revolutionary, controversial, and masterly, saxophonist and composer Ornette Coleman electrified the jazz world with his first recordings. Born in Fort Worth, Texas, and largely self-taught, Coleman played in rhythm-and-blues bands and settled in Los Angeles in 1951, where he first recorded in 1958. Following his New York debut in 1959, his iconoclastic albums of 1959-1961 helped shape the direction of jazz for the next two decades. A sporadic performer, since the early 1960s he has created several works for symphony orchestra based on his "harmolodic" theory.

COLEMAN, William T., Jr.
1920-

Graduated first in his Harvard Law School class despite the interruption of service in the Amry Air Corps (1943-1945), he became the second African-American to hold a U.S. cabinet post. He was a partner in a prestigious Philadelphia law firm (1956-1975), specializing in corporate, transportation, and civil rights law. He is remembered for his work in *Brown v. Board of Education* (banning school segregation) and *McLaughlin v. Florida* (allowing interracial marriage). He served as U.S. secretary of transportation under President Gerald Ford (1975-1977), then practiced corporate law with O'Melveny & Meyer in Washington.

COLES, Honi (Charles)
1911-1992

Regarded as one of the great virtuosos of tapdancing, Coles was a link between the first generation of American tapdancers and the revival that followed his own rediscovery in the 1970s. While he was growing up in Philadelphia he learned from observing the famous Nicholas Brothers and other tapdancers, and by 1931 he was dancing in New York City with the Three Millers. He went on to dance with the Lucky Seven Trio and Cab Calloway's band; while with the latter, he teamed with Cholly Atkins, and the two would be tap partners for another 25 years. They joined the army during World War II, then returned to dance in New York and at famous theaters and clubs across the U.S.A. and Europe. Coles and Atkins also appeared with many of the great jazz bands and in 1949 performed a show-stopping routine in *Gentlemen Prefer Blonds*. Coles was famous not only for the speed and complexity of his dancing but also for his sophisticated elegance. For about two decades following 1956, when tapdance was in decline with mass audiences, Coles became a choreographer and consultant, but by 1979 he was dancing again on major New York stages. He won a Tony as the best featured actor in a musical for his role in *My One and Only* (1982); he also appeared in the movies *Dirty Dancing* and *The Cotton Club*. In his later years he gave master workshops in tapdancing, taught black dance and history at major universities, and was the recipient of many awards.

William T. Coleman in 1987.

COLTRANE, John
1926-1967

Since his death the most influential and imitated tenor saxophonist in jazz, Coltrane was born in Hamlet, North Carolina, and received his formal music training in Philadelphia. Influenced by Charlie Parker, he worked as a journeyman with many jazz masters, including Dizzy Gillespie, Johnny Hodges, Miles Davis, and Thelonious Monk. Following his acclaimed albums *Giant Steps* and *My Favorite Things* (1960), he began leading his own groups, touring constantly until his illness and death from liver cancer. His instrumental mastery, spiritual intensity, and ferocious quest for musical self-renewal made him one of the most revered and controversial artists in America.

CONE, James Hall
1938-

A revolutionary theologian and educator, Cone was born in Fordyce, Arkansas. He earned his Ph.D. at Northwestern University. He has taught at a number of colleges and universities but has spent most of his career at Union Theological Seminary in New York City. He is best known for his writings on black liberation theology in books such as *Black Theology and Black Power* (1969), *A Black Theology of Liberation* (1970), and *God of the Oppressed* (1975). He also published an impressively thorough comparison of the lives and ideas of Martin Luther King, Jr. and Malcolm X in *Martin and Malcolm in America: A Dream or a Nightmare* (1991).

CONYERS, John, Jr.
1929-

An outspoken member of the U.S. House of Representatives, he is the son of an autoworker. After service in the U.S. Army (1950-1954) he earned his law degree from Wayne State University (1958). As a Democrat representing his Michigan district in Congress since 1965, he was a founder, and is now senior member, of the Congressional Black Caucus and is chairman of the Government Operations Committee. He succeeded in establishing the Martin Luther King federal holiday and has campaigned frequently for the African-Americans. His so-far unsuccessful efforts include securing reparations for descendants of slaves, becoming mayor of Detroit, and dropping the death penalty in drug bills. Although somewhat abrasive, at times when others have chosen a more restrained approach to issues of civil rights he has never been afraid to take controversial stands.

ABOVE: John Coltrane in 1962.
BELOW: John Conyers in 1987.

Will Marion Cook *c.* 1900.

Sam Cooke in 1964.

COOK, Will Marion
1869-1944

Classically trained as a concert violinst at Oberlin College, Ohio, and in Germany, he is best known as a composer for the African-American musical theater in New York. Throughout the 1890s and 1900s he composed for Bert Williams, the leading black comic. His Broadway success, *Clorindy, the Origin of the Cakewalk* (1889), was the first produced entirely by African-American artists. His many works include *In Abyssinia* (1906) and a collection of Negro songs (1912). He toured Europe with his chiefly ragtime Southern Syncopated Orchestra until 1919; therefter he freelanced, influencing Duke Ellington's work.

COOKE, Sam
1931-1964

Blessed with one of the finest voices in recording history, singer and songwriter Cooke merged gospel music with secular themes and provided the foundation for soul music during his own transformation from gospel to pop star. The son of a Baptist minister from Clarkesdale, Mississippi, and raised in Chicago, he began performing with his siblings (the Soul Children) and sang with the Highway QCs and the Soul Stirrers (1951-1956) before scoring his firt pop hit, "You Send Me," in 1957. With the success of his grittier "Chain Gang" (1960) Cooke dominated the charts, influencing singers from Otis Redding to Bob Marley. He was shot to death in a Los Angeles motel in 1964. His exquisite "A Change is Gonna Come" (1965) was a hit posthumously.

COSBY, Bill
1937-

One of the best known, most challenging – and highest paid – entertainers in the world, Cosby was born in Germantown, Pennsylvania. He served in the U.S. Navy before completing high school and then went to Temple University on an athletic scholarship. While in college he began performing at New York's Gaslight Cafe with a stand-up comedy act. Leaving college to pursue an acting career, he first came to national attention with his appearances on TV telling humorous-but-serious stories of his own life. In 1965 he began the TV series *I Spy*; his role as a CIA agent made him the first African-American to star in a dramatic TV series. From 1972 to 1984 Cosby hosted a children's cartoon show called *Fat Albert and the Cosby Kids*, which gained him popularity with young audiences. He chose to pursue his interest in children and education and earned both an M.A. and Ed.D from the Unviersity of Massachusetts. In 1984, increasingly prominent and thus able to set his own terms, Cosby left *Fat Albert and the Cosby Kids* and launched the hugely successful *The Cosby Show*. The weekly TV series was a positive depiction of an African-American middle class family and the first such show to move wholly into the mainstream of television. A spin-off from this show, *A Different World*, also produced by Cosby, enjoyed considerable success. Cosby has never found quite the right movies for his talents, but he has written best-selling books and has been one of the highest paid spokespersons for a variety of products. He has used his wealth to support numerous humanitarian, educational, and cultural causes.

CUFFE, Paul (b. Paul Slocum)
1759-1817

Born in Cuttyhunk Island, Massachusetts, to a free black father and a Native American mother, Cuffe started his career as a sailor. In 1780 he and his brother John argued in a court case to the effect that they should not have to pay taxes since they could not vote; this led Massachusetts to pass a law in 1783 giving African-Americans the same voting rights as white males. Cuffe prospered in the shipping business, and by 1806 he owned

three ships, land, and more than one house. He served as a minister among the Quakers of Westport, Connecticut. He formed the Friendly Society to encourage the resettling of African-Americans in Africa and led a voyage to Sierra Leone in 1815 to advance this cause.

CULLEN, Countee
(b. Countee L. Porter)
1903-1946

Born in Maryland and raised by Rev. and Mrs. Frederick Cullen, his adoptive parents, young Cullen showed promise as a poet while still at New York University (A.B. 1925) and Harvard (M.A. 1926). A prominent figure in the Harlem Renaissance of the 1920s, he spent six years in Paris after winning a Guggenheim fellowship in 1928. Before his untimely death he published one novel *One Way to Heaven* (1932), edited the magazine *Opportuntiy*, and taught in junior high school in New York City (1934-1946). Cullen spoke out reluctantly on racial issues, preferring that readers see his work as transcending race.

LEFT: Bill Cosby (right) in 1990.
BELOW LEFT: Paul Cuffe.
BELOW: Countee Cullen in 1925.

D

DANDRIDGE, Dorothy
1923-1965

One of the first African-American actresses to receive star billing in Hollywood, Dandridge was born in Cleveland, Ohio; her mother was the actress, Ruby Dandridge. She sang and danced as a child, appearing on radio and making her screen debut when she was 14 years old – a small role in *A Day at the Races* (1937). She eventually rose to stardom with her roles in *Carmen Jones* (1954) and *Porgy and Bess* (1959). Her life and success ended early when she went bankrupt, due to a bad financial investment, and she died of a drug overdose.

BELOW: Dorothy Dandridge in 1954.

ABOVE: Angela Davis speaks at a civil rights rally in Raleigh, N.C., in 1974.

DASH, Julie
1951-

This independent filmmaker became the first African-American woman since Kathleen Prettyman to have directed a feature film when her *Daughters of the Dust* was released in 1991. She grew up in a housing project in Queens, New York City, but her father was a Gullah – that is, an African-American from the South Carolina Sea Islands. In the late 1960s Julie Dash attended a film workshop in Harlem and then went on to take a degree in film from the City College of New York. She then studied at the American Film Institute in Los Angeles, and by 1978 she had completed two short films – *Four Women* and *Diary of an African Nun* (the latter based on a short story by Alice Walker). Her 1982 film *Illusions* was named the Best Film of the Decade by the Black Filmmaker Foundation. Relocating to

Georgia, she produced several more short films before obtaining a grant from the Guggenheim Foundation to conduct research on the distinctive Gullah culture; this was incorporated into her original script for *Daughters in the Dust*. Highly acclaimed for her vivid depiction of the Gullah culture at the turn of the 20th century, as well as her ability to convey the memories and heritage of African-American women, Dash is regarded as one of the most promising new American filmmakers.

DAVIS, Angela Y.
1944-

A radical philosopher, Angela Davis has contributed to increasing political and civil rights for American citizens. Born in Birmingham, Alabama, she received her A.B. degree from Brandeis and her Masters from the University of California at San Diego. Politicized through the Black Panther Party, the Southern Non-violent Coordinating Committee, the Che Lumumba group and the Communist Party, she successfully challenged the California state law forbidding Communists from teaching at state universities. Later charged with conspiracy in the case of the Soledad Brothers murder trial, she received international support for her case and was acquitted in 1970. She founded

Gen. Benjamin Davis, Jr., in 1954.

the National Alliance Against Racist and Political Repression, and continues to teach at San Francisco State University and lecture widely. Her books include *Women, Race and Class* (1980) and *Women, Culture and Politics* (1984).

DAVIS, Anthony
1951-

A graduate of Yale University (1975), he is a composer and facile jazz pianist. He co-founded Advent, a free-jazz group, with trombonist George Lewis (1973), and played in trumpeter Leo Smith's New Delta Ahkri band (1974-1977) and with violinist Leroy Jenkins (1977-1979). His opera *X*, based on the life of Malcolm X, was produced in Philadelphia (1985) and New York (1989). Among his recordings are *Of Blues and Dreams* (1978) and *Hidden Voices* (with flutist James Newton, 1979). His improvisational compositions feature complex, atonal lines and simplicity achieved through repetition.

DAVIS, Benjamin Oliver, Jr.
1912-

Son of General Benjamin Oliver Davis, Sr., Davis, Jr., was graduated from West Point (1936) and was one of the first African-Americans admitted to the Air Corps and pilot training. He organized the all-black 99th Fighter Squadron in World War II. Active in the Korean War, he be-

came the first African-American major-general (1959) and lieutenant-general (1965). He was chief of staff of the U.S. forces in Korea (1965-1968). He retired from the military in 1970 and became the director of public safety for Cleveland, Ohio (1970-1971). He served as the assistant secretary of the U.S. Department of Transportation from 1971 to 1975.

Gen. Benjamin Davis, Sr., in 1944.

DAVIS, Benjamin Oliver, Sr.
1887-1970

Born in Washington D.C., Davis attended Howard University (1897-1898) and joined the U.S. Army at the start of the Spanish-American War. During his long army career (1898-1948) he saw combat in three wars and taught military science and tactics at both Wilberforce University and Tuskegee Institute. In 1940 he was promoted to brigadier general, the first African-American to reach general's rank. He was assistant inspector general of the army from 1945 to 1948.

ABOVE: Ossie Davis (left) and Spike Lee in *Do the Right Thing* (1989).
OPPOSITE: Miles Davis in 1990.

DAVIS, Miles
1926-1991

One of the foremost jazz musicians of the century, trumpeter Miles Davis – known internationally to his fans simply as ''Miles'' – set styles in demeanor and sartorial elegance as well as in music. Born to a well-to-do professional family in Alton, Illinois, he was raised near St. Louis and began playing trumpet in local bands. After classical studies at The Juilliard School in New York City (1944) he played in Charlie Parker's innovative bebop quintet until 1948. Miles remained in the vanguard of jazz exploration from 1949 to 1969, developing and advancing several contrasting styles informed by his distinctive, brooding trumpet voice. These included cool jazz, as exemplified in his album *Kind of Blue* (1959); hard bop; modal jazz; fusion; and innovative orchestral collaborations with arranger Gil Evans. The young talent he attracted and cultivated in his bands included such giants as John Coltrane, Cannonball Adderley, Bill Evans, and Herbie Hancock. The electrified jazz of his final two decades alienated much of his original audience, but his instrumental mastery continues to enthrall and inspire new generations of listeners and performers.

DAVIS, Ossie
1917-

Davis, who was born in Cogdell, Georgia, has been a successful stage, film, and TV actor since the late 1940s. Between 1938 and 1941 he attended Howard University, from which he received an honorary doctorate in 1973. His first stage appearance was in *Jeb* (1946); young actress Ruby Dee was also in the play, and they married in 1948. Some of Davis's best-known Broadway roles were in Lorraine Hansberry's *Raisin in the Sun* and his own play, *Purlie Victorious*. His films include *Cotton Comes to Harlem, Black Girl*, and *The Joe Louis Story* (1953). He has been seen frequently on television, his first appearance being in *The Emperor Jones* in 1955. He testified before a 1962 Congressional committee investigating racial discrimination in show business and in 1975 represented African-Americans at the World Festival of Black and African Arts and Culture.

DAVIS, Sammy, Jr.
1925-1990

Best known in later years for his appearances in Las Vegas and on TV, the diminutive Davis's extraordinary versatility and vitality epitomized the best of old-time vaudeville. Born in New York City to vaudeville dancers, he began performing at the age of four and starred in the first of his 20-odd movies at age six. Coached by legendary tap-dancer Bill ''Bojangles'' Robinson, he starred with his father and his adopted uncle in the popular song-and-dance Will Mastin Trio, in which he performed as a singer, dancer, impersonator, and instrumentalist. After Davis returned from his army service (1943-1945) the trio experienced phenomenal success. In 1954 Davis released the first of 40 solo records; in that year he also lost an eye in an automobile accident. He subsequently drew fire from some critics for his conversion to Judaism (1956) and his marriage to white

Sammy Davis, Jr., plays, as Dean Martin and Frank Sinatra look on.

actress Mai Britt. Billed as the "world's greatest entertainer," he made a stunning Broadway debut in *Mr. Wonderful* (1956), opening the door to more films. A phenomenal solo act by the late 1950s and a core member of Frank Sinatra's "Rat Pack" clique, his success on stage, screen, and records peaked into the early 1970s. After brief time out, he returned to the stage in the 1980s, touring North America with Sinatra and Dean Martin in 1988 and Europe with them, as well as Liza Minnelli, in 1989.

DE CARAVA, Roy
1919-

Known for 40 years' photographs of the people of Harlem, he first studied architecture and sculpture at Cooper Union (1938-1940), then painting and printmaking at the Harlem Art Center (1940-1942). From work as a commercial artist (1944-1958), he pursued freelance photography with magazines such as *McCall's, Look, Newsweek*, and *Life* (1959-1968 and after 1975). He was a contract photographer for *Sports Illustrated* (1968-1975). He won the first Guggenheim fellowship awarded to an African-American photographer (1952). His photos in *The Family of Man* (1955) toured the world. Since 1975 he has taught at Hunter College.

DEE, Ruby
1923-

A distinguished actress, Dee met her future husband and frequent acting-partner, Ossie Davis, when they appeared in the play *Jeb* in 1946; they married in 1948. By then Dee had already appeared in *South Pacific* and several other Broadway productions. Her many movies include *No Way Out, Edge of the City, Raisin in the Sun*, and *The Balcony*. She has also acted in a number of Shakespearean roles and was the first African-American actress to have major roles at the American Shakespeare Festival in Stratford, Connecticut.

DELANY, Martin Robison
1812-1885

This precursor of twentieth-century African-American militancy was born to a free black woman and an enslaved father in Charles Town, Virginia (now in West Virginia). The family moved to Pennsylvania in 1823, and in 1831 young Delany apprenticed himself to a doctor in Pittsburgh. He founded an African-American magazine, *Mystery* (1843-1847), and worked on behalf of the abolitionist cause. He was admitted to the Harvard Medical School in 1850 but was soon forced out because of his classmates' protests. Now convinced that African-Americans could never attain full equality in the United States, he began to consider resettling in Canada or Latin America. In 1859 he went to Africa to seek land there, and that same year published a novel, *Blake, or the Huts of America*, about a slave insurrection. During the Civil War he helped organize all-black regiments for the Union Army, and in 1865 he became the first African-American to obtain the rank of major. After the war he held several federal offices in Charleston, South Carolina, and ran unsuccessfully for lieutenant-governor of the state (1874). With the end of the Reconstruction period, he moved to Xenia, Ohio, but he continued to speak out for the rights of African-Americans.

DELLUMS, Ronald V.
1935-

Born in Oakland, California, Dellums served in the Marine Corps before attending San Francisco State College (A.B., 1960), and the University of California at Berkeley (M.A., 1962). He worked as a psychiatric social worker in Berkeley before his election, as a Democrat, to the U.S. House of Representatives in 1972. He has been a harsh critic of U.S. military policy and a strong advocate of civil liberties. In 1983 he became chairman of the Subcommittee on Military Installations and Facilities, and in 1988 he was elected to chair the Congressional Black Caucus. In 1993 he became the first African-American to chair the House Armed Services Committee.

Rep. Ron Dellums became Chairman of the House Armed Services Committee in 1993.

DEPRIEST, James Anderson
1936-

A composer and critically acclaimed conductor and the nephew of Marian Anderson, he attended the University of Pennsylvania (B.S., 1958; M.A., 1961) and the Philadelphia Conservatory of Music (1959-1961). He composed several ballet scores (1960-1965). Stricken with polio while touring the Far East for the U.S. State Department (1962), he persevered, conducting in Bangkok (1963-1964). He won the Mitropoulos conducting competition in 1964, and in the late 1960s held conducting positions in Rotterdam, Washington, D.C., and Quebec. In 1980 he became director of the Oregon Symphony. He has also published two volumes of poetry (1987, 1989).

Rep. and Mrs. Oscar Depriest in 1929, when he was the only black Congressman.

DEPRIEST, Oscar Stanton
1871-1951

The son of freed slaves, DePriest was born in Florence, Alabama. He moved north and worked as a painter and decorator in Chicago. He became a real estate broker and was the first African-American to serve on Chicago's City Council (1915-1917). He served in the U.S. House of Representatives (1929-1935), where he fought against the Jim Crow laws. Failing of election in 1934 and 1936, he returned to the real estate business and served again on Chicago's City Council (1943-1947).

DIDDLEY, Bo (b. Otha Ellas McDaniel)
1928-

One of rock 'n' roll's earliest African-American stars and a major influence on music, guitarist Diddley was born in McComb, Mississippi. He worked as a street-corner gospel and blues singer before recording for Chess records in Chicago in 1955. Touring widely and making numerous TV appearances through the mid-1960s, his popularity as a recording artist gradually waned, but he has remained a vital concert performer. Inducted into the Rock 'n' Roll Hall of Fame in 1987, the irrepressible rock pioneer returned to TV as a rock icon in commercials.

ABOVE: Mayor David and Mrs. Dinkins at the time of his election in 1989.

DINKINS, David
1927-

The first African-American mayor of New York City, Dinkins was born in Trenton, New Jersey, and practiced as a lawyer before entering politics in 1966. He worked his way up in New York City Democratic Party politics, serving for years as an assemblyman, on the Board of Elections, as a city clerk, and then (1986-1989) as the president of the borough of Manhattan. He was elected mayor in 1989 and served his term amidst heightened racial tension in the city. Despite his strong support from African-American and white liberal communities, he lost the election in 1993.

DIVINE, Father (b. George Baker)
?1877-1965

ABOVE: Father Divine, at a celebration in one of his "Heavens" in 1937.
RIGHT: Fats Domino in 1956.

Born near Savannah, Georgia, he began preaching about 1900 and became an important advocate for racial justice. He founded his first "heaven," or communal dwelling, in 1919. During the Depression his Peace Mission provided food and housing to thousands of people in Harlem and throughout the U.S. His movement featured communal living; vows of morality, celibacy, and charity; and racial equality. It grew to include 178 "heavens," mostly in New York and Philadelphia. By the 1960s it owned property worth $10 million, but its value declined soon after Divine's death.

DIXON, Dean
1915-1976

A conductor widely admired in Europe, he studied violin and conducting at The Julliard School (1932-1939), earned an M.A. at Columbia University (1939), and founded the New York Chamber Orchestra (1938) and the American Youth Orchestra (1944). Eleanor Roosevelt helped him become the first African-American to conduct the New York Philharmonic (1941). In Europe he led the Göteborg Symphony (1953-1960), the Hessian Radio Orchestra (1961-1970), and the Sydney (Australia) Symphony (1964-1967). In 1970 he conducted summer concerts of the New York Philharmonic in Central Park. He made his final home in Switzerland in 1974.

DOMINO, Fats (Antoine)
1928-

An archetypal New Orleans singer and pianist who cut his teeth in his home town honky tonks, Domino was one of the first African-American rhythm-and-blues artists to achieve mainstream white acceptance. "The Fat Man" (1950) was his first million-selling record. He headlined rock 'n' roll shows between 1954 and 1968 on the strength of such hits as "Ain't That A Shame" (1955), "Blueberry Hill" (1956), and "Blue Monday" (1957). Since the

1970s his public appearances have been mostly confined to New Orleans. He received a Grammy Lifetime Achievement Award in 1987 and in 1993 released a Christmas album, his first recording in many years.

DOUGLASS, Frederick
(b. Frederick Augustus Washington Bailey)
1817-1895

An editorial in the *Washington Post* on Douglass's death said that he "died in an epoch which he did more than any other to create." Born into slavery to a mother of African-American descent and a white father, he escaped from his Baltimore shipyard apprenticeship in 1838 and fled to New Bedford, Massachusetts. There he took the name Douglass, was befriended by abolitionist William Lloyd Garrison, and became active in the abolition movement. In 1841, after giving a fiery speech to the Massachusetts Anti-Slavery Society, he found himself in great demand as a speaker. His skills as an orator won him the sobriquet the "cataract that roared."

In 1845 he published the autobiographical *Narrative of the Life of Frederick Douglass, an American Slave*; its elegant prose astonished readers who knew that Douglass was self-taught. The book received enormous attention and, fearing that a bounty hunter might capture him and return him to his master, Douglass sailed for England, where he lectured widely and earned enough money to purchase his freedom when he returned to the United States in 1847. Settling in Rochester, New York, Douglass embarked on a career as an editor and publisher, co-founding the abolitionist paper *North Star*, which he edited from 1847 to 1851, when he changed its name to *Frederick Douglass's Paper*. In 1859 he again fled the United States, this time to Canada, after being implicated in John Brown's raid on Harper's Ferry. He returned to the United States during the Civil War and worked to open military service to African-Americans, influencing President Lincoln to found the 54th and 55th Massachusetts Negro regiments. After the Civil War, Douglass held a series of government appointments: assis-

tant secretary to the Santo Domingo Commission, marshal of the District of Columbia (1887-1881), district recorder of deeds (1881-1886), and ambassador to Haiti and chargé d'affaires for Santo Domingo (1889-1891). He resigned his ambassadorship in protest against the exploitation of the impoverished island by U.S. business interests. In 1881 he published an updated version of his autobiography, *Life and Times of Frederick Douglass*. Standing well over six feet tall, Douglass loomed over his contemporaries literally as well as figuratively. Dedicated to equal rights for African-Americans, he spoke out forcibly for equal rights for women after the Civil War, proclaiming that "Right is of no sex." His energy was prodigous: in his seventies he began to learn French, and he gave his last speech (to the National Council of Women in Washington, D.C.) on the day he died. On learning of Douglass's death, one awed contemporary asked, "Were ever so many miracles crowded into a single life?"

Frederick Douglass, flanked by Senators Blanche Kelso Bruce and Hiram Revels.

HEROES OF THE COLORED RACE.

Rita Dove in 1992.

DOVE, Rita
1953-

The first African-American poet laureate of the United States, Dove was born in Akron, Ohio. She took her A.B. at Miami University (Ohio), did a year's postgraduate study in Germany, and earned her M.F.A. at the University of Iowa. While in Germany she met her husband, Fred Viebahn, a writer. She became serious about her poetry in college and went on to win high acclaim for her work, including a Pulitzer Prize for her *Thomas and Beulah* (1987). She taught at a number of universities throughout the 1980s and in 1989 joined the faculty of the University of Virginia, where she remains today. In 1993 she was named the Library of Congress's poet laureate.

DRAKE, St. Clair
1911-1990

Known as co-author of *Black Metropolis* (1946), a landmark study of Chicago's ghetto, he was a widely esteemed sociologist and cultural anthropologist. His studies on Pan-African topics, urban anthropology, and race relations theory gained him international honors, awards, and appointments. He taught at Dillard University (New Orleans, Louisiana; 1935-1936); Roosevelt University (Chicago; 1946-1968); the University of Liberia (1954); the University of Ghana (1958-1961); and Stanford University (1969-1976), where he became the first permanent director of African and Afro-American Studies. He advised African leaders and helped develop Peace Corps training programs, advocating interracial harmony and nonviolent social change.

DREW, Charles
1904-1950

The man who discovered the modern processes for preserving blood for life-saving transfusions, Charles Drew grew up in a solid but poor African-American family in a Washington D.C., ghetto. His intelligence and athletic skill won him a scholarship to Amherst College, where he was captain of the track team, the starting halfback on the football team, and an honors student. Upon graduation in 1926 he was awarded the Messman Trophy, given to the graduating senior deemed to have brought the most honor to the college. For the next two years Drew taught and coached at Morgan College (now Morgan State) in Baltimore, Maryland, to earn money to attend the medical school at McGill University in Montreal, Canada. There he became increasingly interested in the general field of medical research and in the specific problems of blood transfusion. After graduation from McGill in 1932 Drew did his three-year residency at Montreal General Hospital before joining the faculty of Howard University in 1935. In 1938 he took a two-year break from Howard to pursue a D.Sci. degree at Columbia University. His dissertation was on the topic of what was to be his most important work: the preservation of blood plasma, which Drew referred to as "baked blood." Back at Howard, Drew was appointed head of the department of surgery, a position he held until his death in a car crash in 1950.

St. Clair Drake *c.* 1965.

During the last decade of his life Drew continued his pioneering research into the separation and preservation of blood. In 1940-1941 he spent time in New York City as director of the American Red Cross blood donor project, spearheading the Plasma for Britain program. This important war effort led to his being appointed head of the U.S. National Blood Bank program when the U.S. entered World War II in 1941. Furious at the official government policy that mandated that whites' and African-Americans' blood would be given only to members of their respective races, he resigned from his post and returned to Howard. In 1944 he became chief of surgery at Freedmen's Hospital in Washington, D.C., where his presence encouraged other young African-Americans to enter the field of medicine.

Dr. Charles Drew c. 1941.

DU BOIS, W.E.B.
(William Edward Burghardt)
1868-1963

Born in Great Barrington, Massachusetts, he became the most respected and effective spokesperson for the full rights of African-Americans in the decades before World War II. His public school headmaster in Great Barrington recognized Du Bois's great potential and persuaded the local Congregational Church to send the youth to college. In 1888 Du Bois earned an A.B. degree at Tennessee's Fiske University, where he had his first experience of overt racial prejudice. Returning to Massachusetts, in rapid succession he earned a second A.B. (1890) and an M.A. (1891) at Harvard and then spent two years studying at the University of Berlin (1892-1894) before becoming the first African-American to earn his Ph.D. from Harvard (1895). Du Bois taught

W.E.B. Du Bois in 1928.

Greek and Latin at Wilberforce University (1894-1896) and, thereafter, sociology at the University of Pennsylvania (1896-1897) and Atlanta University (1897-1910; 1933-1944). Throughout his life Du Bois combined an illustrious academic career with his work for full rights for African-Americans. He is perhaps best-known for his work in founding the National Association for the Advancement of Colored People in 1909 and helping it to become the country's single most influential organization for African-Americans. Over the years Du Bois served in various capacities at the NAACP: he held office continuously from 1909 to 1948 as director of publicity and publications except when he chaired the department of sociology at Atlanta University (1933-1944). Throughout, Du Bois published widely and prolifically. One of his most influential books was *The Souls of Black Folks* (1903), a collection of essays in which he stated that "the color line" posed twentieth-century America's greatest challenge. In the same book he argued – directly against the beliefs of Booker T. Washington – for the creation of a black elite, which he called the "talented ten percent." This elite, Du Bois felt, would win social equality for African-Americans by winning the respect of powerful educated whites. Over the years, Du Bois was often disheartened by African-Americans' lack of progress. In 1916 this led him to urge those interested in civil rights to vote for the socialist presidential candidate, and after

W.E.B. Du Bois (standing) in the office of the NAACP magazine *Crisis*.

World War I he turned from socialism to Marxism. Frustrated by the slow progress in civil rights at home, he increasingly looked abroad, espousing the cause of Pan-Africanism, for which he won the NAACP's highest annual prize, the Spingarn award, in 1920. But in 1934 he resigned from the NAACP to protest their goal of accommodation with white society. During the McCarthy era Du Bois's radical views led to an investigation by the Justice Department, which accused him of being a foreign agent. Du Bois was acquitted, but he lost his passport (1952-1958). Increasingly disillusioned with life in the United States, he visited Europe and the Soviet Union (where he was awarded the Lenin Peace Prize in 1959) after he regained his passport. In 1961 he announced that he had joined the Communist Party and emigrated to Accra, Ghana, at the age of 93. Two years later he died there, shortly after becoming a naturalized citizen.

As the passions he aroused by endorsing communism have subsided, Du Bois has been increasingly honored.

DUNBAR, Paul Lawrence
1872-1906

The son of former slaves, Dunbar was a precocious child who began to write poems when he was only a boy of six in Dayton, Ohio. When Dunbar was 12 his father died, and he and his mother supported themselves by delivering laundry. He was graduated from high school (the only African-American in his class), where he was president of the school literary society and editor of the school newspaper. Unable to attend college, he sought work in journalism, but no jobs were available for African-Americans, and he had to settle for a job as an elevator operator. In 1893 he published his first book of poetry, *Oak and Ivory* (1893). His second volume, *Majors and Minors* (1895) caught the eye of critic William Dean Howells, who wrote the introduction to Dunbar's *Lyrics of Lowly Life* (1896). For

Undated portrait of Paul Lawrence Dunbar.

a number of years, Dunbar toured both the United States and England giving readings. He was one of the first African-American writers widely read by whites.

DUNHAM, Katherine
1912-

Katherine Dunham has been called the "mother of Afro-American dance." Born in Chicago, she attended the University of Chicago, where she did her undergraduate and graduate work in anthropology, earning a Ph.D. Her interest in anthropology was not merely scholarly, and field trips to the Caribbean (especially Haiti) and Brazil filled her with the desire to blend traditional European dance forms with African dance forms and rituals. She founded her own dance company in 1930 and during the 1930s she was the dance director for the Works Progress Administration's Chicago theater project. Her first commercial success was the musical *Cabin in the Sky* (1940), in which she performed and for which she had done the choreography. After World War II she toured Europe, America, the Caribbean and South America with her troupe. In 1967 concerns for inner city youth led her to found a performing arts center and free dance school in East Saint Louis. In 1979 she recived the Albert Schweitzer Music Award. Her involvement in dance and social issues continued: in 1992 she went on a hunger strike to protest the U.S. deportation of Haitian refugees.

Katherine Dunham *c.* 1950. Famous as the "mother of Afro-American dance," she is also known for her social activism.

EDELMAN, Marian Wright
1939-

A prominent children's rights activist and attorney, Edelman was born in Bennettsville, South Carolina. Early in her career she worked with the National Association for the Advancement of Colored People as a legal defense fund attorney. In 1968 she founded the Washington Public Policy Research Center. She is perhaps best known for her work with the Childrens Defense Fund, which she started in 1973. Her work in the area of children's rights has linked her with Hillary Clinton, both as a friend and a professional associate. She has recently published *The Measure of Our Success: A Letter to My Children and Yours* (1992).

EDWARDS, Harry
1942-

A sociologist and sports consultant, he played basketball and threw the discus as an undergraduate at San Jose State College (California.) He received his M.A.

BELOW: Marian Wright Edelman in 1992.

(1966) and his Ph.D. (1972) from Cornell University. He urged African-American athletes to boycott the 1968 summer Olympics to protest South Africa's apartheid system. He joined the faculty of the University of Californa at Berkeley in 1970, receiving tenure in 1977. His books include *Revolt of the Black Athlete* (1969). He has been a consultant for football, bas-

ABOVE: Harry Edwards in 1968.

ketball, and baseball teams and is popular on TV and on the lecture circuit, promoting fairness for minorities in sport.

ELDERS, M. (Minnie) Joycelyn
1933-

The first African-American ever to hold the position of United States Surgeon General, Elders was born in a poor family in Schaal, Arkansas. She was certified as a physical therapist after joining the army in 1952 and received her medical degree (1960) from University of Arkansas Medical School in Little Rock. She taught at UAMS and became a professor of pediatrics and then a certified pediatric endocrinologist. She was appointed the director of Arkansas Department of Health in 1987 and then, in 1993, was named United States Surgeon General by President Clinton. In that role she has been steadfast in her support of both abortion rights and AIDS funding.

ABOVE: Duke Ellington (at the piano) and band in 1945

ELLINGTON, Duke (Edward Kennedy)
1899-1974

Celebrated during his lifetime for his keyboard virtuosity and his internationally famous Duke Ellington Orchestra, the touchstone of big band jazz for almost half a century, Duke Ellington is now recognized as one of the major American composers of the twentieth century. Born in Washington, D.C., where his father was a White House butler, Ellington began studying painting and piano at the age of six and received his nickname "Duke" from a boyhood friend. In 1914 he began playing ragtime piano at a Washington cafe and wrote his first composition, "Soda Fountain Rag". He won a poster contest sponsored by the National Association for the Advancement of Colored People in 1917 and left high school to oper-

ate his own sign-painting company, but declined a scholarship to Pratt Institute in order to devote himself exclusively to music. In 1923 he moved to New York, where his trio, The Washingtonians, made its first recordings. In 1927 he premiered the Duke Ellington Orchestra at Harlem's Cotton Club. In 1933, already established as one of the world's foremost jazz composers and bandleaders through his numerous radio broadcasts and recordings, Ellington lead his orchestra on its first European tour. Between 1930 and 1942 he created most of his signature compositions, including "Sophisticated Lady," "Don't Get Around Much Anymore," "Mood Indigo," and "In a Sentimental Mood". He premiered *Black, Brown and Beige* at Carnegie Hall in 1943 and continued to introduce extended works there annually through 1948. One of the few jazz orchestra leaders to keep

his band intact during the early 1950s, following his 1956 appearance at the Newport Jazz Festival his popularity underwent a dramatic renewal. He was the first African-American composer to write a soundtrack for a major Hollywood film, *Anatomy of a Murder* (1959). (He had already made many movie appearances, beginning in 1930.) In the 1960s and 1970s he wrote large-scale suites as well as liturgical music for cathedral concerts in the U.S., England, and Germany. Ellington's numerous honors include the Presidential Medal of Freedom (1969). He was the first jazz musician inducted into Sweden's Royal Academy of Music (1971). He continued touring with his band until shortly before his death, by which time he was recognized as a national treasure.

Ralph Ellison in 1964.

ELLISON, Ralph Waldo
1914-1994

Ellison's first – and only – novel, *Invisible Man* (1952) made his reputation, winning the National Book Award for fiction and becoming both a best seller and a durable classic portrait of the alienation of African-American men. Ellison was born in Oklahoma City, Oklahoma, and studied music at the famous Tuskegee In-stitute before his interests in the Arts and literature led him to settle in New York City in the late 1930s. There he met Richard Wright, whose protégé he be-came. Wright introduced him to many authors he had not previously read, in-cluding T.S. Eliot, whose poetry made a profound impression on Ellison. In 1955 the American Academy of Arts and Letters gave Ellison the Prix de Rome, and he spent several years living in Italy. Thereafter, he taught at a number of American colleges and universities, in-cluding Bennington College, Rutgers University, and New York University, where he was the Albert Schweitzer Pro-fessor in the Humanities (1970-1990). His many honors include the Medal of Free-dom, presented by President Nixon in 1969, the Langston Hughes Medallion of the City College of New York (1984), and the National Medal of Arts, awarded by President Reagan in 1980. In addition to the novel that made his reputation, he published several collections of essays, in-cluding *Shadow and Act* (1964) and *Going to the Territory* (1986).

EVERS, James Charles
1922-

A prominent civil rights leader, Evers was born in Decatur, Mississippi. He served in the Korean War, then lived in Chicago in the late 1950s and early 1960s, where he ran a nightclub. The assassination of his brother Medgar in 1963 prompted his re-turn to Mississippi, and he took over Med-gar's post as field director of the National Association for the Advancement of Colored People in Mississippi. In 1969 he was elected mayor of the town of Fayette, Mississippi, making him the first African-American mayor of a racially mixed Southern town. Later he ran unsuccess-fully for governor and for the U.S. Senate. In 1973 he was re-elected mayor.

EVERS, Medgar Wiley
1925-1963

An effective civil rights leader, Medgar Evers was born in Decatur, Mississippi, and joined the National Association for the Advancement of Colored People in 1954. That same year he became the NAACP field secretary in Mississippi. He traveled the state helping African-Americans to register for voting and urging boycotts of racist merchants. In 1963 he was assassinated, and his death spurred both a more energized struggle in Mississippi for civil rights and faster Con-gressional action on anti-discrimination legislation. (His alleged murderer, a white racist named Byron de la Beckwith, went free after two juries in the 1960s could not agree on a decision, but Beckwith was tried again and convicted in 1994.)

Medgar Evers, with Roy Wilkins (left), is arrested during a 1963 protest.

Louis Farrakhan, controversial leader of The Final Call to the Nation of Islam.

FAGAN, Garth
1941-

Widely admired as a dance teacher and choreographer, he was born in Jamaica and began dancing with that island-nation's National Dance Company. After a spell with the Dance Theater of Detroit, he began to teach dance at the State University of New York at Brockport (near Rochester). By 1970 he had formed some of his African-American students into an amateur dance group, the Bucket Dance Theater, which soon was exciting audiences with its mix of modern dance and Afro-Caribbean traditions. Fagan went on to gain acclaim for such works as *Griot New York*, a group of dances to compositions by Wynton Marsalis.

James Farmer (left) and Jackie Robinson at a 1964 political rally.

FARMER, James
1920-

A charismatic civil rights activist, he founded the Congress of Racial Equality (CORE) in 1942 and was its national director (1961-1966). During the early 1960s he led Freedom Riders in desegregating interstate bus terminals and deliberately serving consequent prison terms. He led a national adult literacy project (1966), wrote *Freedom When?* (1965) and an autobiography (1985), and served as executive director of the Coalition of American Public Employees (1972-1982). Best known for popularizing nonviolent direct action, he received 17 honorary doctorates and became a professor at Mary Washington College in 1985.

FARRAKHAN, Louis
(b. Louis Eugene Walcott)
1933-

Little in his boyhood indicated that Farrakhan would become such a fervent and outspoken leader, but his life changed when, as a young man, he met Malcolm X and became a member of the Nation of Islam. Born in the Bronx section of New York City, Farrakhan grew up in Roxbury, Massachusetts, where the discrimination that he experienced made him think that African-Americans could not earn equality in white America. After his conversion to Islam, Farrakhan was initially close to Malcolm X, but in 1963, when Malcolm left the movement, Elijah Muhammad appointed Farrakhan to be his national representative. In 1975 Muhammad's son announced that whites would be allowed to join the Nation of Islam, something that Farrakhan totally opposed. Consequently, Farrakhan left the Nation of Islam and formed a new movement, the Final Call to the Nation of Islam. Since then Farrakhan has worked for black separatism, which he feels can best be advanced by strengthening the economic power of the black community. Often accused of being anti-white and anti-semitic, largely because of his fiery speeches, he has consistently maintained that he is not a racist. In 1989, when he spoke (along with the Reverend Al Sharpton) at the funerals of Yusef Hawkins, an African-American youth killed by a gang of white hooligans in the Bensonhurst section of Brooklyn, he appealed to the common experience of suffering shared by

Jews and African-Americans. "We say," Farrakhan said, "as the Jews say: Never again. Never again. Never again." But, so far, such small peace offerings have failed to satisfy most of his critics.

FAUSET, Jessie Redmon
1886-1961

In recent years Fauset's novels, including *There is Confusion* (1924), have been "rediscovered" and praised for their portraits of strong, independent African-American women. After graduation, Phi Beta Kappa, from Cornell University in 1905, Fauset studied at the Sorbonne in Paris. This was the beginning of her life-long interest in black Francophone writers. During the 1920s she was active in the Pan-African movement, edited a children's magazine, *The Brownie's Book*, and served as literary editor of the National Association for the Advancement of Colored People's magazine *Crisis* (1919-1926). Over the years she supported herself by teaching in high school, as well as at Hampton Institute in Hampton, Virginia. She is credited with having played an important editorial role in nurturing the writings of authors such as Claude McKay, Countee Cullen, and Langston Hughes.

FITZGERALD, Ella
1918-

A celebrated and influential vocalist famous for her exceptionally clear tone and instrument-like improvisatory scat solos, Fitzgerald was born in Newport News, Virginia, and raised in Yonkers, New York. After winning first prize in an amateur night contest at Harlem's Apollo Theatre (1934) she worked with Chick Webb's big band, scoring her first hit with "A-Tisket, A-Tasket" (1938) and leading the band for two years after Webb's death in 1939. In 1946 she was a featured soloist in the Jazz at the Philharmonic series. During the 1950s her increasingly commercial recordings included a series of collections of standards by Gershwin, Cole Porter, and others ("Songbooks"). She also began her famous collaborations with Louis Armstrong and recorded outstanding work with the Oscar Peterson Trio. During the 1960s she continued performing with small groups and big bands, notably with Duke Ellington in 1966. She sang with symphony orchestras throughout the world in the 1970s and remained an active performer TV and recordings.

OPPOSITE: Ella Fitzgerald (left) in 1952.

Christian Fleetwood in 1864.

FLEETWOOD, Christian Abraham
1840-1914

Born in Baltimore, Maryland, to free African-American parents, Fleetwood was graduated from Ashmun Institute (later Lincoln University). He enlisted in the Union Army (1863), was promoted to sergeant-major, and was awarded the Congressional Medal of Honor for heroism at the battle of Chafin's Farm (1864). He was commanding officer of the Sixth Battalion of the D.C. National Guards (1887-1892), and he taught military science at the Colored High School Cadet Corps (1888-1897). In his retirement he was a choirmaster and, with his wife, was active in the social life of Washington, D.C.

FLIPPER, Henry Ossian
1856-1940

The first African-American to be graduated from West Point, Flipper suffered much from prejudice and jealousy. Born in Thomasville, Georgia, to enslaved parents, Flipper endured four years of harrassment in order to receive his diploma from the U.S. Military Academy (1877). Fellow officers subsequently accused him of theft, and he was court-martialed and discharged (1882). He pursued a long and honorable career as a mining engineer, an author, and a translator of Spanish land grants in the West, but his efforts to win reinstatement were fruitless. Long after his death the army finally changed the discharge from dishonorable to honorable (1976).

FLOOD, Curt (Curtis Charles)
1938-

When Flood sued major league baseball in 1970 he lost the case in the Supreme Court on a technicality but ushered in a new financial era for professional ballplayers. Traded by the Cardinals to the down-and-out Phillies, Flood refused to go. His request for free agency was denied, so he filed a lawsuit on the grounds of anti-trust violations. Flood had been named to the All-star squad three times and had played in three World Series for the Cardinals. He batted over .300 six times, and earned seven consecutive Gold Glove Awards.

Curt Flood in 1968.

Rube Foster *c.* 1925

FORTUNE, Timothy Thomas
1856-1928

A journalist and activist who spent his life in advancing the position of African-Americans, he was born into slavery in Marianna Township, Florida. Freed in 1865, he grew up observing the failures of the Reconstruction. In 1876 he moved to Washington, D.C., but after being unable to afford Howard University, he turned to working for the *People's Advocate*, an African-American newspaper. In 1880 he moved to New York City, where he founded, worked on, or edited several newspapers – his most notable association being with *The New York Age* (1884-1887, 1891-1907). He is credited with coining the term "Afro-American" as a substitute for "Negro," and he was president of the Afro-American League (1890-1893). From 1909 to 1916 he edited periodicals in various Eastern seaboard cities, and in 1917 he became secretary of the Negro Welfare Bureau of New Jersey. He edited *The Negro World* (1923-1928) for Marcus Garvey's cause. During his long career he was associated with virtually every prominent African-American leader, from Frederick Douglass and Booker T. Washington to Marcus Garvey, and although he was sometimes criticized for not being militant enough, he helped to lay the foundations for many of the concepts, movements, and organizations that have influenced later generations of African-Americans.

FOSTER, Rube (Andrew)
1879-1930

Overcoming childhood illness and parental objections, Foster became an outstanding pitcher, a shrewd manager, and the dominant executive of Negro Leagues baseball. He developed the Leland Giants into the team with the best record ever, 123-6 in 1910. Foster established the Negro National League in 1920 in order to organize finances and improve gate receipts in black baseball. It operated in the Midwest from 1920 to 1931, with Foster as its president until 1926. He was elected to the Baseball Hall of Fame in 1981.

FOXX, Redd
(b. John Elroy Sanford)
1922-1991

A comedian who became one of the highest paid actors in television, he was famous as Fred Sanford in the TV series "Sanford and Son" (1972-1977). For many years he had played the black vaudeville circuit in Chicago and New York. His X-rated scatalogical humor limited bookings in the 1950s, but his party records sold over 20 million copies, and he later played the Las Vegas nightclubs. He appeared in a movie, *Norman, Is That You?* (1976) and in another TV situation comedy "My Buddy" (1978). After a lengthy absence from TV and many battles with the IRS, Foxx aired a new TV sitcom, "The Royal Family," in 1991. Initial ratings were high, but after just seven episodes Foxx suffered a fatal heart attack on the set.

Redd Foxx, as Fred Sanford in the TV series *Sanford and Son*, in 1972.

ABOVE: Aretha Franklin in 1993.

FRANKLIN, John Hope
1915-

He was the first African-American to be president of the American Historical Association (1978-1979). With degrees from Fisk University (A.B., 1935) and Harvard (M.A., 1936; Ph.D., 1941), he joined the faculty of Howard University in the year of his major work, *From Slavery to Freedom: A History of Negro Americans* (1947; sixth edition, 1988). He was chairman of the history department at Brooklyn College (1956-1964) and a professor at the University of Chicago (1964-1982) and at Duke (1982-1985). Throughout his life he has been the recipient of many honors and awards.

FREEMAN, Morgan
1937-

One of the new wave of African-American actors to break into Hollywood, Freeman was born in Memphis, Tennessee, to a working-class family and grew up in Chicago and Mississippi. He was in the Air Force and went to Los Angeles City College before he made his Broadway debut in 1967 in an all-black production of *Hello, Dolly!* He later appeared on the children's television show *The Electric Company* and in the 1980s both did award-winning theater work and won fame in such films as *Street Smart*, *Driving Miss Daisy*, and *Glory*.

BELOW: Morgan Freeman and Jessica Tandy win Golden Globe Awards in 1990.

FRANKLIN, Aretha
1942-

America's "Queen of Soul," born in Memphis, Tennessee, began singing in her Detroit clergyman father's – the famous Baptist preacher the Reverend Clarence L. Franklin – choirs and gospel revues as a child. Encouraged to use her gospel roots at Atlantic records, her searing "I Never Loved a Man the Way I Love You" (1967) and subsequent soul hits established her international fame. After a fallow period she returned to triumphant stardom with major hits for Arista Records in the 1980s. She was the subject of the TV special *Aretha!* (1986) and of the documentary *Aretha Franklin: Queen of Soul* (1989). In 1990 her flamboyant performances sold out Radio City Music Hall in New York City.

GARVEY, Marcus (Mosiah), Jr.
1887-1940

A fiercely driven visionary, Marcus Garvey created the most popular black nationalist movement of the first half of the 20th century: his tenets influenced African-American people for years after he died. He was born in St. Anns Bay, Jamaica where he worked as a printer. For a short time he worked in Costa Rica and

Marcus Garvey in 1936.

Panama, and he traveled extensively elsewhere in Latin America. He then lived in London, where he learned about the Pan-African movement. He returned to Jamaica and there founded the Universal Negro Improvement Association (sometime between 1911 and 1914). In 1916 he moved to New York City and started promoting his "Back to Africa" program to resettle African-Americans in Africa, as well as an economic program for people of African descent to take control of their destiny. In 1918 he founded a newspaper, *Negro World*, which by its second year had a subscription base of 50,000. In 1920 he held a 31-day international convention of people of African descent, where he presented both his Declaration of Rights for blacks the world over and his plan to colonize Liberia with African-Americans. Liberia rejected his proposal because of rumors that he was actually trying to take control of the country. In 1922 he married his second wife, Amy Jacques, a moving public speaker and leading figure in UNIA. In order to fulfill his visions of economic independence for blacks, he formed the Black Star Line, a shipping company that was to be an economic base for trade and transportation between

Africa and the black Diaspora. Financially naive, he surrounded himself with people who took advantage of his ignorance. Although his message had wide appeal to the masses of black people, elite blacks such as W. E. B. DuBois disagreed with his programs and showy methods. His business ventures were failing, and the U.S. government charged him with using the mail to defraud prospective investors. Later evidence has shown that the charges were politically motivated. Sentenced to five years in prison, his sentence was commuted in 1927 after he served two years. He was deported, and never returned to the United States. After an unsuccessful try in Jamaican politics, in 1935 he moved to London, where he spent the remainder of his eventful life.

ABOVE: Henry Louis Gates, Jr.

GATES, Henry Louis, Jr.
1950-

Gates, winner of a MacArthur "genius" award, is one of the first African-Americans to become an academic "superstar." After graduation from Yale in 1973 he attended Cambridge University in England, from which was the first African-American to receive a Ph.D. (1979). He returned to Yale to teach and soon earned a reputation as a "literary archaeologist" for his work in unearthing, editing, and publishing forgotten African-American texts. One of his most important discoveries established that Harriet Wilson, author of *Our Nig*, was in fact an African-American, and not, as previously thought, a white woman. In 1985 Gates moved to Cornell, where he was the W.E.B. Du Bois professor of literature.

In 1990 he moved to Duke University but left after only a year for Harvard. Gates has published in both scholarly and popular publications, including the *Southern Review* and the *New York Times Book Review*, and in recent years has spoken out on issues of immediate concern to the African-American community.

GIBSON, Althea
1927-

One of the dominant female tennis-players in the world during the 1950s, she was born in Silver, South Carolina, but grew up in New York City. She began playing tennis in the early 1940s but did not emerge on the national scene until she was a college student at Florida Agricultural and Mechanical University. In 1957 and 1958 she won the British women's singles title at Wimbledon (where she was presented to Queen Elizabeth), as well as the U.S. national singles title. She retired in 1958 and went on to play professional golf. She was inducted into the International Tennis Hall of Fame in 1971.

BELOW: Althea Gibson (with Manhattan Borough President Hulan Jack) in 1957.

ABOVE: Josh Gibson *c*. 1940.

GIBSON, Josh (Joshua)
1911-1947

A tremendous gate attraction in Negro League baseball during the 1930s and 1940s, Gibson was known for his home run power. His batting average topped .400 at least twice. Combining with Buck Leonard, Gibson led the Homestead Grays to nine straight pennants (1937-1945). The Hall of Fame (1972) catcher handled every type of pitch, from the spitball to the shineball. When, in 1946, Jackie Robinson became the first black to be signed by the Major Leagues, Gibson was 35 years old and understandably disappointed at having been passed over.

GILLESPIE, Dizzy (John Birks)
1917-1993

One of the fathers of modern jazz and as great an influence on trumpeters as Charlie Parker has been on saxophonists, Gillespie's brilliant, long career included leading a 16-piece band on a State Department-sponsored international tour (1956) that marked the first occasion jazz received official recognition and support from the U.S. government. Born in Che-

raw, South Carolina, Gillespie became a leading exponent of the new bebop after working with the swing bands of Teddy Hill, Cab Calloway, and Earl Hines (1937-1941). His recordings with Charlie Parker in February 1945 are the first bebop classics. His goatee, horn-rimmed glasses, and beret became symbols of jazz and of alternatives to mainstream culture. In the late 1940s he incorporated Latin elements in to American jazz, and by the 1970s his worldwide lectures and performances with groups large and small made him America's ambassador of jazz. Gillespie received innumerable national and international honors. In 1978 he was a featured performer at President Jimmy Carter's White House. His numerous compositions include "A Night in Tunisia" and "Salt Peanuts".

RIGHT: Charles Gilpin (undated photo).
BELOW: Dizzy Gillespie in 1991.

GILPIN, Charles Sidney
1878-1930

Called the dean of African-American actors, he was born in Richmond, Virginia, and for two decades traveled with vaudeville troupes in between odd jobs. He first won acclaim in drama and opera with the Pekin Stock Company in Chicago (1907). Beginning in 1916, he managed the all-black Lafayette Theatre Company in Harlem. His first Broadway role (1919), as William Custis in John Drinkwater's *Abraham Lincoln*, led to his title role in Eugene O'Neill's *The Emperor Jones* (1920-1924). He was among the first African-Americans to play such major roles on Broadway.

GIOVANNI, Nikki
(Yolande Cornelia, Jr.)
1943-

A poet and activist, Giovanni was born in Knoxville, Tennessee. She received her A.B. in history from Fisk University (Tennessee) and did postgraduate work at more than six colleges and universities. She went on to teach at a number of schools, including Rutgers University and Mount St. Joseph on the Ohio. She has gained considerable recognition for her poetry and writing and has made a number of television appearances over the years on talk shows, including the "Tonight Show". Much of her poetry deals with intensely personal themes; she has often drawn on jazz and blues for her rhythms, a fact which makes her public readings particularly impressive. She is also known as an African-American activist who has been vocal on family and gender issues. In 1985 she was elected into the Ohio Women's Hall of Fame.

GLOVER, Danny
1947-

This well known and versatile actor was born in San Francisco, California, and earned his bachelor's degree in economics from San Francisco State University. He worked in the mayor's office in San Francisco before joining the American Conservatory Theatre's Black Actor Workshop. He acted on stage before breaking into the movies, where he gained critical acclaim with his role as the abusive husband in *The Color Purple* (1985). Since then, he has been able to reach a wide range of audiences via such box office hits as *Lethal Weapon* (1987) and politically charged films such as *Bopha* in 1993.

ABOVE: Nikki Giovanni in 1973.
LEFT: Danny Glover (right), with Mel Gibson, at the '93 MTV Movie Awards.

GOLDBERG, Whoopie
(b. Caryn Johnson)
1955-

One of the most popular actresses of the 1980s and 1990s, Goldberg was born in New York City, where she began acting professionally at the age of eight. In 1974 she moved to California and co-founded the San Diego Repertory Theater. In 1984 director Mike Nichols wrote for, and directed her in, a solo Broadway show, *Whoopi Goldberg*. The next year, she made her film debut in *The Color Purple*. In 1990 she won an Academy Award for her supporting role in *Ghost*, and other successful film roles have followed. She has made numerous appearances in television series and specials and has in addition hosted her own TV talk show, *The Whoopie Goldberg Show* (1992-1993).

OPPOSITE: Berry Gordy (bearded), with Diana Ross, in 1971.

GORDY, Berry, Jr.
1929-

He is a record producer who, by founding Motown Records, helped make African-American music part of the popular music industry. Born in Detroit, Gordy wrote songs as teenager and worked in the auto industry and as a boxer. After his songs became rhythm-and-blues hits for Jackie Wilson in New York City in the 1950s he returned to Detroit and founded Motown in 1959. Through such outstanding artists as Smokey Robinson, Marvin Gaye, Diana Ross, and the Jackson Five, his "Motown Sound" became hugely successful. His produced *Lady Sings the Blues* (1972) and other films after 1970. He sold Motown Records in 1988.

Louis Gossett, Jr., with his 1983 Oscar.

GOSSETT, Lou (Louis), Jr.
1936-

An award-winning actor, Gossett was born in Brooklyn, New York, and received his A.B. from New York University. He made his Broadway debut in 1953 in *Take a Giant Step* and moved into films in the early 1960s. His movie credits include *A Raisin in the Sun* (1961), *The Choirboys* (1977), and *Diggstown* (1992). He won best supporting actor at the Academy Awards in 1983 for his role in *An Officer and a Gentleman*. He has also had a successful career on television since the 1970s, and in 1977 he won an Emmy for his role in *Roots*.

GRAVELEY, Samuel
1922-

Born in Richmond, Virginia, Graveley became the first African-American U.S. Navy midshipman (1944), the first to be commissioned an ensign in World War II, the first to command a U.S. Navy ship (1961), and the first to rise to the rank of rear admiral (1971). He was graduated from Virginia Union University (1948) and served in the Korean War. A specialist in naval communications, he ultimately became the director of the Defense Communications Agency (1978-1980). He retired as a highly decorated vice-admiral in 1980. He then became a consultant to defense contractors and served on the boards of several corporations.

GRAY, William Herbert, III
1941-

This prominent member of the U.S. House of Representatives had an earlier career as a Baptist minister. Born in Baton Rouge, Louisiana, he studied at Drew Theological Seminary and Princeton Theological Seminary. He preached in New Jersey and in Philadelphia (1964-1978). As a Congressman from Philadelphia (1979-1991), Gray served as chairman of the House Budget Committee (1985-1989) and then as Democratic whip (1989-1991) — the first African-American to hold such an influential position in the leadership of the Congress. In 1991 he retired from Congress to become president of the United Negro College Fund.

GREGORY, Dick
1932-

One of the country's best-known comedians in the 1960s, Gregory first used his talent to highlight racial prejudice and then turned from humor to political activism. Born in Saint Louis, Missouri, during the Depression, Gregory, like so many talented African-Americans of his generation, went to college on an athletic scholarship. Although Southern Illinois University named him the outstanding athlete of the year in 1953, he left after two years and entered the army. In the army he soon found work as a comedian in Special Service shows; when he left the army, he moved to Chicago, where his big break came in 1961 in a fill-in appearance for an ailing comedian at the Playboy Club. Gregory was so good that his impromptu appearance won notices in *Time* magazine. That publicity in turn led to

Dick Gregory in 1977.

coast-to-coast bookings, and he seemed well on his way to enormous success when he began to concentrate on protests (including hunger strikes) concerning injustices to African-Americans. Once, when told that he should consider the possibility that he could do more for racial equality as a comedian than as an activist, he reportedly replied "They didn't laugh Hitler out of existence, did they?" In 1966 Gregory ran for mayor of Chicago and in 1968 for president of the United States. In the 1980s Gregory drew on his experience with fasting to found Dick Gregory Health Enterprises, Inc., designed to help the overweight. He continues to speak out on a wide variety of political and social issues.

GUMBEL, Bryant
1948-

In 1982 Gumbel became the first African-American co-host of NBC's popular "Today" program. He had broken into journalism in 1972, writing for the monthly *Black Sport* and working as a sports commentator for KNBC-TV in Los Angeles. In 1976, the year in which he became KNBC's sports director, he won the first of several Emmy Awards. From 1980 to 1982 he was the sports correspondent for the "Today" show, a position he held until he became its co-host. In 1986 he was voted the Best Morning TV News Interviewer by the *Washington Journal Review*'s annual poll.

H

Alex Haley receives a 1989 honorary degree as President Bush looks on.

HALE, Clara (Mother) McBride
1904-1993

Orphaned herself at the age of 16, Hale first began to take in foster children to support along with her three children when she was widowed in her 30s. She raised more than 40 foster children and was thinking of retiring when, in 1969, she was given her first drug-addicted baby by a young woman who had been put in touch with Mother Hale by her daughter, Dr. Lorraine Hale. In 1970, when she was 66, she founded Hale House for drug-addicted babies. Her many awards included the Medal of Freedom, awarded by President Reagan in 1985, and the Salvation Army's Booth Community Service Award and Leonard H. Carter Humanitarian Award (1987).

Mother Clara Hale in 1988.

HALEY, Alex
(Alexander Murray Palmer)
1921-1992

To most people, Alex Haley and *Roots: The Saga of an American Family* (1976) are almost synonymous. *Roots* was the saga of Haley's own family, which he traced back to Kunta Kinte, brought from Gambia to America as a slave in 1767. First the book and then the incredibly successful television miniseries (1977) gave African-Americans a vivid sense of their heritage, as well as making countless white Americans realize that they had no monopoly on worthy ancestors. Born in Ithaca, New York, Haley grew up in Tennessee and then studied at the Elizabeth City (North Carolina) Teachers College (1937-1939) before entering the U.S. Coast Guard. While in the Coast Guard (1939-1959), he worked as a journalist. He then supported himself as a freelance writer after returning to civilian life. In 1965 he collaborated on *The Autobiography of Malcolm X*, which brought him national attention. He spent most of the next decade working on *Roots*. *Roots* brought Haley many awards, including the Spingarn Medal, the highest annual award of the National Association for the Advancement of Colored People and a special Pulitzer prize (1977). The revelation that *Roots* was a mixture of fact and fiction did not diminish the book's standing as an important milestone in African-American historiography.

HAMER, Fannie Lou
1917-1977

The youngest of 20 children of Mississippi sharecroppers, she worked as a girl and young woman as a cotton sharecropper. Despite her lack of formal education, she entered the civil rights movement in the 1960s and was one of the founders of the interracial Mississippi Freedom Democratic Party, which challenged white supremacy in Mississippi. In 1964 she ran for Congress on the MFDP "Freedom

Ballot," received more votes than her white opponent, Congressman Jamie Whitten, but saw her election invalidated by the state. Her words "I'm sick and tired of being sick and tired" voiced the impatience of many African-Americans in the 1960s with the slow progress of civil rights. In 1969 she founded the Freedom Farm Corporation, created to offer scholarships and to help poor families raise food and livestock, and for the remainder of her life she she continued the fight to transform the South into a safe and just place for African-Americans to live.

HAMMON, Jupiter
?1720-?1800

The first known African-American writer published in America, Hammon was born a slave, worked as a clerk, and may have been educated by English missionaries. His poem *An Evening Thought, Salvation by Christ, with Penitential Cries* appeared in 1761, when he was a slave of the Lloyd family of Long Island, New York. In 1776, after the British invaded Long Island, Hammon fled along with the Lloyds to Hartford, Connecticut. In addition to his poetry (almost all on religious subjects), Hammon wrote *An Address to the Negroes of the State of New York*, which he delivered to the African Society of New York City in 1786. The influential speech was published in 1787 and ran through three editions. Though neglected for many years, his reputation was revived in 1970 with the publication of *America's First Negro Poet: The Complete Work of Jupiter Hammon of Long Island*.

ABOVE: W.C. Handy (undated photo).
LEFT: Lionel Hampton in 1944.

HAMPTON, Lionel
1909-

After drumming in midwestern bands as a teenager, Hampton introduced the vibraphone into jazz on a recording session with Louis Armstrong (1930) and has remained the dean of vibes and a legendary showman ever since. Born in Louisville, Kentucky, "Hamp" came to prominence with Benny Goodman's bands in the late 1930s and recorded extensively with the leading soloists of the day. He led his own bands from 1940 until the 1990s, apprenticing such players as Charlie Mingus, Dexter Gordon, Wes Montgomery, Clifford Brown, and Quincy Jones. Based in Manhattan in recent years, he has been a mentor to young musicians.

HANDY, W.C.
(William Christopher)
1873-1958

Much celebrated in his later yeas as "The Father of the Blues" (the title of his 1941 autobiography), bandmaster and cornetist Handy was among the first composers to fix the blues idiom on paper. Born in Florence, Alabama, he began notating examples of the rural blues he encountered while touring with minstrel groups. Handy composed (or held copyright on) numerous classic blues songs, including "Memphis Blues" (1911), "St. Louis Blues" (1914), and "Beale Street Blues" (1916). He founded one of the first African-American-owned music publishing businesses (1918). He combined performing and recording in New York City in the 1920s and 1930s with publishing management.

Lorraine Hansberry in 1959.

HANSBERRY, Lorraine
1930-1965

Although she died just as her career as a writer was taking off, Lorraine Hansberry and her work remain models of the new voice for African-Americans in the theater. Born in Chicago, Illinois, she experienced her father's legal fight to move the family into a formerly-restricted white neighborhood. She studied art at Chicago's Art Institute, the University of Wisconsin, and in Mexico before moving to New York City in 1950 to concentrate on writing. Her first full-length play – financed, produced and directed by African-Americans – was *A Raisin in the Sun* (1959); it made her the youngest writer and first African-American ever to win the New York Drama Critics Circle Award. *A Raisin in the Sun* was made into a movie in 1961 (and in 1973 into a musical, *Raisin*) and remains a widely read and performed work. She died of cancer soon after her second play, *The Sign in Sidney Burstein's Window*, opened on Broadway. Her husband, Robert Nemiroff, brought out some of her other writings posthumously, including the play *Les Blancs* (1970) and the book, *To Be Young, Gifted and Black* (1969); the latter was adapted as a play.

HARPER, Frances Ellen Watkins
1825-1911

This poet and social reformer was born free in Baltimore, Maryland, when it was still a slave city. She published her first volume of poetry early in her life (1845), then taught sewing for a while before continuing her career as a poet. In the same year that her second volume of poetry was published, 1854, she gave her first anti-slavery lecture. By the end of the decade she had become the most poular African-American poet in the Union. In 1864 she returned to lecturing on social issues and helped to found the National Association for the Advancement of Colored Women

(1896). The most prolific African-American author of her time, during her career she published poetry, articles, a short story, a novel, and a travel book.

HARRIS, Barbara Clementine
1930-

In 1989 Harris was elected suffragan bishop of the Episcopal diocese of Massachusetts, thus becoming the first woman bishop in the 450-year history of the Anglican Church. Before her ordination as a priest in 1980 Harris worked in public relations and was board member of the Pennsylvania Prison Society. Since her election, in addition to managing Boston's Cathedral of Saint Paul, she has traveled world-wide, speaking out on issues such as racism, women's rights, and multi-culturalism. She has maintained her interest in prison reform and represents the Episcopal Church on the board of the Prisoner Visitation and Support Committee, a ministry in federal and military correctional institutions.

HARRIS, Patricia Roberts
1924-1985

Born in Mattoon, Illinois, Harris was graduated from Howard University (1945) and was first in her class at George Washington University School of Law (1960). During her career she established many "firsts": she was the first female black ambassador (to Luxembourg) during 1965-1967, the first black dean of an American law school (1969), and the first female black cabinet member (secretary of housing and urban development 1977-1980). She ran, but lost to Marion S. Barry, in a tough race for mayor of Washington, D.C., in 1982.

HASTIE, William Henry
1904-1976

In 1949 Hastie became the first African-American jurist to be appointed to be judge on the U.S. Circuit Court of Appeals. Born in Knoxville, Tennessee, Hastie was perhaps the country's best-known African-American legal figure after Supreme Court Justice Thurgood Marshall. After graduation from Amherst College (1925), Hastie went on to study law at Harvard University, where he received both a bachelor of law degree (1930) and a doctorate in jurisprudence (1933). He worked briefly for a private law

OPPOSITE: Bishop Barbara Harris in 1989.

Robert Hayden *c.* 1965.

firm and then as an attorney at the U.S. Department of the Interior and in the district court of the Virgin Islands. He then served as dean of the law school at Howard University (1939-1946). During his tenure at Howard, he also served briefly (1940-1943) as a consultant on race relations to the secretary of war, but he resigned in protest against discrimination against African-Americans in the military. In 1946 he was appointed governor of the Virgin Islands, and three years later President Truman elevated him to the United States Court of Appeals for the Third Judicial Circuit, a position he held until his retirement in 1971.

HAWKINS, Coleman
1904-1969

One of the great saxophone masters of the twentieth century, Hawkins pioneered the use of the tenor saxophone in jazz during his years with the Fletcher Henderson Orchestra (1923-1934). Born into a middle-class St. Joseph, Missouri, family and educated in music in Chicago and Topeka, Kansas, Hawkins gained an international reputation in Europe (1934-1939) and returned to the U.S. at the outbreak of World War II. The 1940s were in some respects his most creative years, but his understanding of harmony made him a vital player throughout the bebop revolution, and he remained a prolific recording artist and concert performer until the mid-1960s. His "vertical improvising,' exemplified in his classic recording of "Body and Soul" (1939), laid the groundwork for the styles of John Coltrane, Sonny Rollins, and other postmodernists.

HAYDEN, Robert
1913-1980

One of the best-known African-American poets during the mid-twentieth century, Hayden twice won the prestigious Hopwood Award for poetry (1938, 1942), as well as a Ford Fellowship (1954) and the Grand Award for Poetry at the First World Festival of Negro Arts in Senegal, Africa (1965). Over the years he taught at Fisk University in Nashville, Tennessee, and at his alma mater, the University of Michigan (1969-1980). His work during the 1930s for the Federal Writers' Project on African-American history and folklore had a lasting influence on his own writings, which include *A Ballad for Remembrance* (1962), *Selected Poems* (1966), and his most highly acclaimed work, *Night Blooming Cereus* (1972).

Roland Hayes in 1930.

HAYES, Roland
1887-1977

A tenor world-renowned for German lieder, French songs, and Negro spirituals, he was born of former slaves in Goergia. After studies at Fisk University and in Europe he debuted in Boston (1917) and toured the U.S., then studied in London (1920) and toured Europe. In 1924 he performed 80 concerts in the U.S.A. and in 1925 was awarded the Spingarn Medal for "most outstanding achievement among colored people." He gave command performances for King George V in England and for Queen Mother Maria Christina in Spain and taught at several universities.

ABOVE: Bishop James Healy *c.* 1875.
OPPOSITE: Coleman Hawkins *c.* 1945.

HEALY, James Augustine
1830-1900

The first African-American to be ordained as a Roman Catholic priest and to become a bishop, Healy was born near Macon, Georgia; his mother was a freed slave, his father a white plantation owner. Healy studied in Quaker schools in the North, then was graduated from Holy Cross College (1849) as a Catholic convert; he continued his religious studies in Montreal, Canada, and Paris, France, where he was ordained in 1854. He served as a pastor and then as an administrator in the Boston archdiocese before being appointed bishop of Portland, Maine (1875-1900), where he oversaw the building of many new churches and was known for his eloquence. His brother, Patrick F. Healy (1834-1910), also became a Catholic priest and, after teaching philosophy at Georgetown University (1866-1969), became that institution's first black president (1873-1882).

HENDRIX, Jimi (James Marshall)
1942-1970

A leading performer of 1960s psychedelic music and one of the guitar players of the century, the gifted Jimi Hendrix was among the few African-American musicians to attain superstar status in rock. Born in Seattle, Washington, after apprenticeships with Little Richard, Ike and Tina Turner, and the Isley Brothers, he formed the Jimi Hendrix Experience with two white Englishmen in London and recorded his first hit album, *Are You Experienced?*, in 1966. Hendrix was a major recording and concert artist until his accidental death by drug overdose, and he is still a major influence on guitarists.

Undated lithograph of Josiah Henson.

HENSON, Josiah
1789-1883

A minister and activist, Henson was born in Charles County, Maryland and was sold into slavery in his childhood. While still in slavery he managed to become a Methodist preacher and a land superintendent. In 1830 he escaped with his family to Ontario, Canada, where he attempted vainly to establish a community for African-Americans who had also escaped slavery. Disappointed in his efforts, he returned to the American South to help liberate other African-Americans from slavery. In 1849 he published his autobiography, and his life story is the basis for one of the narratives used by Harriet Beecher Stowe in her 1851-1852 anti-slavery novel *Uncle Tom's Cabin*.

HENSON, Matthew Alexander
1866-1955

One of the first two Americans to reach the North Pole, Henson had to wait 35 years before he received the recognition he deserved. Born on a farm in Charles County, Maryland, he went to sea when he was about 12. In 1887 he met Robert E. Peary, then a lieutenant in the U.S. Navy and already committed to exploring the Arctic region. Henson began as Peary's personal assistant, but during the next 20 years, as Peary continued his explorations of Greenland and tried to reach the North Pole, Henson played an increasingly important role as the driver of the dog sleds and righthand man on Peary's expeditions. The culminating moment came on

Matthew Henson *c.* 1910.

April 6, 1909, when Henson, Peary, and four Eskimos were the first known humans to reach the North Pole. In 1913 President Taft appointed him clerk of the New York Customs House (1913-1933), but his importance in the discovery of the North Pole was not fully acknowledged by Congress until 1944. He subsequently was awarded the Gold Medal of the Geographical Society of Chicago, and both presidents Truman and Eisenhower praised his contribution to exploration.

HICKS, James L.
1915-1986

Born in Akron, Ohio, Hicks studied at Howard University and rose from private to captain in the U.S. Army during World War II. A pioneer in black journalism, he worked with The *Afro-American* in Baltimore and was a top editor of *The Amsterdam News* (1955-19667, 1972-1977), which he helped to build into one of the most important newspapers directed towards African-Americans. He was the first African-American to cover the United Nations and the first African-American journalist sent to cover the Korean War. He ended his distinguished career as editor of *The New York Voice* (1977-1985).

HIMES, Chester Bomar
1909-

Himes is probably best-known for the series of crime novels written between 1957 and 1980 featuring the African-American detective "Grave Digger" Johnson. Himes's studies at Ohio State

University (1926-1928) were cut short when he was convicted of armed robbery (1928) and spent six years in prison. After his release he worked at various jobs (including journalism) before moving to Europe after World War II (he lived in France and Spain). While his early novels, such as *Lonely Crusade* (1947), look at racial issues in contemporary American, many of his later works were lighter in tone. His autobiography, *The Quality of Hurt*, was published in 1973.

HINES, Earl Kenneth "Fatha"
1903-1983

Hines's "trumpet-style" melodies, improvised with the right hand, freed the piano from the constraints of ragtime and early stride style and made him the seminal jazz pianist of the 1920s and the "Fatha" of modern jazz piano. Born into a musical family in Duquesne, Pennsylvania, and educated in the classics, after moving to Chicago (1924) he showcased his innovative virtuosity in celebrated solo and ensemble recordings with Louis Armstrong and Jimmy Noone (1927-1928) and led influential big bands at Chicago's Grand Terrace Ballroom from 1928 to 1940. His units of the 1940s featured Charlie Parker, Dizzy Gillespie, and Sarah Vaughan. He toured internationally into the 1970s and performed in the San Francisco Bay area until his death.

HINES, Gregory Oliver
1946-

Best known for contributing to the revival of tapdancing as a respected performance art, he was born in New York City, and by the age of five he was tapdancing with his brother, Maurice, Jr., as the Hines Kids. In their teens they became the Hines Brothers and later (1963-1973), with their father as a background percussionist, they toured widely as Hines, Hines and Dad. Tiring of the routine, he settled in California and formed the jazz-rock group Severance. Returning to New York, he began to appear as a dancer in Broadway shows such as *Eubie!* (1978) and *Sophisticated Ladies* (1981) (although he had made his debut as a child tapdancer in 1954 in *The Girl in Pink Tights*). He has been nominated for three Tony awards and in 1992 won best actor in a musical for his role in *Jelly's Last Jam*. He has also had a successful Hollywood career, usually incorporating his dancing into his roles in such films as *Cotton Club* (1984), *White Nights* (1985), and *Tap* (1989). He has also

ABOVE: The brass section of the Earl Hines Orchestra in 1938.
LEFT: Gregory Hines (right) in 1982.

done some singing, but he remains most admired for his having reinvigorated traditional tapdancing with his own, often improvised and always sophisticated, routines.

HOLIDAY, Billie
(Eleanora Fagan)
1915-1959

The most famous and influential singer of the swing era and one of the most celebrated singers in American history, the legendary "Lady Day" is equally famous for her tortured personal life. Born into extreme poverty to teenage parents in Baltimore, Maryland, she was abandoned by her father when he left home to follow his own musical career. After she and her mother moved to Manhattan (1928) and her mother became ill, she turned to prostitution but could not tolerate the abuse to which she was subjected. She failed to get work as a dancer, but she did land work as a singer, a skill she had never cultivated.

ABOVE: Benjamin Hooks in 1992.
OPPOSITE: Billie Holiday in 1946.

She also began a lifelong addiction to heroin. Discovered the year after her singing debut by producer John Hammond, the series of recordings she made with small groups between 1933 and 1942, featuring some of the finest players of the day, including Lester Young and Teddy Wilson, established the preeminence of her unique high, resonant voice, with its subtle speechlike inflection. She sang with Count Basie's orchestra for a year (1937) but suffered racial mistreatment with Artie Shaw's white band and quit to lead her own units. Her recording of "Strange Fruit" (1939), about lynching, was a *cause célèbre*; her song "God Bless the Child," about the poverty of her youth, is a perennial standard. She appeared in films, but she was arrested several times on narcotics charges and was imprisoned and prevented from performing in New York. She continued recording and singing in public, however, until her death.

HOOKER, John Lee
1917-

Known internationally for his hypnotic guitar riffs and growling vocals, Hooker was born in Clarksdale, Mississippi, and began his career in Detroit. The release in 1948 of his "Boogie Chillun," the biggest of his hit records, established Hooker's brand of electric country blues as a perennial source of "Boogie" material for younger blues and rock musicians of all races. Constantly touring, and unusually successful for a "deep blues" artist, Hooker often appears in concerts and on records with leading rock figures. He was inducted into the Rock 'n' Roll Hall of Fame in 1991.

HOOKS, Benjamin Lawson
1925-

He achieved recognition as the first African-American to serve on the Federal Communications Commission (1972-1977); he sought to increase the number of black-owned and -operated radio and TV stations. A lawyer and minister, he was pastor of the Middle Baptist Church of Memphis, Tennessee (1956-1972), a savings and loan officer (1955-1969), and the first African-American judge to serve in the Shelby County (Tennessee) Criminal Court (1965-1968). Always active in civil rights, he succeeded Roy Wilkins as executive director of the National Association for the Advancement of Colored People (1977-1993) and produced several TV shows on racial issues.

HORNE, Lena
1917-

Born into a prominent Brooklyn, New York, family, singer, actress, and celebrated beauty Horne began in show business as a chorus girl at Harlem's Cotton Club at the age of 16. Within two years she became a popular singer with Noble Sissle's band (1935), making her Broadway debut in *Blackbirds of 1939*. After recording with Charley Barnet, Teddy Wilson, Artie Shaw, and Henry Levine, she began her solo recording career with RCA (1941) and became the first African-American signed to a long-term Hollywood movie contract (MGM, 1942-1950). But after *Stormy Weather* (1943), the title tune of which became her signature song, her refusal to play stereotyped roles limited her appearances to musical numbers which were edited out for movies distributed in the South. Enrolled by her grandmother in the NAACP when she was two years old and always outspoken against racism, she was blacklisted in the 1950s but managed to appear on Broadway in *Jamaica* (1957) and to continue her TV, radio, and nightclub performances in Europe and the U.S. She published her autobiography, *Lena*, in 1965. In recent years she has concerned herself with many progressive causes. Her award-winning Broadway show *Lena Horne: The Lady and Her Music* (1980-1981) recapitulated her career.

HOUSTON, Charles Hamilton
1895-1950

A prominent lawyer and advocate for African-Americans' rights, Houston was born in Washington, D.C., where his father was a lawyer. He was graduated from Amherst College (1915), served in France as an officer in World War I, and then received his law degree from Harvard Law School in 1922. He returned to Washingotn to practice law with his father before becoming vice dean, then dean, of the law school at Howard University (1929-1935). Having already taken part in various important civil rights cases, he became the special counsel for the national Association for the Advancement of Colored People (1935-1940). After returning to private practice, he nevertheless remained a member of NAACP's legal committee (1940-1950). He argued several important cases before the U.S. Supreme Court and was especially noted for testing the constitutionality of "gentlemen's agreements" that kept minorities from purchasing real estate in many areas.

HOUSTON, Whitney
1963-

One of contemporary America's most popular singers, she was born into a musical family in East Orange, New Jersey. Trained largely by her mother, the singer Cissy Houston, Whitney was singing in the New Hope Baptist Choir by the time she was 11 and in her mother's nightclub act by the time she was 15. Within a few years she was supplementing her burgeoning musical career by becoming a top fashion model for *Glamour* and *Seventeen* magazines. She recorded her first single ("Hold Me," with Teddy Pendergrass) in 1984 and her first album, *Whitney*, in 1985,

Langston Hughes *c.* 1945.

the same year in which she won the first two of her numerous American Music awards and the first of her several Grammy awards. Many other honors would follow, including *Billboard's* Artist of the Year award (1986). She has also appeared in a feature film, *The Bodyguard* (1992). Among her best-known hits are "Greatest Love of All," "Saving All My Love for You," "Didn't We Almost Have it All?" and "I'm Your Baby Tonight".

HUGHES, Langston
(James Mercer)
1902-1967

One of the original writers of the Harlem Renaissance movement and long a presence in the African-American community, Hughes was born in Joplin, Missouri. In 1921 he began studies at Columbia University but left after a year. Although several early poems had gained him some acclaim, he went off to work on a freighter and traveled to Africa that way, then later lived in Paris and Rome. Returning to the U.S., he was graduated from Lincoln University in 1926, publishing his first volume of poetry, *The Weary Blues*, that same year. Also in 1926, Hughes published a critical essay, "The Negro Artist and the Racial Mountain," which became a defining piece for the Harlem Renaissance movement. During the next four decades he continued to write in a number of forms – novels, poetry, short stories, plays, autobiographies, and non-fiction. He had always sought to meld poetry with music, and he wrote the lyrics for the musical *Street Scene* (1947) and the play that developed into the opera *Troubled Island* (1949). His most frequently performed stagework is *Black Nativity* (1961), which dramatizes the birth of Christ with gospel music. In 1942 he began a column in a Chicago newspaper that introduced his character, "Simple," an African-American Everyman who wittily comments on the ironies besetting black people's lives. He eventually published five volumes of his "Simple Stories." Amazingly prolific, admirably versatile, and a man capable of hearty humor as well as bitter criticism, he fell in and out of favor with the public, but the best of his work promises to survive. His loving and insightful depiction of everyday black life has prompted many public schools to use his work as an introduction to the study of black literature.

HUNTER-GAULT, Charlayne
1942-

Hunter-Gault's interest in journalism began in 1961 when she observed the journalists covering the story as she and Hamilton Holmes became the first African-American students to integrate the University of Georgia (A.B. 1963). After graduation she worked at *The New Yorker* (1963-1967) and *The New York Times* (1968-1978) before joining the staff of the *MacNeil/Lehrer Report* on PBS (1978). In 1983 she became a national correspondent for the expanded MacNeil/Lehrer News Hour. Since then, she has traveled widely for the program, filing reports from around the world. Her publications included articles in *Essence*, *Ms.*, *Life*, and *The Saturday Review* and her autobiography, *In My Place* (1992).

HURSTON, Zora Neale
1903-1960

A writer and anthropologist, Hurston was born in Eatonville, Florida, a self-governed African-American town. Growing up in Eatonville shaped Hurston's later work and attitudes, for she was influenced by both the oral tradition alive there and the independence of the African-American community. She studied at both Howard University and Barnard, where she earned her A.B. in 1928. While at Howard University she had published her first two short stories, launching her writing career. She published a number of novels and anthropological studies over the years, her most successful novel being *Their Eyes Were Watching God* (1937). She chose to write most often about African-American traditions and culture rather than explicitly about racism. Her interest in African-American folklore led her to pursue a graduate degree in anthropology at Columbia University, and she spent many years studying the folklore of the South, as well as that of Haiti, Bermuda, and Honduras. In her later life she became a controversial figure in the African-American community, as she grew increasingly conservative. She even questioned the value of the Supreme Court decision in *Brown vs. The Board of Education*: "How much satisfaction can I get from a court order for somebody to associate with me who does not wish me near them?" In 1948 she was arrested on child molestation charges; although she was cleared of all charges, hostile elements in African-American press magnified her troubles, and she was both personally and professionally devastated. She spent the last decade of her life working at various small jobs and at her death was buried in an unmarked grave. In the 1970s Alice Walker located her grave and erected a stone marker for her. Her work has been revived in recent years and is now widely read, and she has influenced many writers.

HYMAN, Earle
1926-

A stage actor drawn to classic roles, he studied at the Actors Studio in New York, played Othello frequently abroad, and appeared in ten other roles with the American Shakespeare Theatre. Since 1957 he has taught acting in New York. He had a memorable part in the first hit of the American Negro Theatre, *Anna Lucasta* (1944-1945), and similar triumphs in *Mr. Johnson* (1956), *Driving Miss Daisy* (1989), and *Pygmalion* (1991). He has also appeared in American movies and on TV (eg., "The Cosby Show"). Well known for his roles in European productions, he won the State award in Oslo, Norway, for *The Emperor Jones*.

Charlayne Hunter-Gault in 1961.

INNIS, Roy (Emile Alfredo)
1934-

A controversial civil rights activist, Innis was born in St. Croix, Virgin Islands, and moved to Harlem in 1946. A graduate of the City College of New York, in 1963 he became a member of the Congress of Racial Equality and in 1968 became CORE's president. He was an advocate of community development corporations and was involved in a number of African-American business groups. Often surrounded by criticism from within the civil rights movement, he was forced to pay $35,000 to CORE in 1981 following an investigation by the New York Attorney General's office for alleged misuse of funds. In the 1980s he ran unsuccessfully for Congress.

Roy Innis (2nd from right) in 1968.

JACKSON, Jesse Louis
1941-

One of the most outspoken and influential leaders in the civil rights struggle, Jackson was born in Greenville, South Carolina, to a sharecropper from Alabama. An athlete in high school, he turned down the opportunity to play professional sports because of the persistent prejudices that gave white players more money and more opportunity. He did his undergraduate study at the Agricultural and Technical College of North Carolina and studied for the ministry at Chicago Theological Seminary, eventually becoming an ordained Baptist minister. He had been involved in the struggle for integration since his college years, and in 1967 he was named the head of Operation Breadbasket, a program of the Southern Christian Leadership Conference intended to boost African-American economic prospects via the strategic use of boycotts and picketing. After finishing his schooling he worked to integrate schools and housing in Chicago through the Chicago Freedom Movement. An assistant to Martin Luther King, he was at King's side at the time of his assassination in 1968. In 1971, after some differences with SCLC, he founded the organization People United to Save Humanity, focusing his efforts in Chicago. In 1972 he successfully challenged Mayor Richard Daley's group of delegates to the Democratic National Convention. He later founded the Rainbow Coalition and used it as a base for his candidacy in the 1984 and 1988 Democratic presidential primaries. He was a strong presence in both elections, forcing issues, such as economic justice, world hunger, and disarmament, that might otherwise have been ignored; although he finished a strong second to the eventual Democratic nominee, Michael Dukakis, in 1988, he had moved into the forefront of American public life by building on the efforts of a diverse support base. Extending his concerns beyond those limited to the African-American community, he has worked for everything from freeing Americans held hostage in the Middle East to showing up on picket lines in various labor actions. Known to millions of TV viewers as the host of *Both Sides with Jesse Jackson*, he remains one of the most influential African-American figures in public life.

OPPOSITE: Rev. Jesse Jackson at the 1992 Democratic National Convention.

Mahalia Jackson in 1954.

JACKSON, Mahalia
1911-1972

Credited with inspiring generations of gospel singers and introducing gospel music to international audiences, Jackson was born in New Orleans and was raised a Baptist. After moving to Chicago she joined the Johnson Gospel Singers (1928) and Thomas A. Dorsey's group from the mid-1930s to late 1940s. Her 1947 million-selling recording of "Move Up a Little Higher" earned her the sobriquet "queen of gospel" and opened the door for radio, TV, and European appearances. She sang at President John F. Kennedy's inauguration and Martin Luther King, Jr.'s funeral, but she steadfastly avoided secular songs and venues.

JACKSON, Maynard Holbrook, Jr.
1938-

Born in Dallas, Texas, Jackson was graduated from Morehouse College (1956) and North Carolina Central State School of Law (1964). He was a successful encyclopedia salesman (1958-1961) before he became a lawyer. He made an unsuccessful run for the U.S. Senate (1968) and then became vice-mayor (1970-1974) and mayor (1974-1982) of Atlanta – the first African-American mayor of a major Southern city. Although he had been criticized by some who said he represented middle-class rather than working-class African-Americans, Jackson was again elected mayor of Atlanta in 1990, serving until 1992. He has subsequently continued to be an influential force in Democratic politics in Georgia.

JACKSON, Michael
1958-

Capitalizing on his brilliant success as a child star, Michael Jackson's even more spectacular success as an adult has made him an entertainment phenomenon. Born in Gary, Indiana, he achieved great fame singing with his older brothers in the popular Motown Records group The Jackson Five. After his first solo hits in the early 1970s, he began producing and songwriting in 1976. In 1979 Jackson's first solo Album, *Off the Wall*, a collaboration with arranger/producer Quincy Jones, firmly established his adult career. His second solo album, *Thriller* (1982), sold over 30 million copies and made him an international superstar. Known for the unusual choreography and elaborate special effects of his concert performances, Jackson became a tabloid staple for his unusual offstage behavior, which included extensive reconstructive plastic surgery, friendship with showbiz celebrities such as Elizabeth Taylor, and an exotic, reclusive lifestyle. His ambiguous sexual persona did not help his cause when he faced allegations of sexual abuse of minor boys in 1993, but no criminal charges were filed.

BELOW: Michael Jackson in 1993.

JACKSON, Reggie
(Reginald Martinez)
1946-

The final game of the 1977 World Series – when Jackson blasted three home runs for the Yankees, each on the first ball pitched to him – is indelibly etched in the memories of those who saw it. In 27 Fall Classic games "Mr. October" batted .357 and slugged .755, the latter mark being the all-time best in the major leagues. In the dozen seasons from 1971 to 1982 the three teams that had Jackson on the roster won a total of ten division crowns and five world championships. Hall of Famer (1993) Jackson is sixth on the all-time home run list, and has four home run crowns, as well as a Most Valuable Player Award (1973). Intelligent and articulate, Jackson carried a big stick, but did not speak softly. His arguments with club owners and managers were legendary, but, in the end, he always delivered what they wanted most.

JACKSON, Shirley Ann
1946-

A distinguished theoretical physicist, she made important contributions to science's understanding of the ways in which elementary particles interact: charge density waves, polaronic aspects of electrons, and semiconductor strained-layer superlattices. Crediting her father and high school teachers for their encouragement, she became the first African-American woman to earn a Ph.D. from the Massachusetts Institute of Technology (1973). She worked at the Fermi National Accelerator Laboratory (1973-1976) and in Geneva, Switzerland, before moving to AT&T Bell Laboratories (1976-). A trustee of MIT and Rutgers University, she promoted science and women's roles on many national committees.

JAMAL, Ahmad (b. Fritz Jones)
1930-

Important among mainstream jazz pianists for his popular trio work and definitive interpretive arrangements, Jamal exerted considerable indirect influence through the more famous Miles Davis, who admired and promoted elements of his lean style and his use of space and adopted much of his repertoire, including "Ahmad's Rhumba," "Autumn Leaves," and "But Not For Me". Born in Pittsburgh, Pennsylvania, Jamal performed professionally during high school and toured with George Hudson's Orchestra before achieving fame with his 1950s trios and recordings. Though now in his sixties, he has continued his recording and touring into the 1990s.

JAMES, Daniel, Jr. "Chappie"
1920-1978

Born in Pensacola, Florida, James attended Tuskegee Institute and joined the Army Air Corps in 1943. He served as a fighter pilot and instructor. He flew 101 combat missions in the Korean War and rose steadily in the ranks during the Vietnam War. In 1975 he was named commander of the North American Air Defense Command and was promoted to the rank of four-star general, the first African-American to reach that rank. He served in that capacity from 1975 to 1978, when he died of a heart attack.

JAMISON, Judith
1944-

Choreographer and director of the Alvin Ailey American Dance Theatre, she gained fame and many honors as a physically commanding yet deeply spiritual dancer. Agnes de Mille recognized her talents at the Philadelphia Dance Academy in 1964. She danced with the American Ballet Theatre, then joined Alvin Ailey as principal dancer (1965-1980) and dancer-choreographer (1980-1989), touring worldwide and succeeding Ailey as artistic director in 1989. She extended the company's assistance to underprivileged youth. Apart from Ailey, she performed in the Broadway musical *Sophisticated Ladies* (1980) and directed the Jamison Project (1988-1989).

General "Chappie" James in 1978.

Al Jarreau in 1979.

JARREAU, Al (Alwin)
1940-

One of the foremost jazz and scat singers of his generation, multi-Grammy-Award-winner Jarreau's vocal pyrotechnics represent expansions upon the improvisational attitude and vocalizing of bebop. Born in Milwaukee, Wisconsin, he holds a masters degree in psychology. After achieving success in late-1960s San Francisco jazz clubs, he began recording in 1975 and toured Europe in 1976, winning his first Grammy in 1977 for his first popular hit, "We're in This Love Together" (1981). Combining jazz, soul, and pop in increasingly commercial proportions, and with a remarkable ability to "sing" numerous instruments and sounds, his concerts continue to be impressive tours-de-force.

JEMISON, Mae C.
1956-

The first African-American woman astronaut, a physician and educator, she appeared in dance and theater productions and earned degrees in both chemical engineering and African-American studies at Stanford University (1977) before receiving her M.D. from Cornell (1981). A Peace Corps medical officer in West Africa between 1983 and 1985, she then joined CIGNA Health Plans in Los Angeles, still pursuing her goal. In 1987 the National Aeronautics and Space Administration chose her for astronaut training, and she first entered space on September 12, 1992. Active in health-oriented associations, she was given a teaching fellowship at Dartmouth College in 1993.

JOHNS, Vernon
1892-1964

Although not as well known as some other civil rights leaders, Johns inspired many of them. Born in Prince Edward County, Virginia, and largely self-educated, as a boy he memorized much of the Bible and learned enough German, Latin, and Greek to gain admission to Oberlin College in Ohio. After his matriculation in 1918 he went on to the graduate school of theology at the University of Chicago. He soon gained fame as a scholar and preacher among his fellow African-Americans, but, thanks to his volatile temperament and unpolished manner, he seldom retained fixed jobs for very long and was effectively an itinerant preacher throughout the 1920s and 1930s. He did, however, hold two prestigious posts: president of the Virginia Seminary and pastor of the historic First Baptist Church in Charleston, West Virginia. Finally, in 1948, he was chosen to be pastor of the Dexter Avenue Baptist Church, the oldest of the all African-American churches in Montgomery, Alabama. He soon unsettled both his conservative middle-class congregation, as well as the white people of Montgomery, with his unconventional and outspoken ways, openly challenging the Jim Crow laws that kept African-Americans second-class citizens, selling farm produce from a truck in front of the church, and preaching disturbing sermons such as "Segregation After Death" and "It's Safe to Murder Negroes in Mont-

Mae C. Jemison in 1987.

gomery". He was forced to resign in 1952 (and was succeeded by a young Martin Luther King, Jr.) but continued both to preach and to lecture. He also continued his struggle for rights for African-Americans, in 1956 becoming co-founder (with Reverend Fred Shuttlesworth) of the Alabama Christian Movement for Human Rights (later to become the Southern Christian Leadership Conference). In 1960 he headed the Maryland Baptist Center in Baltimore, Maryland, which provided adult education to African-American preachers, but again his outspokenness led to his dismissal. He held no other major position in the few years of life that remained to him.

JOHNSON, Jack (John Arthur)
1878-1946

In becoming the first African-American heavyweight boxing champion of the world, Johnson not only had to overcome many obstacles but then paid dearly for his success. Born in Galveston, Texas, he was small and skinny as a boy. When he was a young man he rode the rails and traveled the country, supporting himself in a series of odd jobs and boxing as an amateur before becoming a professional in 1899. After rising through the ranks he was denied his bid for the heavyweight championship in America, but he finally obtained it by knocking out Tommy Burns in Sydney, Australia, in 1908. Many white Americans resented seeing an African-American rise so high in heavyweight boxing, but Johnson successfully defended his title against a series of "great white hopes," most notably James J. Jeffries, who came out of a six-year retirement in 1910. Outside the ring Johnson's self-confident manner and flamboyant life style – most particularly his relations with white women – led to his constantly being under fire, and in 1913 he was convicted of violating the Mann Act. He fled abroad and in 1915 lost his title to Jesse Willard in Havana, Cuba, by a knockout in the 26th round. Johnson returned to the U.S. and served a 10-month sentence. After his release he boxed in exhibition matches, turned to operating night clubs, and ended up working in carnivals. His career record was 78 wins (45 knockouts), 8 losses, and 12 no-decisions. He was inducted into the Boxing Hall of Fame in 1954. He was the subject of the play (1968) and movie (1970) *The Great White Hope*, both starring James Earl Jones.

OPPOSITE: Jack Johnson in 1931.

James Weldon Johnson (undated photo).
OPPOSITE: Magic Johnson in 1992.

JOHNSON, James Weldon
1871-1938

Johnson, one the most prominent African-Americans in the early decades of the century, was born in Jacksonville, Florida, and got his A.B. at Atlanta University before taking a law degree at Columbia University. In 1897 he became the first African-American to be admited to the Florida bar. Although he was deeply involved in the life of the African-American community in Jacksonville, where he organized a system of secondary education for blacks, his love of the theater led him to move to New York City in 1901. There, along with his brother, J. Rosamond Johnson, and Bob Cole, he formed a song-and-dance troupe that toured both in America and Europe. With his brother he wrote more than 200 songs, including "Under the Bamboo Tree" and "The Congo Love Song," but their best-known song was "Lift Every Voice and Sing," originally written for Jacksonville schoolchildren to perform at a Lincoln's Birthday celebration. The song, which begins "Lift every voice and sing/Till earth and heaven ring,/Ring with the harmonies of liberty . . ." soon became known as the "black national anthem". President Theodore Roosevelt, for whom Johnson campaigned during the presidential election of 1904, appointed him consul to Venezuela (1906) and Nicaragua (1909). He served in Nicaragua during the difficult period of the revolution of 1912 and helped to mediate between the insurgents and the Nicaraguan government. Shortly there-

after the Democrat-controlled U.S. Senate rejected his appointment as consul to the Azores. Johnson resigned from the consular service, returned to the United States, and took up yet another career: writing books. His novel *Autobiography of an Ex-Colored Man*, published anonymously in 1912, was followed in rapid succession by *50 Years and Other Poems* (1917), *The Book of American Negro Poetry* (1922), *God's Trombone* (1927), his best known book of poetry, *Saint Peter Relates an Incident of the Resurrection* (1930), and *Along This Way* (1933). Somehow he also found time to serve as field secretary (1916-1921) and executive (1921-1930) of the National Association for the Advancement of Colored People and to campaign for passage of the Dyer Anti-Lynching Bill. He spent his last years writing and teaching. After his death, as the result of an automobile accident in 1938, his home at 187 West 135th Street in New York City was named a National Historic Landmark.

JOHNSON, John Harold
1918-

For many years he was said to be the richest African-American in America, but Johnson's true stature rests on his creation of a publishing empire that provided an inspiration for generations of African-Americans. Born in Arkansas, Johnson grew up with his mother and stepfather after his father's death in 1924. When the family moved to Chicago, Johnson attended DuSable High School, where he was an excellent student and active in extracurricular activities. After two years at the University of Chicago, he attended the Northwestern School of Commerce before going to work for the Supreme Liberty Life Insurance Company. In 1942 he began the *Negro Digest*, modeled on the *Reader's Digest*, and thus launched the Johnson Publishing Company. His next venture was *Ebony* (1945), like *Life* a pictorial magazine but one focusing on African-Americans. *Ebony* undeniably promoted a middle-class life style and would receive its share of criticism for its espousal of what some considered "white" values and its lack of militancy. But it has also been praised for opening up the possibilities of a distinct area of African-American publishing and creating a vast readership. Also, its advertising, by featuring both standard products meant for all Americans as well as special products meant specifically for African-Americans, opened up new economic

horizons for African-American enterpeneurs while providing readers with a new sense of their community. Additionally, it provided many white Americans with their first, impressive glimpse of that community. The great success of *Ebony* allowed Johnson to launch more publications – including *Jet, Ebony, Jr.* and *Ebony Man* – and also to move into radio and television. He was the first black to receive the most coveted award in magazine publishing, the Henry Johnson Fisher Award (1972). He eventually became the chairman and chief executive officer of the Supreme Life Insurance Company and served on the boards of directors of numerous other businesses. He has also been a trustee for organizations such as the United Negro College Fund.

JOHNSON, Judy (William Julius)
1900-1989

Considered the Negro Leagues' top third baseman of the 1920s and 1930s, Johnson was also valued for the steadying influence he exerted on his teammates. His club, the Hilldales, played in the first two Negro League World Series. In the 1924 contest Hilldale lost to the K.C. Monarchs, but Johnson led both teams in batting (.341). In 1925 the teams met again, this time Hilldale winning. After his playing career Johnson scouted and coached for the Philadelphia Athletics, and in 1975 he was inducted into the Baseball Hall of Fame.

JOHNSON, Magic (Earvin, Jr.)
1959-

Three times the National Basketball Association's Most Valuable Player and three times the postseason MVP, Johnson's magical moments started in the most important basketball game in television history. Johnson and his Michigan State team faced Larry Bird and the Indiana State squad for the National Collegiate Athletic Association title in 1979. The dramatic game was televised nationally and is credited with reestablishing the public's interest in basketball. As a pro, Johnson led Los Angeles to five National Basketball Association titles, including 1980, when he replaced injured teammate Kareem Abdul Jabbar at center. The all-time leading assist-maker in NBA history, Johnson ended his career in 1991 with the announcement that he had tested positive for HIV, the virus that causes AIDS. He has become active in AIDS education and has served on the President's Council for AIDS Research.

Rafer Johnson in the decathlon during the 1960 Olympic Games in Rome.

JOHNSON, Rafer Lewis
1934-

Skilled in several sports, Johnson earned a scholarship to the University of California at Los Angeles, where he became a track star. He earned the Silver Medal in the 1956 Olympic decathlon, then took the decathlon Gold Medal at the 1960 Olympic Games, setting a new world record of 8,392 points. Named the Associated Press Athlete of the Year in 1980, Johnson served on the 1984 Olympic Committee. He still serves on the board of the Amateur Athlete Union, and is active in the Special Olympics.

JOHNSON, Robert
1911-1938

Singer-guitarist-composer Johnson is the most celebrated of Mississippi Delta bluesmen. Born in Hazelhurst, Mississippi, he played juke joints and street corners throughout the Deep South before recording the 29 songs (1936-1937) upon which his legend rests. In 1990 a CD reissue of these songs became a million-seller. His songs were already familiar to pop and blues audiences through the recordings of both traditional blues artists and The Rolling Stones. In popular folklore Johnson's impassioned genius is ascribed to a deal with the devil. He was poisoned at the age of 27 by a jealous girlfriend.

JOHNSON, Sargent (Claude)
1888-1967

A sculptor, ceramist, and printmaker, he was born in Boston but was mostly based in San Francisco, where he died. He studied at the California School of Fine Arts, the Boston School of Fine Arts, and the A. W. Best School of Art in San Francisco. He enjoyed considerable success working in terracotta, porcelain enamel, mosaic tile, and polychrome wood. Among his better-known works were "Head of a Negro Woman" and "Neptune's Daughter". He exhibited nationwide, but his work was probably best known in San Francisco. After his death in 1967, his work became prized nationwide, and it is now represented in over 50 public and private collections. He received many medals, awards, and prizes, beginning in 1925.

JOHNSTON, Joshua
1765-1830

Formerly enslaved in Baltimore, he became the first African-American portrait painter. His work, which is classed among the early American "primitives", in fact steadily increased in sophistication throughout his lifetime and may have been influenced by his famous contemporaries, Baltimore artists Charles and Rembrandt Peale. All but two of his 30 known subjects were white. Typical of his style was inclusion of Sheraton furniture, detailed attention to lace and hair, wonderfully sobersided children, and an unmistakable sympathy toward his sitters. His success went unnoticed for over a century, but in the 1960s his work was exhibited in 20 major U.S. museums.

JONES, Bill T.
1952-

A celebrated dancer and choreographer, he is known for his exciting stage presence and complex choreography. The son of migrant farmers, by 1973 he had co-founded the American Dance Asylum with Arnie Zane, Lois Welk, and Jill Becker. His 1979 concerts with Sheryl Sutton brought great acclaim. In 1982 he and longtime dancing partner Arnie Zane formed their own company, creating such productions as *History of Collage* (1988). After Zane's death Jones produced *Last Supper at Uncle Tom's Cabin/The Promised Land* (1991). He continues to create dance that confronts issues of race, politics, and sexual preference.

for which he won a Tony Award in 1969. He has also appeared in many movies, including *Dr. Strangelove* and *Conan the Barbarian*. In addition, his was the unforgettable voice of Darth Vader in the hugely popular *Star Wars*. His many honors include membership in the Theater Hall of Fame (1985), the Emmy Award for *Gabriel's Fire* (1991), and the National Medal of the Arts (1992).

JONES, Quincy Delight, Jr.
1933-

Known as the producer of important records for entertainment celebrities such as Michael Jackson and Frank Sinatra, Jones's spectacular success in the pop record industry was preceded by a distinguished career as a jazz musician, arranger, and conductor. Born in Chicago, he was first interested in arranging by a teenage friend, Ray Charles, in Seattle. Jones subsequently played trumpet and arranged for Lional Hampton (1951-1953) and for various artists on numerous jazz recordings before becoming musical director on Dizzy Gillespie's international big band tour of 1956. He worked for Barclay Records in Paris (1957-1958) and led an all-star band for the European production of Harold Arlen's blues opera *Free and Easy* (1959). In New York he composed and arranged for Count Basie, Dinah Washington, and Sarah Vaughan, and, while an executive at Mercury Records, he started producing his own pop-oriented records. Beginning in the mid-1960s, he composed over 50 scores for movies and television, opening many doors for African-American musicians in Hollywood. He founded his Qwest Productions in 1975.

ABOVE: James Earl Jones in *Othello*, 1982.
RIGHT: Quincy Jones in 1991.

JONES, James Earl
1931-

Jones's deep, resonant voice has made him one of the country's best-known actors. The son of an actor, Jones was raised by his grandparents on their Mississippi farm, studied at the University of Michigan (A.B. 1953), fulfilled his military service in the army, and then headed for New York to pursue his acting career. He has appeared in more than 50 plays and is perhaps best-known for his *Othello* and for his performance as the heavyweight boxing champion Jack Johnson in the Broadway hit *The Great White Hope*,

Scott Joplin (undated photo).

JOPLIN, Scott
1868-1917

Joplin was almost as famous in his day as he is now, but he was largely forgotten until his compositions were used in the soundtrack of the poular movie *The Sting* in 1973. A self-taught itinerant pianist, he was born in Texarkana, Texas. After studying music at the George R. Smith College in Sedalia, Missouri, in 1896 he

Barbara Jordan in 1987.

began to notate compositions that he and his fellow musicians created in the gamey venues in which they made their livings. Eventually, working with music publisher John S. Stark of Sedalia, he began to receive credit and income for his "rags." After the huge success of his "Maple Leaf Rag" (1899) Joplin toured throughout the Midwest as the "King of Ragtime," performing on the piano such of his own compositions as "The Easy Winners" (1901) and "The Entertainers" (1902). After settling in Harlem he tried to legitimize ragtime music, but the failure of his *Treemonisha* (1915), an ambitious opera based on folk-music themes and never performed until 1972, is credited with causing his premature death.

JORDAN, Barbara
1936-

After earning a J.D. at Boston University in 1959, Jordan returned to her native Texas to practice law. In 1966 she became the first African-American to be elected to the state senate since 1883. In 1972 she was elected president pro tempore of the legislature and was named Governor for a Day. In 1972 she was elected to the U.S. House of Representatives, where she sponsored legislation on voting rights and workers compensation. In 1976 she was keynote speaker at the Democratic National Convention. Ill-health forced her resignation from politics in 1978, and

she is now a professor at the Lyndon B. Johnson School of Public Affairs at the University of Texas at Austin.

JORDAN, June
1936-

A poet, novelist, and educator, Jordan is of Jamaican parentage but was herself born in New York City. Since studying at Barnard and the University of Chicago, she has taught at many colleges and universities around the U.S., including Sarah Lawrence College, Yale University, and the State University of New York at Stony Brook. She is a writer, having published more than ten volumes of poetry (including *New Days: Poems of Exile and Return*, 1973), as well as essays (*On Call: Political Essays*, 1985) and children's books (including *Fannie Lou Hamer*, 1972, and *His Own Where*, 1971). Much of her work has dealt with the pain black women often have to undergo in order to establish their identities. She is also a regular columnist for *The Progressive Magazine*. She received a Rockefeller grant in 1969, and in 1984 she won an award for international reporting from the National Association of Black Journalists.

JORDAN, Michael Jeffrey
1963-

A seven-time scoring leader in the National Basketball Association, Jordan was the most visible and popular African-American athlete of the early 1990s. He was also the most highly paid, earning more than $60 million per year. Following a championship collegiate career (he took North Carolina to the top in 1982, then won Player of the Year honors in 1984) Jordan became the most exciting player in the NBA. Four times the NBA named him Most Valuable Player, a title also bestowed on him by the Chicago Bulls in three consecutive championship series (1991-1993). An excellent all-round athlete, Jordan golfs in the low 80s. After the murder of his father he was understandably uncertain about his future. His sudden retirement from basketball in the fall of 1993 stunned sports fans, but left him free for such projects as the construction of golf entertainment centers. In 1994 he was given a minor-league contract with the White Sox, though how serious he was about starting a professional baseball career was unclear.

OPPOSITE: Michael Jordan being fouled as he goes for the hoop in a 1989 game.

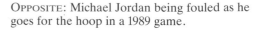

Vernon Jordan in 1992.

JORDAN, Vernon Eulion, Jr.
1935-

Born in Atlanta, Georgia, Jordan would become one of the most influential figures in the civil rights movement in the 1960s and 1970s. After graduation from De Pauw University (1957) and Howard Law School (1960) he returned to his native Georgia, where he practiced law. It was Jordan who forced his way through a mob of whites to escort African-American Charlayne Hunter-Gault to enroll at the University of Georgia. In 1962 he became field secretary for the Georgia branch of the National Association for the Advancement of Colored People. His most important work in the 1960s was as director of the voter education project of the southern regional council. More than 2 million African-Americans were registered between 1964 and 1968; not surprisingly, during these years the number of elected African-Americans rose from 72 to 564. From 1970 to 1972 Jordan served as executive director of the United Negro College Fund before becoming executive director of the Urban League in 1972. Again, Jordan concentrated on voter registration while maintaining the League's traditional commitment to community service. A skilled politician, Jordan kept the door open between the League and the Nixon administration, although he may have been more at ease during the presidency of his fellow Georgian, Jimmy Carter. Despite their personal friendship, Carter came in for some harsh criticism from

Jordan in 1977 when the weak economy prompted Carter to advocate cutbacks in some human service programs. In 1980, after delivering a speech in Fort Wayne, Indiana, Jordan was wounded by a rifle bullet fired by an as-yet-unknown sniper. He recovered fully but resigned as head of the Urban League the next year and resumed his law practice. In 1992 he became an important member of President Clinton's transition team and has maintained close ties to the Clinton administration.

JOYNER-KERSEE, Jackie
(Jacqueline)
1962-

Sometimes called "the world's greatest female athlete," Jackie Joyner-Kersee was born in East St. Louis, Illinois. She led her high school basketball team to two straight titles and was named to the All-State team three times. She was also the Illinois state champion in the 400-meter sprint and the long jump. While attending the University of California at Los Angeles she trained for the rugged heptathlon, in which she had to compete in seven track and field events. She took the silver medal in the 1984 Olympics in the women's heptathlon. When she won the gold medal in that event in the 1988 Olympics she set new Olympic records for the women's heptathlon in total points. She also set a record for the 100-meter sprint and won the gold medal in the long jump. In an amazing display of both persistence and skill, she took the gold again in the heptathlon at the 1992 Olympics and also won the bronze in the women's long jump. In addition to her triumphs as an athlete, she has also written children's books.

JULIAN, Percy Lavon
1899-1975

The grandson of a slave, he became well known for his work on soya proteins and the structures of steroids. He earned his M.A. from Harvard (1923) and his Ph.D. in organic chemistry from the University of Vienna (1931). Between 1920 and 1964 he taught at several universities, including Fisk, DePauw, Howard, Lincoln, Northeastern, and Oberlin. In 1935 he synthesized physostigmime, used to treat glaucoma. Directing research for the Glidden Company (1936-1954), he developed scores of soybean derivatives, notably cortisone and soy lecithin. He established Julian Laboratories (1954), headed the Julian Research Institute (1964-1975), and contributed to African-American civil rights groups.

JUST, Ernest Everett
1883-1941

Known as the "Black Apollo of Science" for his dignified bearing, he was educated at Dartmouth (A.B., 1907) and the University of Chicago (Ph.D., 1916). A marine zoologist and cell biologist, he also began studies at the Woods Hole (Massachusetts) Marine Biological Laboratory in 1909 and returned there during summers for the next 20 years. His principal appointment was at Howard University (1907-1941), though lack of facilities and recognition led him to pursue research in Europe for a time. He is known for demonstrating the cancer-producing effects of ultraviolet radiation on cells.

Jackie Joyner-Kersee in Tokyo in 1991.

before joining the Potomac Electric Power Company as counsel in 1976. Despite her involvement in local politics, which included serving as Democratic national committeewoman from the District of Columbia (1977-1980), her 1990 bid to be mayor was widely regarded as a longshot. Since her election, she has concentrated heavily on such issues as crime and public safety.

KING, B.B. (Riley B.)
1925-

One of the best-known blues performers and the first to enter the pop mainstream, singer and guitarist King remains a blues giant whose distinctive guitar voice has served as a primary model in rock. Born into a sharecropping family in Itta Bena, Mississippi, after work as a Memphis disc jockey ("The Beale Street Blues Boy" became "B.B.") he released rhythm-and-blues hits (1949-1962) and toured continuously for nearly 30 years. He was the first bluesman to tour the U.S.S.R. and to appear regularly in Las Vegas and on network TV. King was inducted into the Rock 'n' Roll Hall of Fame in 1987.

Rev. Martin Luther King, Jr., in 1965.

KING, Martin Luther, Jr.
(b. Michael L. King)
1929-1968

The most influential leader in twentieth-century African-Americans' struggle for civil rights, King was born in Atlanta, Georgia. Both his father and his maternal grandfather were Baptist ministers at Ebenezer Baptist Church in Atlanta, providing a strong religious tradition for King. He attended the Atlanta public schools and was graduated with his A.B. from Morehouse College in 1948, when he was 19 years old. He went on to Crozer Theological Seminary (in Chester, Pennsylvania), where he was the first African-American to be elected president of the student body there. He was graduated from Crozer in 1951 at the top of his class and went on to get his Ph.D. from Boston University in 1955. King met Coretta Scott while in Boston, and his father married them in 1953. By this time an ordained minister, King took the pastorate of the Dexter Avenue Baptist Church in Montgomery, Alabama, in 1954 and quickly became involved in the civil rights movement. With the 1954 U.S. Supreme Court decision in *Brown vs. The Board of Education*, the struggle against segregation laws heated up in the South, and King soon found himself in the forefront of a boycott of Montgomery's segregated buses (1955-1956). The boycott led to another Supreme Court decision in 1956 declaring Alabama's bus segregation laws unconstitutional. Following this triumph King was made president of the newly

KELLY, Sharon Pratt
1944-

The first African-American woman to be elected mayor of the nation's capital, Pratt was educated in Washington, D.C., where she earned her A.B. (1965) and J.D. at Howard University. In the 1970s she was an associate at the firm of Pratt and Queen and was on the faculty of Antioch College,

B.B. King in 1990.

guitar is famous for using his riveting voice to sing himself out of prison, where he was discovered by pioneering folklorist John Lomax. The hundreds of songs he recorded for Lomax formed the corner-stone of the Library of Congress folklore archives. He moved to New York City in 1938 and there pioneered live folk music on network radio and recorded for Columbia Records.

LEE, Canada
(b. Leonard Canegata)
1907-1952

A boxer, jockey, and violinist, he found his greatest fame as an actor. He grew up in Harlem, left home when he was 14, and won over two hundred fights (1925-1930) before gaining attention as Blacksnake in a revival of *Stevedore* (1934). After work-ing with African-American theater troupes, he achieved success as Bigger Thomas in *Native Son* (1941), and as Cali-ban in *The Tempest* (1945). He appeared as George in *Set My People Free* (1948) and in four movies, including *Cry, the Beloved Country* (1952). He was black-listed during the 1950s for association with communists.

BELOW: Canada Lee (center) in the 1946 Broadway play *On Whitman Avenue*.

ABOVE: Director Spike Lee (left) with Magic Johnson in 1992.

LEE, Spike (Shelton Jackson)
1957-

Born into a middle-class family, Lee, like his father and grandfather before him, attended Morehouse College in Atlanta. While there he bought his first super-B camera and began experimenting with filmmaking. After graduation from More-house in 1979 Lee won a summer intern-ship at Columbia Pictures in Burbank, California. He then studied filmmaking at the New York University Film School (M.A. 1982). When his first film was vetoed by the Screen Actors Guild in 1984 Lee unsuccessfully sued the guild for racism, losing some $40,000. The follow-ing year he made his first hit, *She's Gotta Have It*, filmed in 12 days for $175,000. *School Daze* (1988), *Do the Right Thing* (1989), *Mo' Better Blues* (1990), and *Jungle Fever* (1991) followed in rapid suc-cession. In 1992 Lee departed from his usual low-budget approach to produce *Malcolm X*, which was widely regarded as sparking a nation-wide revival of interest in the slain Black Muslim leader. In addition to his film work Lee has made commercials and music videos, has taught a course in film at Harvard University (1992-1993), and supports the efforts of young African-American filmmakers with a scholarship fund at his alma mater, the New York University Film School.

LEWIS, Carl (Frederick Carlton)
1961-

Known for several years as the "fastest man in the world" for his records in the 100-meter dash – his personal best came in

Carl Lewis in the 1992 Olympics.

1991 with 9.86 seconds – Lewis had won attention while still a student at Houston University. In 1984, at the Los Angeles Olympics, Lewis became the first athlete since Jesse Owens to win four gold medals in one Olympics: the 100-meter dash, the 200-meter dash, the long jump, and the 100-meter relay. Lewis went on to win two more gold medals in the 1988 Seoul games (100-meter dash and the long jump) and another gold medal for the long jump in the 1992 Olympics. (Lewis's gold for the 1988 100-meter dash was awarded after Canadian Ben Johnson's victory was overturned when his post-victory urine test revealed he had illegally used steroids.) Although his intense manner sometimes

makes him seem arrogant or remote, Lewis nonetheless has won the respect and admiration of his peers, who consider him one of the finest track and field athletes of all time.

LEWIS, Edmonia
?1845-?1911

Part African-American and part Chippewa Indian, she was raised in Albany, New York, and attended Oberlin College (1859-1862) before becoming a sculptor of the Neoclassic school. After training in Boston she visited France and settled in Rome, producing both portrait busts of eminent Americans and subjects drawn from her racial heritage. Especially cited are "Old Indian Arrow Maker and His Daughter", "Haggar," and "Freedwoman". She wrote: "I have strong sympathy with all women who have struggled and suffered." She exhibited in Boston (1865), in San Francisco (1873), and at the Philadelphia Centennial Exposition that was held in 1876.

LEWIS, John Aaron
1920-

Best known as pianist and musical director of the Modern Jazz Quartet (1952-1974; 1981-), Lewis was a major composer in the "Third Stream" movement, which explored the fusion of jazz and classical elements. Born in La Grange, Illinois, and raised in Albuquerque, New Mexico, he worked as pianist and arranger for numerous bandleaders (1945-1951) including Dizzy Gillespie, Charlie Parker, Miles Davis, Illinois Jacquet, and Lester Young. Long active in jazz education, he has composed for motion pictures and ballets and has become known in recent years for energetic, masterly soloing.

LEWIS, Reginald
1942-1993

A lawyer and international financier, he was a high-flyer known for his $985-million acquisition of the Beatrice Companies in 1987. He was graduated from the Harvard Law School in 1968 and specialized in venture capital with two New York law firms. He became rich through the controversial $50-million sale of his McCall Pattern Company (1987), which went into Chapter 11 reorganization. Merrill Lynch halted a stock offering of his TLC Beatrice in 1990, but, still undaunted, he continued to pursue ventures in Eastern Europe.

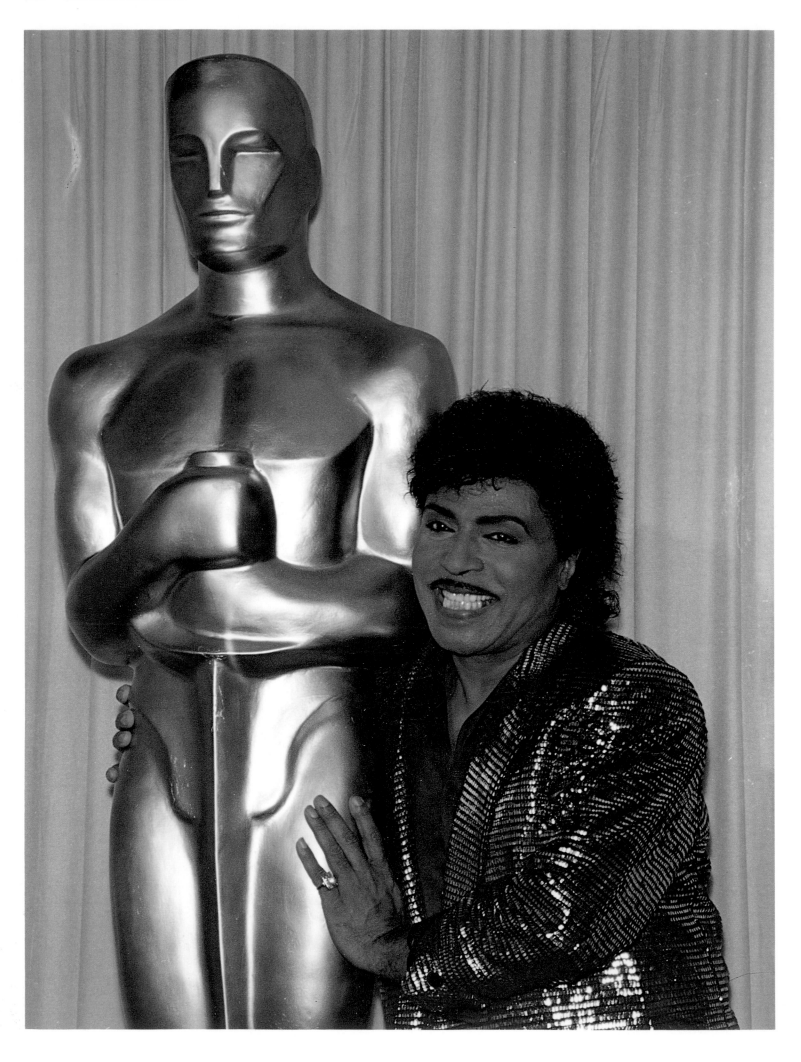

OPPOSITE: Little Richard gives Oscar a hug at the 1988 Academy Awards.

LITTLE RICHARD
(b. Richard Wayne Penniman)
1935-

The most flamboyant star of early rock 'n' roll, Little Richard's histrionic singing and manic piano playing made his name synonymous with the genre. His three-million-selling single "Tutti Frutti" (1956) became the official rock song of his native Georgia in 1989. Born in Macon, he had performed in choirs, gospel shows, and medicine shows until he began recording in 1952. A phenomenal success in the late 1950s, he retired to the ministry, then returned to rock in 1963 and toured England with the Beatles and the Rolling Stones. He has been equally engaged in music and religion ever since. He was an inductee of the Rock 'n' Roll Hall of Fame in 1986.

BELOW: Pop Lloyd (undated photo).

LLOYD, Pop (John Henry)
1884-1965

Lloyd's contemporaries, including Babe Ruth and Honus Wagner, considered him the greatest baseball player they ever saw. Describing his often sensational fielding technique, Cuban fans called him *el Cuchara*, "the scoop". An expert batsman as well, he was already in his thirties when the Negro National League was formed, yet he played in it for a dozen years and hit .564 in 1928, leading the league in home runs at the age of 44. He was elected to the Baseball Hall of Fame in 1977.

LOCKE, Alain Leroy
1886-1954

An influential teacher, editor, and writer, Locke was the first African-American to attend Oxford University as Rhodes Scholar (B. Litt., 1910). After studying at the University of Berlin he took up a teaching post at Howard University in 1912. He remained there until his death, except for year spent at Harvard to complete his Ph.D. studies in 1918. In 1925 he edited the influential anthology *The New Negro: An Interpretation*, and in the following years he published widely on African-American art, literature, and culture. At the time of his death he left a mass of unpublished works-in-progress, much of which was edited by his colleague, Margaret Just Butcher, and published as *The Negro in American Culture* (1956, 1972).

Louis Lomax (right) interviewing in 1958.

LOMAX, Louis E.
1922-1970

Born in Valdosta, Georgia, Lomax earned degrees from American University (1944) and Yale University (1947). He was a newspaperman (1941-1958) and a news commentator with Metromedia Broadcasting (1964-1968), but he was primarily a free-lance writer. He was an important commentator upon the movement toward African-American integration into white society; during the struggles of the 1960s he freely criticized both sides. His works include *The Reluctant African* (1960) and *When the Word is Given* (1963), and in 1970 he was at work on a three-volume history of African-Americans when he was killed in an automobile crash.

LORDE, Audre Geraldin
1934-1992

Lorde was born and raised in New York City. She attended the University of Mexico (1954), Hunter College (A.B., 1959), and Columbia (M.L.S., 1961). Settling in the Virgin Islands, Lorde taught in many schools, including Hunter College in New York City. An activist and lesbian feminist, Lorde became a highly regarded poet and writer. Her works include *Zami: A New Spelling of My Name* (1982), her "biomythography" *Sister Outsider* (1984), and *A Burst of Light* (1988).

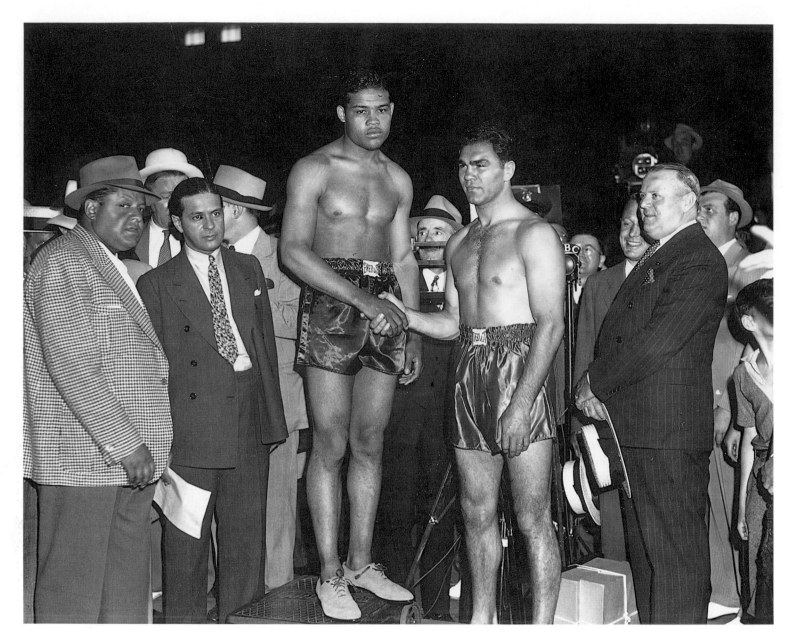

Joe Louis (center) and Max Schmeling before their second fight, in 1938.

LOUIS, Joe (b. Joe Louis Barrow)
1914-1981

Joe Louis still holds the record for the longest reign as heavyweight boxing champion: 11 years, eight months, and seven days. During that time he fought 25 title fights – more than the combined total of the eight title holders who had preceded him. Louis, who was born in Lafayette, Alabama, was only four when his sharecropper father died. His mother remarried, and when Louis was 16 the family moved to Detroit. It was in Detroit that Louis first began to box, winning 50 out of 59 fights as an amateur before turning professional in 1934. In 1935 he had his first big fight, against former champion Primo Carnera, who was attempting a comeback. Louis knocked out Carnera in the sixth round and earned the nickname "The Brown Bomber." In the next few years Louis knocked out two more former champions, Max Baer and Jack Sharkey, and met his only defeat at the hands of Max Schmeling, who knocked him out in the 12th round. In 1937 Louis got his shot at the title, taking on champion James J. Braddock, whom he put away in the eighth round. The next year, he met Schmeling again and won the fight in the first round. In 1941 Louis defended his title an amazing six times in six months. In 1947 Louis won a disputed decision over Jersey Joe Walcott. Six months later the fighters met again, and Louis won by a K.O., but he retired from the ring in 1949. Attempts at a come-back in the 1950s were unsuccessful. In 1978 his autobiography, *Joe Louis: My Life*, was published. Louis's last years were a sad falling off from the great days when his awesome skills had made him rich and famous – poor financial management left him impoverished and forced him to to work as a "greeter" in Las Vegas casinos and to rely on charity from wealthy friends – but he never lost his essential dignity.

LOWERY, Joseph E.
1924-

A softspoken and unassuming Methodist clergyman, he became a civil-rights activist and president of the Southern Christian Leaderhsip Conference (1977-). His first congregation was at Warren Street, Birmingham (1952-1961). In Atlanta he was minister of St. Paul (1964-1968), Central United Methodist (1968-1986), and Cascade United Methodist Church (1986-1992). In 1979 he led an SCLC factfinding mission to meet with leaders of the Palestine Liberation Organization. He reinstituted SCLC's Operation Breadbasket to encourage reinvestment within the African-American community. He promoted anti-apartheid action and the Voting Rights Act of 1982.

M

MALCOLM X (b. Malcolm Little)
1925-1965

One of the most controversial figures in the civil rights movement and one of the best-known advocates of what would come to be called "black power," Malcolm's career was cut short by an assassin. Malcolm's minister father died in Michigan when Malcolm was a boy of 6; Malcolm later said that his father had been murdered by racists, but other accounts say that his death was accidental. Shortly after her husband's death, Malcolm's mother had a nervous breakdown, and her eight children were placed in institutions and foster homes. At the age of 15 Malcolm headed east, settling in Boston, where he supported himself with odd jobs, including shining shoes and pimping. In 1943 he moved from Boston to New York City, where he began to sell drugs and led an increasingly marginal life. In 1946 he received a ten-year prison sentence for burglary. Prison transformed Malcolm's life: he became a follower of Elijah Muhammad's Nation of Islam movement, and upon his parole in 1952 he was ordained as a minister, taking the name Malcolm X. His militant stance and his depiction of whites as "blue-eyed devils" won him considerable press coverage and a good deal of suspicion from the white community. He seemed in many ways the antithesis of Dr. Martin Luther King, Jr., the prophet of non-violence. In 1963 he was ostracized from the Nation of Islam after he characterized President John F. Kennedy's assassination as an instance of the "chickens coming home to roost." He then formed the Organization of Afro-American Unity and continued to work for black rights. In 1964 he made a pilgrimage to Mecca, converted to orthodox Islam, and took the name El Malik el Shabazz. At the time of his death he seemed

to be moderating his hostile view of whites somewhat. Nonetheless, he spoke in the months before his death of his fear that he might be assassinated by opponents in the Nation of Islam or forces in the U.S. government. (His assassin was apparently a member of a dissident black group, though some mystery still remains about the event.) His influential *Autobiography of Malcolm X* (1965) was co-authored by *Roots* author Alex Haley, and many of his speeches were published posthumously. Spike Lee's film *Malcolm X* (1992) helped to spark a renewal of interest in both the man and his political philosophy.

MARSALIS, Wynton
1961-

Born and raised in a New Orleans family of famous musicians (including pianist father Ellis and saxophonist brother Branford), Wynton Marsalis' mastery of the trumpet in both jazz and classical forms

Malcolm X in 1963.

earned him Grammy awards for recordings in both fields in 1984. After a stint with Art Blakey's Jazz Messengers (1980-1982), during which he established himself as an outstanding interpreter and champion of classical acoustic jazz styles, he led a succession of small ensembles. His numerous recordings and constant touring schedule have made him one of the most visible American musicians and a preeminent exponent of jazz as America's classical music. Marsalis conducts numerous clinics to introduce public school students to jazz and to encourage their pursuit of jazz as a career. In recent years he has turned increasingly to composition, with both short and extended works reflecting his veneration of Duke Ellington and his interest in early jazz styles. In 1993 *The New York Times* called him "the most important jazz musician working, both politically and musically."

Thurgood Marshall in 1992.

MARSHALL, Thurgood
1908-1993

The son of a sleeping car porter, Marshall was both a prominent civil rights activist and the first African-American U.S. Supreme Court Justice (1967-1991). Born in Baltimore, Maryland, Marshall at first studied dentistry as an undergraduate at Lincoln University, but then he went on to Howard University to study law. After being graduated at the top of his law school class in 1933 he began to practice in Baltimore, where he became a counsel for the National Association for the Advancement of Colored People in 1936. Two years later he became chief counsel for the NAACP, a position he held until his appointment to the U.S. Court of Appeals in 1961. As chief counsel at the NAACP he argued and won 29 of the 32 important civil rights cases he handled – matters ranging from voting rights to desegregated transportation. In 1950 he became director-counsel of the NAACP's Legal Defense and Education Fund. The case that is most closely associated with him – and which he himself regarded as his most important case – was *Brown v. Board of Education* (1954), which overturned *Plessy v. Ferguson* (1896) and made illegal the "separate but equal" education that had perpetuated segregation and inferior education for African-Americans. In 1961 President John F. Kennedy named him to the U.S. Court of Appeals, an appoint-

ment vigorously opposed by many of the Southern Senators in Kennedy's own Democratic party who blocked Marshall's confirmation until 1962. While the appointment was hanging fire, Kennedy sent Marshall as his personal representative to the independence ceremonies in the new West African republic of Sierre Leone. In 1965 President Lyndon Johnson appointed Marshall U.S. solicitor general, a post he held until 1967, when President

Johnson elevated him to the U.S. Supreme Court. During his long tenure on the Supreme Court, Marshall consistently voted with the liberal block, in particular opposing the death penalty and any discrimination based on race or sex. He was also a strong advocate of the rights of criminal defendants. In his later years Marshall became increasingly isolated as conservative justices appointed by presidents Richard Nixon and Ronald Reagan took their places on the bench. Despite failing eyesight, he resisted the idea of retirement until 1991, when ill-health led to his resignation. In retirement, Marshall often spoke of his sorrow at the revived conservatism of the Supreme Court.

MATZELIGER, Jan Ernst
1852-1889

This inventor of a machine that revolutionized the shoemaking industry of the world was born in Paramaribo, Dutch Guiana (now Surinam). He emigrated to the United States at the age of 18 and lived in Philadelphia before settling in Lynn, Massachusetts, in 1877. While working in shoe factories in Lynn he set about, on his own time, to invent a shoe-lasting machine – one that attaches the upper leather portion of the shoe to the inner sole. He took out his first patent on this in

Jan E. Matzeliger (below left) and a drawing of his lasting machine (below).

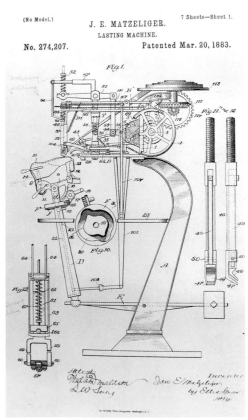

1883 and over the years would receive five more patents for improvements. Unfortunately, he was only given stock in the company that manufactured his machine and never profited much before his premature death from tuberculosis. His machine eventually doubled the wages of shoe workers in the United States and greatly reduced the price of shoes.

MAYNARD, Robert Clyve
1937-1993

Maynard was one of three journalists chosen to question Gerald Ford and Jimmy Carter in their 1976 campaign debate. He had taken up journalism when he quit school to work for *New York Age*, an African-American weekly, and soon thereafter (1961) he went to work for the *York* (Pennsylvania) *Gazette*. At the *Washington Post* he became the first black national correspondent (1967) and an associate editor (1972). In 1979 he became the first African-American to edit a major daily paper, then the first to own one – the *Oakland* (California) *Tribune* (1983-1992). He was also a Pulitzer Prize juror. The unstinting help he gave to minority youth prompted some people to call him "the Jackie Robinson of publishing."

ABOVE: Willie Mays *c*. 1965.

BELOW: Robert C. Maynard in 1976.

MAYS, Willie Howard
1931-

The most exciting baseball player of the 1950s and 1960s, the "Say Hey Kid" compiled statistics that include 660 home runs, 3,283 hits, and 338 stolen bases, while dazzling fans with his play in center field. A catch he made while playing for the New York Giants in the 1954 World Series is often cited as the best outfield play ever: sprinting with his back turned to home plate, Mays made an over-the-shoulder catch near the 475-foot sign on the outfield wall; whirling, he fired the ball to second base, preventing the runner on first from advancing. His prowess in the outfield won him Gold Glove awards for eleven consecutive years and enabled him to set fielding records at both the career and league levels. Mays was a star at the plate as well as in the field. He led the league in home runs four times, won the National League batting title in 1954, and was named the league's Most Valuable Player twice (in 1954 and again in 1965). During his 25-year professional baseball career

Mays played for the Negro League Birmingham Black Barons, the National League New York Giants, the San Francisco Giants, and the New York Mets. He received baseball's highest honor in 1979, when he was elected to the Baseball Hall of Fame in his very first year of eligibility.

MCCOY, Elijah
1843-1929

This ingenious inventor – who may have inspired the expression "the real McCoy" – was the son of African-Americans who fled from slavery to Canada. He was born in Ontario, Canada, but after the Civil War his family moved back to the United States and settled (1870) in Ypsilanti, Michigan. He evidently studied mechanical engineering in Scotland, but on returning to Michigan he could only get a job as a fireman on the railroad. His work at constantly oiling the moving machinery led him to invent a "drip cup," (patented

Hattie McDaniel wins an Oscar in 1940.

in 1873) still widely used to provide a steady supply of oil to moving machinery. He continued improving his basic invention, obtaining 57 patents for devices that improved the automatic lubrication process, which was important in the development of rail and ship transportation. He also took out patents on 15 other inventions. By 1920 he was able to open his own manufacturing company.

MCDANIEL, Hattie
1895-1952

Famous as the first African-American to win an Academy Award – as a supporting actress in *Gone With the Wind* (1939) – McDaniel was born in Wichita, Kansas, the daughter of a Baptist preacher. She began her career as a band vocalist, going on to be the first African-American woman to sing on American radio. In addition to making numerous movies in the 1930s and 1940s, she was on many radio shows and later on TV, but in keeping with contemporary conventions she was usually cast as a servant.

ABOVE: Bobby McFerrin in 1989.

MCFERRIN, Bobby
1950-

Using his body as a percussion instrument, improvising in vocalese, employing a fluid, four-octave range, circular breathing, and a peculiar repertoire of sounds and genres, McFerrin considers himself a "healer" and "a channel for fun". Born in New York City to classical singers and educated at The Juilliard School, after work as a journeyman pianist, with encouragement from John Hendricks he perfected a unique unaccompanied vocal style of wordless improvisations and vocal acrobatics and began performing lengthy impromptu concerts involving audience participation (1983-1988). Following the release of his four-Grammy-award-winning album *Simple Pleasures* (1988), featuring the hit "Don't Worry, Be Happy," he moved beyond his jazz audience to mainstream acceptance and began exploring vocal regions ever more varied and unpredictable.

MCKAY, Claude
(b. Festus Claudius McKay)
1889-1948

This writer and poet was born in Sunny Ville, Jamaica, and had published two volumes of poetry before coming to the

United States in 1912. He studied at Tuskegee Institute in Alabama and then at Kansas State before moving to New York City and publishing more poetry under the pseudonym "Eli Edwards". He worked in London for a communist newspaper (1919-1920) before returning to New York and publishing *Harlem Shadows* in 1922, a book of poems that were an influential product of the Harlem Renaissance. He lived in Europe for many years (1922-1934), writing novels and short stories, but he returned to New York City in the mid-1930s and continued to write books, among them his autobiography, *A Long Way from Home* (1937) and a sociological text, *Harlem: Negro Metropolis* (1940).

MCKISSICK, Floyd B.
1922-1991

A civil rights leader and business executive, he won the Purple Heart and five battle stars in World War II, then became the first African-American to earn a law degree at the University of North Carolina (1951). He handled hundreds of civil rights cases (1952-1966) and was legal counsel for the Congress of Racial Equality before becoming CORE's national chairman (1966) and a leading exponent of Black Power. Beginning in 1968, he financed and developed enterprises such as Soul City in North Carolina. His books include *A Black Manifesto* (1966) and *Three-Fifths of a Man* (1968)

RIGHT: James Meredith in 1962.
BELOW: Floyd McKissick (right) in 1966.

MEREDITH, James Howard
1933-

Meredith was born in Kosciusko, Mississippi, and had served in the U.S. Air Force. He was abruptly thrust into the limelight when he became the first African-American to enroll in the University of Mississippi in 1962. The riots that ensued left two dead, and whites were so hostile that he had to be guarded by federal troops until he was graduated in 1963. He was shot on a one-man March Against Fear in Mississippi in 1966 and, although he was able to complete the march, he left the civil rights movement, denouncing non-violence as a tactic, and thereafter attended Columbia University Law School and moved into business. In 1968 he became president of his own company, Meredith Enterprises.

MICHEAUX, Oscar
1884-1951

At various times a farmer, rancher, and Pullman porter, he eventually became the first black producer in the history of American film. Between 1918 and 1940 he produced a distributed in the U.S.A. and Europe over 30 films, many from his own novels, with African-American casts, for African-American audiences. His films focused on the black middle-class and often cast blacks in roles that broke with stereotypes. They included *Within Our Gates* (1920), treating a lynching; *The Exile* (1931), his first "all-talkie" film, touching on interracial love; and *God's Stepchildren* (1938), dealing with degrees of skin color. He sought always to present the truth, but this was sometimes misunderstood. He became bankrupt in the early 1940s.

BELOW: Florence Mills *c*. 1925.

ABOVE: Charlie Mingus in 1960.

MILLS, Florence
1895-1927

A major international star, singer and entertainer, Mills, born in Washington, D.C., was performing by the age of five. After replacing the lead in *Shuffle Along* (1921) she starred on Broadway in musicals such as *Plantation Review* (1922) and *Dixie to Broadway* (1924), as well as in productions in London and Paris. Known for her rendition of "I'm a Little Blackbird Looking for a Bluebird" and for her solo in William Grant Still's orchestral work *Levee Land* (1926), the beautiful, petite, masterly performer was greatly mourned when she died prematurely.

MINGUS, Charles
1922-1979

A passionate virtuoso on the bass and one of the seminal composers of the century, Mingus's volatile genius bridged modern and free jazz, encompassing his own spiritual quest (detailed in his autobiography *Beneath the Underdog*, 1971) and his fierce insistence on civil rights. Born in Nogales, Arizona, and raised in Watts in Los Angeles, following extensive classical and jazz studies he worked with Louis Armstrong, Lionel Hampton, and Red Norvo (1941-1953). He collaborated with major bepob figures, including Charlie Parker, Dizzy Gillespie, and Max Roach. His legendary "Jazz Workshop" bands

schooled such jazz giants as Eric Dolphy and Jackie McLean. The Mingus Big Band, composed of former band members and devotees, continued to perform his works regularly in Manhattan throughout the early 1990s.

MITCHELL, Arthur
1934-

Ballet dancer, choreographer, and artistic director, he was the first African-American to become a full-contract member of the New York City Ballet (1956). In 12 years there, he was best known for dancing in the works of George Balanchine, especially in *Agon* (1957), *Midsummer Night's Dream* (1962), *Don Quixote* (1965), and *Ragtime* (1966). His own choreographed works include *Rhythmetron* (1968), *Fête Noire* (1971), and *Tones* (1974). In 1970 he opened the Dance Theatre of Harlem, created to teach dance, especially ballet, to children.

ABOVE: Thelonious Monk (undated photo). BELOW: Arthur Mitchell (center, wearing shirt) and company in 1973.

MONK, Thelonious
1917-1982

Internationally honored for his unique musical voice and enduring compositions and one of only five jazz musicians ever featured on the cover of *Time* magazine (1964), Monk was a key innovator of modern jazz and a legend among musicians. Born in Rocky Mount, North Carolina, and raised in New York City, he began piano lessons at the age of 11. Working as a sideman for established jazz artists in the early 1940s, he became a principal contributor to the evolution of "bebop". After two years with Coleman Hawkins and a year with Dizzy Gillespie, Monk began leading his own groups in 1947, and for the next seven years he recorded extensively. At the height of his creativity as a composer, this enigmatic, reclusive figure was banned (1951) from performing in New York nightclubs for six years. He continued recording and in 1957 returned to performing with a new quartet featuring John Coltrane. By the beginning of his association with Columbia Records in 1961 many of his compositions had become recognized as standards. He toured nationally and internationally throughout the 1960s (as pianist with the Giants of Jazz in 1971-1972), making his last major public appearance at the 1974 Newport Jazz Festival.

Garrett A. Morgan c. 1955.

MORGAN, Garrett A.
1875-1963

Born in Paris, Kentucky, Morgan moved to Cincinnati (1889) and then to Cleveland (1895). He began his career by repairing and selling sewing machines, and soon he opened his own tailoring shop. He invented a safety hood and smoke protector (1912), which he developed into a gas mask (patented, 1914). He won fame by rescuing workmen trapped in a smoke-filled tunnel (1916), and his gas mask – rejected by Southern states because of his race – protected many American soldiers during World War I. He invented and patented (1923) a three-way automatic traffic signal and founded the *Cleveland Call* (1920), a weekly newspaper. He contracted glaucoma in 1943 and remained nearly blind for the rest of his life.

MORRISON, Toni
(b. Chloe Anthony Wofford)
1931-

A winner of the most prestigious of literary honors, the Nobel Prize, Morrison was born in Lorain, Ohio. She early excelled in school and went on to get her A.B. from Howard University in 1953. She earned her M.A. in English at Cornell (1955) and moved on to teach at Texas Southern University. Then, in 1957, she returned to teach at Howard (included among her students were Houston A. Baker, Jr. and Stokely Carmichael). It was while teach-ing at Howard University that she wrote the short story that would later develop into her first novel. In 1964 she resigned from Howard and took an editing position with Random House; she was soon promoted to senior editor. Encouraged by publishers, she developed the story she wrote at Howard about a young African-American girl who longed for blue eyes into her first novel, *The Bluest Eye* (1970).

In 1973 Morrison published *Sula*, her second novel, which immediately established her as a talented and respected fiction writer. The title character in *Sula* is a strong and resourceful African-American woman, and through her experiences Morrison explores the destruction of traditional African-American culture wrought by violence and discrimination against African-Americans. Morrison's next novel, *Song of Solomon* (1977), was her first to deal directly with the experiences of an African-American man. When, in 1981, Morrison published her fourth novel, *Tar Baby*, she was already well established as a significant American literary figure. Morrison's fifth novel, *Beloved*, a powerful, non-linear narrative that explores the after-effects of slavery, earned her a Pulitzer Prize in 1988. In 1984 Morrison resigned from her position with Random House and became a professor at the State University of New York at Albany. In 1989 she was appointed the Robert F. Goheen Professor of the Humanities at Princeton University. With the publication of her latest novel, *Jazz*, in 1992, Morrison moved into the forefront of American literature, and in 1993 she was awarded the Nobel Prize for Literature, making her the first African-American to earn that honor.

Toni Morrison in 1985.

MORTON, "Jelly Roll"
(Ferdinand Joseph)
1890-1941

A legendary braggart who claimed he had invented jazz in 1902, the much-traveled Morton was an accomplished and influential pianist, composer, arranger, and bandleader. Born in New Orleans, Louisiana, of Creole ancestry, his solo piano style evolved in bordellos and minstrel shows. His Red Hot Peppers, a band of prominent Chicago-based New Orleans musicans, recorded classic examples of New Orleans-style arranging and improvising (1926-1930). His colorful biography,

LEFT: Jelly Roll Morton in 1940.
BELOW: Edwin Moses in the 1984 Olympics.

Mister Jelly Roll (1950), was based on material he related to Alan Lomax for the Library of Congress in 1939.

MOSES, Edwin Corley
1955-

One of the greatest hurdlers in the history of track and field, Moses won the Gold Medal in the 400-meter hurdles in both the 1976 and 1984 Olympics. Three times the nation's top amateur athlete, he was inducted into the Olympics Hall of Fame after he earned the Bronze Medal in the 1988 Games: he had recorded 17 of the 20 fastest times in the 400-meter hurdles, and he won a record 107 consecutive races. During his career as an athlete Moses became an aeronautical engineer.

MOSES, Robert
1935-

Moses was an active leader within the Student Nonviolent Coordinating Committee (1960-1965). In 1964, Freedom Summer, he guided the hundreds of college students who came to Mississippi to assist black people make Mississippi open to black voters. A pacifist, he refused to go to Vietnam, changed his name, and moved to Canada, then to Tanzania. Since his return to the United States, he has started the pioneering Algebra Project that teaches children math by relating it to their personal experiences. After a successful pilot run, and accolades from labor and education experts, Moses brought the Algebra Project to the Delta, and envisions it as a way to make the mathematical and computer world accessible to young black children.

MOTLEY, Constance Baker
1921-

The first African-American woman to become a federal judge, she began as a lawyer for the Legal Defense and Education Fund of the National Association for the Advancement of Colored People. While there (1945-1964), she successfully argued nine NAACP cases before the U.S. Supreme Court, including James Meredith's suit to enter the University of Mississippi. She is considered the chief

Constance Baker Motley in 1965.

courtroom tactician of the civil rights movement. The first African-American woman in the New York Senate (1964) and on a federal bench (1966), she became chief judge (1982-1986) of the southern district of New York. She has received 24 honorary doctorates.

Elijah Muhammad in 1966.

MUHAMMAD, Elijah
(b. Elijah Poole)
1897-1975

Elijah Poole was born in Georgia to former slaves and sharecroppers. About 1930 he joined the Nation of Islam, founded and led by W.D. Fard, who became Poole's spiritual leader. After Fard's disappearance in 1934 Poole emerged as Elijah Muhammad, the divine leader of the Nation of Islam. Muhammad's talent lay in his ability to instill a sense of power and personal worth in black people who had been imprisoned, or addicted, or simply so exploited that they despaired of making a difference in their lives. He espoused a strict code of conduct, as well as physical, spiritual and emotional separation from whites, whom he characterized as devils. Under Muhammad's leadership, the Nation of Islam created separate schools, farms and small businesses, run by and for black people. Many of his teachings live on in Minister Louis Farrakhan's Final Call to Islam, a breakaway group created after Farrakhan quarreled with the more moderate Wallace Muhammad, Elijah Muhammad's son and successor.

children's lunch program, and established an elementary school. In 1968 Newton was convicted of voluntary manslaughter in the killing of a police officer, but the conviction was overturned. While on bail he went to Cuba, where he spent three years (1974-1977). In 1978 his retrial again resulted in a conviction, which was again overturned. That same year Newton was tried for the 1974 murder of a woman: the trial resulted in a hung jury and the charges were dismissed. In the 1980s he earned a Ph.D. from the University of Califonia, but he was arrested first for embezzling (1985) and then for illegal possession of firearms (1987): this time he was convicted and sentenced. He was killed in a drug-related shootout in 1989.

NIXON, Edgar Daniel
1899-1987

Through five decades he led the struggle for civil rights in Alabama, chiefly as founder, president, and activist with the Alabama branch of the Brotherhood of Sleeping Car Porters (1928-1964). In the 1950s he worked to integrate Alabama's public schools. When Rosa Parks was jailed in Alabama for refusing to move to the rear of a Montgomery bus (1955) he provided bail and helped lead the Montgomery bus boycott. He was treasurer of the Montgomery Improvement Association, a group that played a key role in sustaining the boycott. In the 1960s and 1970s he promoted affirmative action programs.

NEWTON, Huey P.
1942-1989

In 1966 Newton joined with Bobby Seale to found the Black Panther Party for Self-Defense, based in Oakland, California. This armed black-nationalist organization attracted many young black people who rejected non-violence as a tactic to counter oppression. Initially formed to monitor the activities of the police who patrolled Oakland's black community, it broadened its scope with a 10-point program to address a variety of social, economic, and political inequalities, set up a

RIGHT: E. D. Nixon (left) in 1956.
BELOW: A "Free Huey" (Newton) protest.

NORMAN, Jessye
1945-

Educated at Howard University, the Peabody Conservatory, and the University of Michigan (M.Mus., 1968), she became a world-renowned soprano. She made her operatic debut in Berlin in 1969; engagements followed in La Scala and Covent Garden. Her American debut was in *Aida* at the Hollywood Bowl (1972) and *Les Troyens* at the Metropolitan Opera (1983). Her rich, full tone impressed audiences worldwide in operas, concert tours, and festivals at Edinburgh, Helsinki, Lucerne, Vienna, Salzburg, Spoleto, and Tanglewood. Her many recordings only hint at a repertoire ranging from Mozart and Wagner to Mahler and African-American spirituals.

ABOVE: Jessye Norman in *Parsifal* in 1991.
RIGHT: Eleanor Holmes Norton in 1972.

NORTON, Eleanor Holmes
1937-

In 1990 Norton became the Congressional representative for the District of Columbia, her native town. She first came to national attention while working for the American Civil Liberties Union, when she defended Alabama Governor George Wallace's right to hold a rally in New York City in 1968. In 1970 she was made head of New York City's Commission on Human Rights, a post she held until President Carter put her in charge of the Equal Employment Opportunity Commission (1977-1981). In 1982 she joined the faculty of Georgetown University.

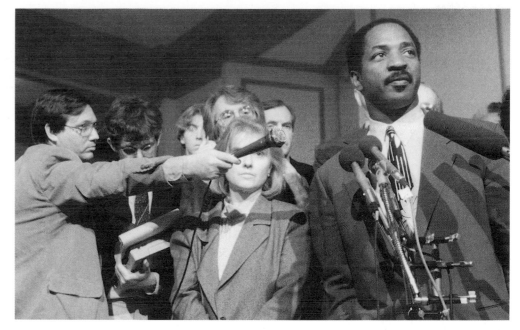

ODETTA (b. Odetta Holmes)
1930-

One of the major figures of the 1950s-1960s folk revival, Odetta became known for her powerful, operatic voice and driving solo acoustic guitar renditions of African-American folk songs, gospel, jazz, and blues. Born in Birmingham, Alabama, she moved to Los Angeles (1937), where her education included vocal and piano lessons. Initially influenced by Bessie Smith, after appearing in the chorus of *Finian's Rainbow* (1949) she opted for a career in folk music, and with the support of Pete Seeger and Harry Belafonte she became a staple of concerts, festivals, TV, and films (and a major influence on Janis Joplin). Since the 1960s her audience has been increasingly international.

King Oliver (back row, with cornet) and his Dixie Syncopators in 1925.

OGLETREE, Charles J., Jr.
1952-

A law professor known for his television commentaries on legal issues, he earned his first two degrees at Stanford University (A.B., 1974; M.A., 1975) before being graduated from the Harvard Law School (1978). He worked with the District of Columbia Public Defender Service as a staff attorney (1978-1982), then returned as deputy director (1984-1985). After adjunct positions in Washington, D.C., area law schools, he joined the faculty of the Harvard Law School (1985-), subsequently becoming director of its Criminal Justice Institute (1990-). Since 1990 he has received many awards for achievement, service, and teaching.

Charles Ogletree (right) in 1991.

OLIVER, "King" (Joseph)
1885-1938

Pioneering jazz cornetist and bandleader Oliver was born in Louisiana and raised in New Orleans, where, in the second decade of the century, he was idolized by the young Louis Armstrong. Known for his use of the mute to manipulate tone color and expand rhythmic interpretation, after he relocated to Chicago (1922) his Creole Jazz Band profoundly influenced Chicago's jazzmen, including Bix Beiderbecke. When Oliver added Armstrong to the band, it became the most innovative and influential small jazz group of the early 1920s.

OWENS, Jesse (James Cleveland)
1913-1980

The tenth child of an Alabama sharecropper, Owens played a pivotal role on an international stage when he won four Gold Medals in the 1936 Olympics in Berlin. He set four Olympic records, exposing Nazi racial theories to international ridicule. A hero after Berlin, Owens found that his Ohio State University education, his 11 world records, and his international acclaim did not help him much in making a living. He went on barnstorming tours, playing baseball with fellow Olympian Mack Robinson (Jackie Robinson's older brother). A frequent and outspoken critic of America's racial policies, Owens eventually emerged as an engaging speaker and leader of youth. Selected as the greatest track and field athlete of the half century in 1950, Owens served on the U.S. Olympic Committee and was awarded the Presidential Medal of Freedom in 1976.

Jesse Owens in the 1936 Olympics.

PAIGE, Satchel (Leroy Robert)
1906-1982

After two decades of prominence in the Negro Leagues, Paige became a 42-year-old rookie in the major leagues (Cleveland) in 1948. In his final game, at age 59, Paige tossed three innings as a starter for the Kansas City Athletics on September 25, 1965. Enduring, lanky, charismatic,

Paige had earned more than $30,000 a year during the 1930s, an amount that reflected his value to his Negro League teams, since it was more than most major league players were paid. He named his pitches: The "two-hump blooper" was a moving change-up, "Little Tom" was a medium fastball, "Long Tom" was a hard fastball, and the "hesitation pitch" was a stupefying delivery during which he paused mid-way. Paige's greatest triumph came in the 1942 Negro World Series, when he pitched and won all four games for the Kansas City Monarchs over the favored Homestead Grays. He was elected to the Hall of Fame in 1971.

PARKER, Charlie (Charles, Jr.)
1920-1955

By 1951 perhaps the most influential jazz musician in the world, Charlie Parker, known to the world simply as "Bird" (or "Yardbird"), was, more than any other musician, the father of bebop and modern

Satchel Paige in 1948.

Saxophonist Charlie Parker (RIGHT) at jazz festival in Paris in 1949.

jazz. Born and raised in Kansas City, Missouri, a center for jazz and blues during the 1930s, Parker dropped out of school at the age of 14 to concentrate on the alto saxophone. He attained such mastery that his playing is still the touchstone for the instrument. His Kansas City-based mentors and models included Buster Smith, Lester Young, Count Basie, and Hot Lips Page. After a season in New York City, he was a featured sideman in the best big bands of the day (1940-1944). In 1945 he led his own group in New York with Dizzy Gillespie, making numerous recordings in the revolutionary bebop style. His career was briefly interrupted by a nervous breakdown, but he returned to the New York scene in 1947 and formed his celebrated quintet, featuring Miles Davis and Max Roach, with which he made many of his most famous recordings. In 1951 the New York police, in response to his legendary heroin addiction, banned him from performing, forcing him into an itinerant career. He was permitted to perform in New York again in late 1953, but he was by then in poor physical and mental health, as well as in debt. He attempted suicide twice in 1954 and then committed himself to Bellevue Hospital. Seven days after his last public performance at Birdland, a Manhattan club named in his honor, he died, felled by his addictions and the problems they had caused him.

Gordon Parks in 1961.

PARKS, Gordon A.
1912-

Best known as a photojournalist, Parks has also produced films on African-American themes, has written books, including *The Learning Tree* (1966) and *Born Black* (1971), and has composed everything from popular songs to symphonies. Born in Kansas, Parks grew up in Saint Paul, Minnesota, but moved to Chicago in 1937 to pursue a career as a photographer. During World War II he served in the Overseas Division of the Office of War Information; his work there won him a job offer from *Life* magazine after the war. In the 1950s and 1960s Parks did a good deal of work on aspects of African-American life for public television, and in the 1970s he moved to Hollywood and produced a number of films, including *Shaft* and *Super Cops*. In 1977 Parks was one of three prominent African-Americans who banded together to purchase *Essence*, the popular magazine for African-American women. Parks's many awards include the Magazine Photographer of the Year in 1961 and the Spingarn Prize, the highest annual award of the National Association of Colored People, in 1972. In 1988 he was one of 12 recipients of the National Medal of Arts, awarded by President Reagan.

Rosa Parks, heroine of the Montgomery, Alabama, bus boycott of 1955-1956.

PARKS, Rosa
1913-

A native of Alabama (she was born in Tuskegee), Parks had briefly attended Alabama State University before moving to Montgomery. There she worked for the Union of Sleeping Car Porters and was the secretary of the local chapter of the National Association for the Advancement of Colored People. She became world famous as the result of her deliberate refusal, on December 1, 1955, to relinquish her bus seat to a white passenger on a public bus in Montgomery. Her resulting arrest helped to trigger the Montgomery bus boycott (1955-1956), which in turn fueled a decade of challenges to segregation ordinances throughout the South. Fired from her job in a department store, she moved to Detroit and became a youth worker. She has since become an outstanding spokeswoman for the cause of civil rights and has been the recipient of many honors, one of the most recent being the 1993 Essence Award, which she shared with Alice Harris, Lena Horne, and Senator Carol Moseley Braun.

PICKETT, Bill
1860-1932

One of the most prominent of the African-American cowboys, Pickett was born on a ranch near Taylor, Texas; his mother was a Choctaw Indian and his father of mixed African-American and European descent. As a horseman and performer at the

P.B.S. Pinchback *c.* 1872.

101 Ranch in Texas, he originated the art of "bulldogging," or steer wrestling, around 1880. He became a star attraction of the 101 Wild West Show, which performed in Mexico, New York City, and England. He died after being kicked and trampled by a horse. In 1994 the U.S. Postal Service issued a stamp in his honor, a tribute somewhat marred by the fact U.S.P.S. had mixed up his picture with that of his brother Ben.

PINCHBACK, Pinckney Benton Stewart
1837-1921

The first African-American to serve as a governor, Pinchback was born in Macon, Georgia, and educated in Ohio. He worked as a steward on Mississippi riverboats during the 1850s. During the Civil War he organized the Corps d'Afrique, a company of African-American volunteers in Union-occupied New Orleans in 1862. As a Republican politician after the war, he served in the Louisiana senate (1869-1872) and was, for 43 days, the governor of Louisiana (1872-1873). He lost contested elections to the U.S. House of Representatives and the U.S. Senate. In 1882 he became surveyor of customs in New Orleans; he earned a law degree, although he did not practice.

PIPPIN, Horace
1888-1946

An early "primitive" painter, he did his first work at the age of 43 and was "discovered" by a companion of illustrator N. C. Wyeth. Despite a right hand immobilized by a wound in World War I, he produced 57 works with characteristic bold patterns, among them "Abe Lincoln's First Book," "Argonne Sector," "The Blue Tiger," "Crucifixion," "Marian Anderson Singing," "Victory Vase," and "Water Boy". His work was exhibited at the Museum of Modern Art (1938), the San Francisco Museum of Art (1942) and the Newark Museum (1971), among others, and at the Carlen Galleries, Philadelphia, since 1940.

POITIER, Sidney
1924-

The first African-American to win an Oscar as best actor, Poitier was born in Miami, Florida, but grew up in the Bahamas. After serving in the U.S. Army, he

OPPOSITE: Sidney Poitier in 1964.

joined the American Negro Theater and debuted on Broadway in 1946. After his first Hollywood movie in 1950 he quickly moved on to one successful film after another, including *The Blackboard Jungle* (1955), *The Defiant Ones* (1958), *Lillies of the Field* (1963) – for which he won his Academy Award – and *In the Heat of the Night* (1967). Poitier was one of the first African-American actors to play dignified leading roles in films that were predominantly white. Thus he played one of the leads in *Guess Who's Coming to Dinner* (1967), perhaps the first movie to depict an inter-racial romance as a respectably middle-class affair. Starting in 1972 Poitier began to direct occasional movies, and in later years he became increasingly open in speaking out for social justice and other progressive causes.

POUSSAINT, Alvin Francis
1934-

A highly respected psychiatrist, Poussaint is best-known for his work on psychological traumas that racism and prejudice impose on many African-Americans. His 1972 book *Why Blacks Kill Blacks* received considerable attention. He has taught at the Harvard Medical School since 1969 and has been associated with Children's Hospital since 1978. In addition to being the author of many scholarly publications, he has served as script consultant to NBC's hugely popular series *The Cosby Show* (1984-1992).

Alvin F. Poussaint in 1992.

Rev. Adam Clayton Powell in 1968.

POWELL, Adam Clayton, Jr.
1908-1972

Through his long career as a minister, Congressman, and social activist, Powell did much to promote the interests of African-Americans. Powell's father, Adam Clayton Powell, Sr., was the pastor of Harlem's Abyssinian Baptist Church and supported many of Marcus Garvey's ideals. The influential Abbyssinian Church boasted the world's largest congregation. Powell grew up in New York City and, after graduation from Colgate University, went on to receive an M.A. from Columbia. Influenced by his father, as well as by the communists of the 1920s and 30s, Powell had a vision of economic justice for all people. During the Depression he ran a relief operation in Harlem that clothed and fed thousands. He also edited black newspapers and organized boycotts to force white merchants to hire blacks. When his father retired from the ministry in 1936 Powell took his place, and used his pulpit to continue his fight for social equality for African-Americans. He campaigned for jobs for blacks at the World's Fair of 1939, fought for improved housing in Harlem, and protested de facto segregation in New York's universities. In 1941 he was elected in a landslide to the New York City Council, and while serving he published the black tabloid, the *People's Voice*. After his election to the U.S. House of Representatives (1944-1971) he continued to fight discrimination, pressing for desegregation in the military and abolition of the Jim-Crow laws separating blacks and whites. During his chairmanship of the influential House Committee on Education and Labor (1960-1967) he sponsored 48 major pieces of legislation, including the minimum wage bill. His blunt speech and lack of diplomacy had earned him some enemies in the House, and in addition, his personal life came under fire, as his three marriages dissolved and it was revealed that he had used public funds to support his love of women and night life. Slowly, his political life unravelled, and in 1966 he moved to the island of Bimini to avoid paying damages in a libel suit. He lost reelection to the House in 1970 and spent much of the rest of his life in Bimini.

POWELL, Bud (Earl)
1924-1966

The most influential bebop pianist of the mid-1940s and a major influence on virtually every jazz pianist ever since, Powell is considered by many the pianist who most fully assimilated the ideas of modern jazz to the keyboard. Born into a gifted New York City musical family, at the age of six he undertook a seven-years study of the European masters. After playing with his older brother's band in his teens he studied the new jazz at Minton's Playhouse under the tutelage of Thelonious Monk. Following work with Cootie Williams (1942-1944) and a hospitalization in 1945 for the mental illness that, complicated by alcoholism, would hamper his work throughout his career, in 1946 he recorded two tracks with Charlie Parker that, along with his own sessions, especially for Blue Note (1949-1951), confirmed his status as a seminal bebop master. In Europe from 1959 to 1964, he played in Paris (1959-1962) and elsewhere, but his chronic mental and physical illnesses gained the upper hand after his return to Manhattan, and he died in 1966.

POWELL, Colin (Luther)
1937-

Born and raised in New York City, where he was graduated from the City University of New York, Powell would go on to become one of the country's best-known figures during Operation Desert Storm, the U.S.-led United Nations offensive against Saddam Hussein's Iraq in 1990-1991. Upon graduation from college in 1958 Powell received a second lieutenant's commission and became a career army officer, serving with distinction in Vietnam. Rising through the ranks and increasingly responsible commands, from 1987 to 1989 he was a presidential assistant for national security in the Reagan administration. As such, he was the highest-ranking African-American in the administration. In 1988 he was nominated to become one of only ten four-star army generals. His responsibilities included the command of all army personnel serving in the mainland United States and the defense of the mainland in the event of enemy attack. During the Reagan years Powell advised the president at summit conferences in both Moscow and

Gen. Colin Powell in Arabia in 1990.

Washington, D.C. In 1989 he became the first African-American to serve as chairman of the Joint Chiefs of Staff, a position he held until he retired from the army in 1993. Although he denied that he had taken retirement because of his profound disagreement with President Bill Clinton's advocacy of ending the military's ban on gays, Powell made no secret of his opposition to the president's policy. Upon retirement he was awarded the Presidential Medal of Freedom (his second such award: President Bush had similarly decorated him after Desert Storm). At the time of his retirement he announced that he intended to concentrate on writing his memoirs and speaking out on issues of national importance.

PRICE, Leontyne
1927-

Leontyne Price, one of the world's best-known sopranos, was born in Laurel, Mississippi, and attended college in Ohio before moving to New York to study music at The Juilliard School. When composer Virgil Thompson saw her in a 1952 Juilliard student production of Verdi's *Falstaff* he was so impressed that he asked her to sing in his *Four Saints in Three Acts*. The same year, she appeared as Bess in a revival of *Porgy and Bess* and two years later demonstrated her versatility when she premiered Samuel Barber's *Hermit Songs* at the New York Town Hall. Her Metropolitan Opera debut came in Verdi's *Il Trovatore* in 1961; although most critics thought that her rich soprano was perfect for Verdi, she proved her versatility when she appeared later in the year in the lighter title role of Puccini's *Girl of the Golden West*. Since then she has had an international career, appearing in the finest opera houses of the world. In 1982 Price appeared at the convention of the Daughters of the American Revolution in Constitution Hall in a concert honoring Marian Anderson, who had been barred from appearing there by the DAR in 1939.

RIGHT: Charley Pride in 1975.
BELOW: Leontyne Price (undated photo).

PRIDE, Charley
1938-

The first African-American star in country music, Pride topped the country charts from 1969 to 1971 with 29 hits. Born to sharecroppers in Sledge, Mississippi, he preferred country music to the blues he heard on the radio, and, after an unsuccessful try-out for professional baseball, he began performing professionally, scoring his first hit in 1966. At first his reputation was based almost entirely on his records, but after some radio success he was accepted by the country market on the strength of his performances and by the early 1970s had become a full-fledged superstar and the recipient of many awards. Now the owner of the cotton farm on which he was born, and still fascinated by baseball, he remains a top country artist.

PRIMUS, Pearl
1919-

Dancer, choreographer, and lecturer, she was a pioneer in developing African-American dance as an art. Born in Trinidad, she was graduated from Hunter College in New York and debuted as the first African-American with the New Dance Group in 1944. Critical acclaim led to Broadway, cross-country tours, and her own company. Her style stressed authenticity, pulsing power, drama, and grace. She studied dance in Africa (1948-1951) and anthropology at Columbia, later earning a Ph.D. at New York University. She has won worldwide honors, including the (United States') National Medal of the Arts (1991).

PROSSER, Gabriel
c. 1775-1800

Born in slavery on the estate of Thomas Prosser in Henrico County, Virginia, Gabriel Prosser became convinced that he was divinely intended to deliver his people from bondage. He organized a large-scale uprising (1,000 persons involved) that was intended to begin on August 30, 1800, and to march on Richmond, Virginia, only six miles away. Prosser's plan was thwarted both because some details of the intended revolt were known to the authorities and because a heavy rain on August 30 caused streams to rise, which isolated the Prosser estate and made coordination impossible. Prosser disbanded his followers and went into hiding. He was apprehended, tried on October 3, and hanged on October 7.

Richard Pryor *c.* 1972.

Blues (1971), *The Bingo Long Traveling All Stars and Motor Kings* (1976), and *Silver Streak* (1976). Simultaneously, he continued a series of live performances that allowed him more freedom of language and subject matter; these proved extremely popular, both on stage and in their taped versions. After almost burning to death in a drug-related incident in 1980 he gave up drugs and worked to persuade others to do the same.

PURYEAR, Martin
1941-

A sculptor, he earned his M.F.A. at Yale in 1971. Among his exotic wood and mixed media pieces are "Greed's Trophy," "On the Tundra," "Pride's Cross," "Sleeping Mews," and "Verve". His work has been shown in traveling exhibitions at major galleries nationwide since 1984, and in solo exhibitions beginning with the Corcoran Gallery (Washington, D.C.) in 1977. He is represented at the Museum of Modern Art (New York), the Art Institute (Chicago), and the Walker Art Center (Minneapolis). He has taught at the University of Illinois at Chicago (1970, 1978-1988).

Pearl Primus in *Rock Daniel* in 1944.

PRYOR, Richard
1940-

One of the most innovative (and often outrageous) comedians of his generation, Pryor effectively retired from performing after developing multiple sclerosis in the late 1980s. Pryor grew up in Peoria, Illinois, in a poor family. Drawing on an old tradition that combines raunchy language with social satire, he began to work as a stand-up comedian in small clubs in the United States and Canada. He was "discovered" by Johnny Carson in 1966, the same year he appeared in his first movie, *The Busy Body*, and from that point on he began to reach more mainstream audiences. A writer as well as a performer, he worked with Mel Brooks on the script of *Blazing Saddles*, and he wrote several Lily Tomlin specials, as well as scripting much material for his own TV specials. He appeared in a number of successful movies, including *Lady Sings the*

RAINEY, Joseph Hayne
1832-1887

Born to enslaved parents in Georgetown, South Carolina, Rainey grew up free and learned the barber's trade. He worked as a barber until 1862, when he escaped from the Confederacy and went to Bermuda. He returned to South Carolina in 1866 and became an active member of the Republican Party. He won a special election in 1870 and served as the first African-American elected to the U.S. House of Representatives (1870-1879). He was an internal-revenue agent in South Carolina (1879-1881) and then worked as a banker and a broker in Washington, D.C.

RANDOLPH, A. (Asa) Philip
1889-1979

Born the son of a minister in Crescent City, Florida, Randolph became one of the most important figures in the American labor movement. After attending school in Florida and studying at the City College of New York, he had to settle for a job as a waiter on a coastal steamship. Unsettled and angered by the ship's inferior conditions for its African-American workers, Randolph spearheaded the first of the many workers' protests that he would organize during his long career. In 1917 he founded the *Messenger*, a magazine whose mission was to encourage African-American workers to unite. During World War I, Randolph worked to unionize African-American shipyard workers in Virginia and elevator operators in New York City. When the war ended he embarked on one of his most successful projects: unionizing the all-black sleeping car porters working on the nation's railroads. In 1925 he founded the Brotherhood of Sleeping Car Porters and served as its president until he stepped

down in 1968. In 1941, after the United States entered World War II, Randolph threatened to lead 100,000 African-American workers on a march to Washington, D.C., to protest the lack of job opportunities in the defense industry. A week before the march was to take place President Roosevelt signed Executive Order 8802 outlawing discrimination in government and defense job hiring. The bill, almost entirely the result of Randolph's work, was the first significant government step in eliminating job discrimination. After the war Randolph worked to end discrimination in the military, making it clear that he would urge African-Americans to boycott the draft if necessary to attain their goals. Again he was successful: in 1948 President Harry S Truman moved to integrate the armed forces. By 1963, when many his age would have been content to rest on their laurels, Randolph worked tirelessly to organize the famous march on Washington at which Martin Luther King gave his "I Have a Dream" speech. The A. Philip Randolph Institute and the A. Philip Randolph Educational Fund in New York City continue

A. Philip Randolph in 1963.

his work for increased African-American participation in labor and government.

RANGEL, Charles Bernard
1930-

An outspoken and influential Congressman, Rangel was born in New York City and served in the Korean War before being graduated from high school in 1953. He earned his law degree from St. John's University in 1960 and practiced law in New York City. In 1965 he served both as counsel to the speaker of the New York State Assembly and as counsel to the President's Commission to Revise the Draft Laws. In 1966 he was elected to the state assembly. As a Democrat, Rangel was elected as Harlem's delegate to the U.S. House of Representatives in 1970 and became an aggressive anti-drug crusader. In 1983 Rangel became chairman of the Select Committee on Narcotics Abuse and Control. He has also been a strong advocate for the homeless and economically disadvantaged.

ABOVE: Charles Rangel in 1989.
LEFT: Otis Redding *c.* 1963.

REDDING, Otis
1941-1967

He was a leading soul singer of the 1960s, and his best work has lost none of its power and influence. Redding was born in Dawson, Georgia, and raised in Macon, where he began his career by imitating Little Richard's manic style. His 1962 hit "These Arms of Mine" established his signature ballad style, and his triumphant performance at Harlem's Apollo Theatre in 1963 confirmed his preeminence among rhythm-and-blues artists. Redding gained mainstream acceptance at the Monterey Pop Festival in 1967 but died that December in a plane crash. Probably his biggest hit, "Dock of the Bay" (1968), was published posthumously.

REED, Ishmael Scott
1938-

One of the most widely-published African-American novelists, Reed first won acclaim when both *Conjure*, his first volume of poetry published in America, and his novel *Mumbo Jumbo*, were nominated for National Book Awards in 1972. Since then, Reed has edited a number of anthologies of African-American poetry, while continuing to write both poems and novels (some published under the name "Emmett Coleman"). After a number of years in New York City, where he was a founder of the alternative newspaper the *East Village Other* (1965), he settled in Berkeley, California, where he was one of the founders of the Yardbird Publishing Company (1971). Many of his novels are satirical, notably *The Terrible Twos* (1982), a political satire, and *Reckless Eye-*

balling (1987), a farcical look at the tense relations between African-American men and black feminists.

REMOND, Sarah Parker
1826-1894

Born in Salem, Massachusetts, to free African-American parents, Remond followed her brother, Charles Remond, into the abolitionist cause. She became an agent (1856) of the American Anti-Slavery Society and lectured both in the United States (1856-1859) and in Great Britain (1859-1865), where she exposed the evils of slavery to British audiences. She returned to the United States for one year but then went to Florence, Italy, where she studied and practiced medicine. She is buried in Rome.

REVELS, Hiram Rhodes
1827-1901

The first African-American to become a U.S. Senator, Revels was born to free parents in Fayetteville, North Carolina. He studied at a number of colleges and seminaries and became an ordained minister of the African Methodist Episcopal Church in Baltimore in 1845. He helped to recruit African-American regiments

RIGHT: Lloyd Richards in 1987.
BELOW: Sen. Hiram Revel's swearing-in.

during the Civil War and began a school for freedmen in St. Louis in 1863. After election to the state senate in Mississippi, Revels was chosen to complete the term of Jefferson Davis in the U.S. Senate. Despite major opposition, he was seated in the Senate in 1870. In his one-year term he fought for several causes, including reinstating African-American legislators barred by the Georgia central assembly, ending school segregation, and increasing cotton production. In the years following his Senate term he was implicated in an election scandal in Mississippi that cost him his pastorate and much of his political support. In time, however, the furor subsided, and he eventually did return to his church at Holly Springs, Mississippi, and taught at Shaw University.

RICHARDS, Lloyd G.
1923-

Actor, stage director, professor, and college dean, he was born in Toronto, Canada, and worked first as a radio and TV actor. He later directed the Great

Lakes Drama Festival and some Broadway productions (including *A Raisin in the Sun* (1959), *Fences* (1987), and *Two Trains Running* (1992)), as well as Off-Broadway plays such as *The Lion and the Jewel* (1977) and television dramas such as *Paul Robeson* (1970). Artistic director for the Eugene O'Neill Theater Center since 1969, and a teacher at the National Theatre Institute since 1970, he was also dean of the Yale School of Drama (1979-1991).

RILLIEUX, Norbert
1806-1894

A prominent engineer and inventor, Rillieux was born in New Orleans, son of a wealthy plantation owner. Fully recognized by his father, he was treated to the advantages of a white youth. He studied engineering in Paris and invented a special steam-based evaporation device for the production of sugar (patented 1843). His return to the United States (1843-1854) finally ended because of continued dis-

Faith Ringgold (front, center) in 1980.

crimination. He returned to Paris, taught at L'Ecole Central, worked as an engineer, and contributed to the deciphering of Egyptian hieroglyphics. His evaporation device remains the basis for vacuum pan evaporators still used today.

RINGGOLD, Faith (b. Faith Willi Jones)
1930-

Painter, soft sculptor, activist, and teacher, she has drawn upon such traditional African-American women's crafts as doll- and quilt-making to attack the notion of white male supremacy in the arts. The cubism of "Between Friends" (1963; about black/white relationships) yielded to pop art in "Die" (1967; depicting a race riot) and moved to political poster art like "Flag for the Moon – Die Nigger" (1969). She began producing fabric figures and masks in 1973, adding performance art in 1986. Bi-coastal, she has been based in Harlem and also teaches at the University of California at San Diego (1984-). Her books include *Tar Beach* (1991).

ROACH, Max (Maxwell)
1924-

Now considered one of the premier drummers of modern jazz, in recent years the internationally acclaimed Max Roach has expanded his role in music to that of educator and professor. Born in New Land, North Carolina, and raised in Brooklyn, New York, Roach attended the Manhattan School of Music and began recording with tenor patriarch Coleman Hawkins in 1943. Over the next four years he performed with many of jazz's greatest figures, including Benny Carter, Dizzy Gillespie, Stan Getz, and Hawkins. From 1947 to 1949 he held the percussion chair in Charlie Parker's innovative quintet. After five more years of free-lance work, including stints with Jazz at the Philharmonic and the Lighthouse All-Stars, he and Clifford Brown co-led one of the most highly regarded groups in modern jazz (1954-1956). Following Brown's untimely death, Roach led a succession of groups while pursuing a wide range of activities as a composer and educator. He has been a professor of music at the University of Massachusetts (1972-1993). An innovator in the use of uncommon meters in jazz and an authority on African percussion, the dean of modern jazz drumming is lionized outside the U.S., where his many honorary degrees and awards include France's having made him a Commander of the Order of Arts and Letters.

ROBERTS, Joseph Jenkins
1809-1876

Although born in Petersburg, Virginia, Roberts spent his adult life in Africa and became the "Founding Father" of Liberia. He migrated to Liberia in 1829 and became governor of the colony there in 1842. After the American Colonization Society gave up all claims to the colony in 1844, Roberts became the first president of the new Republic of Liberia (1847-1856). He won recognition for his country from Britain and France. He was president of the College of Liberia (1856-1876) and served again as president of the Republic (1871-1876). He made two visits to the United States (1844, 1869).

ROBESON, Paul Bustil
1898-1976

According to legend, when actor Paul Robeson was called upon to whistle when he appeared in Eugene O'Neill's play *The Emperor Jones* in 1925, he instead sang –

Actor, singer, and activist Paul Robeson at a recording session in 1933.

and soon found himself the most famous African-American singer of his generation. Born in Princeton, New Jersey, Robeson earned his A.B. at Rutgers University in New Brunswick, New Jersey (1919). At Rutgers, Robeson was an honor student, Phi Beta Kappa, an all-American football player (1917), a 12-letter athlete, and winner of the oratory award. These achievements were all the more impressive at a time when few African-Americans ever attended a university. After graduation from Princeton, Robeson attended the Columbia University Law School, where he earned his L.L.B., but he never practiced law, instead turning to the theater. His first big break came when Eugene O'Neill remembered seeing Robeson in a college performance and asked him to appear in his *The Emperor Jones*. Always one to follow his own star, Robeson turned down the part, but he later accepted a role in O'Neill's play *Taboo*. In *Taboo*, he toured in both the

U.S.A. and in Europe, gaining his first professional stage experience. Next came the starring role in *The Emperor Jones* in 1925. In that same year he had given a widely-acclaimed concert of spirituals, and in 1926 he made a coast-to-coast concert tour and began to make recordings. But the theater remained his first love, and in the next several years he performed in a spectacular series of starring roles – in *Porgy and Bess, Showboat, The Hairy Ape*, and, perhaps most impressive of all, *Othello*. But even as his fame as an actor and singer was reaching its zenith, Robeson's outspoken political views were beginning to raise eyebrows in some quarters. His passionate hostility to Naziism was acceptable to most Americans, but his praise of Russian communism was not and earned him widespread criticism, which culminated, during the McCarthy period, in the government revoking his passport. He regained his passport in 1958 and resumed his international career, returning to the United States in 1963, when ill-health forced his retirement.

ROBINSON, Bill "Bojangles"
(b. Luther Robinson)
1878-1949

Perhaps the greatest tap dancer of all time, called "The King of Tapology," he was one of the first to tap dance on his toes and originated the routine of tapping up and down stairs. He toured the Keith vaudeville circuit (1909-1914) and played the African-American theater circuit. He performed in four Broadway shows (1928-1945) and was the first African-American to star in the Ziegfeld Follies. His many films include *Dixiana* (1930), the first with an original score; *The Little Colonel* (1935), one of four with Shirley Temple; and *Stormy Weather* (1943), where his dance style is best seen.

ROBINSON, Frank
1935-

Hall of Famer Robinson's baseball statistics include 1,829 runs, 528 doubles, and 204 stolen bases. He was a Rookie of the Year, an All-Star 11 times, and Most

ABOVE: Jackie Robinson in 1947.
LEFT: Frank Robinson in 1991.

Valuable Player in both the National (1961) and American (1966) leagues. He was a Triple Crown winner in 1966. In 1975 he became the first African-American to manage in the big leagues; while managing Robinson once put himself into a game and hit a home run to win it. Overall, his managerial record was mixed: he was saddled with poor teams in Cleveland and San Francisco and could not do much with them, but he reanimated the even worse Baltimore Orioles.

ROBINSON, Jackie
(Jack Roosevelt)
1919-1972

Robinson probably played baseball under more intense pressure than any other player has experienced. Not only was he the first African-American in the major leagues in the twentieth century, he was the dominant symbol of the fight for racial integration in the United States in the 1940s. A fine all-around athlete, he was the first four-letter man at the University of California at Los Angeles, where he excelled at football, basketball, and track, as well as baseball. He would have followed in his brother Mack's Olympic footsteps if the 1940 Games had not been canceled due to World War II. In 1947 the Brooklyn Dodgers' General Manager, Branch Rickey, hand-picked Robinson to integrate baseball, and he could not have chosen better. Robinson controlled his emotions and disciplined himself to withstand both physical and verbal attacks, while always being under constant pressure to perform well. Very quickly he worked his way into a key position in the Dodger lineup, and he greatly contributed to the team's six pennant-winning seasons during the years 1947 to 1956. Among his many honors were the Rookie of the Year Award (1947), the Most Valuable Player Award (1949), and a National League batting championship (1949). Robinson was also an outstanding baserunner, and was chosen to play for the All-Star team six times. He was elected to the Baseball Hall of Fame in 1962.

ROBINSON, Randall
1946-

This respected lawyer and lobbyist, born in Richmond, Virginia, was graduated from the Harvard Law School in 1970. He worked for a number of U.S. Representatives before he was awarded a Ford Fellowship. He became the executive director of TransAfrica in 1986, an advocacy organization for people of African descent worldwide. TransAfrica's work focuses on protecting human rights and improving social conditions through political pressure and lobbying. Robinson was one of the most outspoken advocates of the boycott of South Africa during the 1980s and early 1990s.

ROBINSON, Sugar Ray
(b. Walter Smith)
1920-1989

After growing up in Detroit and watching Joe Louis train to fight, Walter Smith moved to Harlem, where he tried to join the Amateur Athletic Union. Told that he was too young to be registered, he used the card of a retired fighter named Ray Robinson. Once in the ring, Sugar Ray moved ahead quickly. He was five times middleweight champ, and he took the welterweight title from Jake LaMota. Robinson closed a 25-year professional career with a bout at the age of 45. He worked with youth groups in Los Angeles until his death.

ROLLINS, Sonny
(Theodore Walter)
1930-

A leading tenor saxophonist in the hard bop style of modern jazz, Rollins's continuing personal evolution and incorporation of calypso, soul, and rock elements have enabled him to remain an influential figure throughout his career. Born in New York City, he recorded and worked with Bud Powell, J.J. Johnson, Thelonious Monk, Art Blakey, Tadd Dameron, Fats Navarro, and, especially, Miles Davis (1949-1955). Following two years with the legendary Clifford Brown-Max Roach quintet, he became a celebrated leader in his own right. Several of his tight compositions (*e.g.* "Oleo," "Doxy," and "Airegin") are jazz standards.

OPPOSITE: Sonny Rollins in 1965.
BELOW: Sugar Ray Robinson (right), 1949.

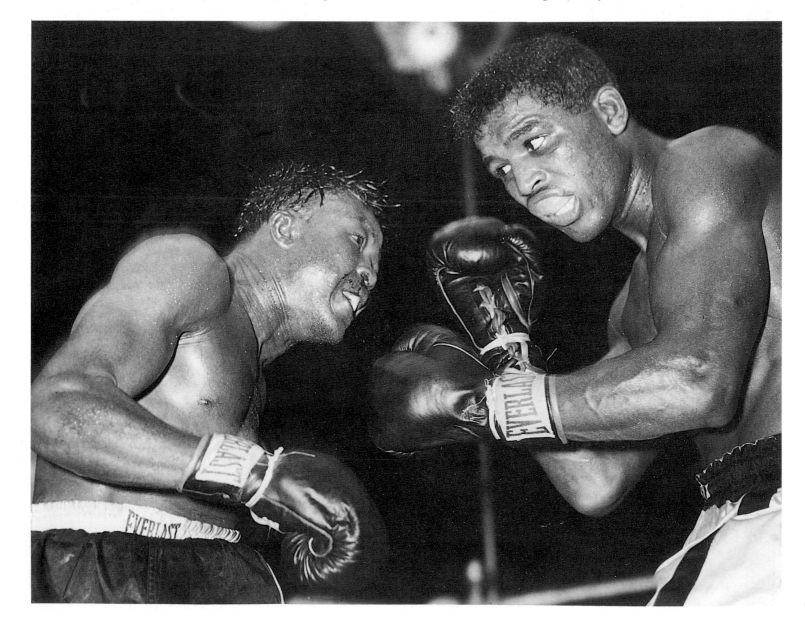

Tribune (1948-1961). In 1961 President John F. Kennedy appointed him to be deputy assistant secretary of state for public affairs. In 1963 he was made U.S. ambassador to Finland, and from 1964 to 1965 he was head of the U.S. Information Agency, the first African-American to hold that post. Since the 1960s he has written a syndicated newspaper column and authored a number of books.

RUDOLPH, Wilma
1940-

Born the 20th of 22 children to a Tennessee family, stricken with polio and scarlet fever as a child, Rudolph became the first American woman runner to win three gold medals in the Olympics (1960).

BELOW: Carl Rowan in 1988.

Diana Ross in 1993 (above) and leading The Supremes in 1967 (opposite).

ROSS, Diana (Diane Ernestine)
1944-

As the lead singer of The Supremes before she began her solo singing and acting career, Ross fronted one of the most successful musical groups in recording history. Born in Detroit, Michigan, she sang backup with the Primettes, who recorded for Lu-Pine (1960) before signing with Motown as The Supremes (1961). Promoted to lead vocalist at the insistence of Motown president Berry Gordy, in 1969 she left the group after 15 consecutive hit singles. "Ain't No Mountain High Enough" (1970) inaugurated a string of lightweight solo pop chart-toppers that lasted into the early 1970s. Ross won an Oscar nomination for her debut movie role in *Lady Sings the Blues* (1972), but her roles in *Mahogany* (1975) and *The Wiz* (1978) drew mixed reviews. Buoyed by disco and disco-pop hits such as "Muscles" (1982), by the middle of the 1980s she was as much media personality as soul singer. Although famous for her TV specials and epic live performances, by the 1990s Ross was still receiving more critical attention for her great past hits packages than for her new releases.

ROWAN, Carl Thomas
1925-

Rowan's distinguished career in journalism began after he got his M.A. in journalism at the University of Minnesota in 1947 and joined the staff of the Minneapolis

After she had contracted polio when she was four she lost the use of her left leg and had to wear a cumbersome leg brace. Her family refused to accept that she would never walk normally and put her on a strict regimen of daily leg massage and exercise. By the time she was eight Rudolph was able to discard her brace and use an orthopedic left shoe. By the time that she was 12 she was able to do without the orthopedic shoe and began to play neighborhood basketball with her brothers. By the time she was 16 Rudolph, nicknamed "Skeeter", was six feet tall and had won a place on Tennessee's all-state high school basketball team. Her great speed on the basketball court led her coaches to encourage her to take up track, and in 1956 Rudolph won a Bronze Medal in the 4×100-meter relay at the Olympics. Her plans to attend college were almost shelved when she became pregnant when she was 18, but coach Ed Temple helped her to enter Tennessee State University on a full track scholarship. In July 1960 she set a new world record for the 200 meters, before going on to the Rome Olympics, where she won the 100-meter dash, the 200-meter dash (Olympic record), and the 400-meter relay (world record). That same year she was voted the United Press Association Athlete of the Year and the Associated Press Association Woman Athlete of the Year. In 1962 she received the Babe Didrickson Zaharias Award for athletic excellence and sportsmanship, before going on to be elected to the Black Sports Hall of Fame (1973), the Women's Sports Hall of Fame (1980), and the U.S. Olympic Sports Hall of Fame (1983). In 1984 she was one of five women chosen by the Women's Sports Foundation as America's greatest athletes. In recent years she has lived in Indianapolis, Indiana, devoting much of her time to work with promising young athletes. Her autobiography, *Wilma*, was published in 1977. She is the creator of the Wilma Rudolph Foundation, an organization designed to encourage and train young athletic hopefuls.

RUSSELL, Bill (William Felton)
1934-

After leading the University of San Francisco Dons to two consecutive National Collegiate Athletic Association basketball titles (1955 and 1956), 6-ft. 9-in. center Bill Russell burst onto the professional basketball scene with a winning reputation. His team, the Boston Celtics, won eleven National Basketball Associa-tion titles with Russell at center. Selected the NBA's Most Valuable Player five times, his battles with scoring ace Wilt Chamberlain were legendary. When Russell led the Celtics as player-coach to the 1968 and 1969 NBA titles he became the first African-American to coach or manage a major professional sport.

RUSTIN, Bayard
1910-1987

One of the most prominent figures in the civil rights movement and a strong propo-nent of non-violence, Rustin was perhaps best known for his long tenure as head of the A. Philip Randolph Institute (1964-1987). Born in Pennsylvania, where he was raised by his grandparents, Rustin was a top student and athlete at this high school. After graduation, encouraged by teachers and his Quaker grandmother, he went on to college, attending first Cheney State College in Pennsylvania and then Wilberforce College in Ohio. In 1936 his growing awareness of inequalities in American society led him to join the Young Communist League, for which he became an organizer two years later. During these years Rustin occasionally earned money by singing in New York nightclubs with such musicians as Lead-belly and Josh White. Nonetheless, it was clear that his real vocation was righting in-equalities; in 1941 he served as youth organizer for A. Philip Randolph's planned march on Washington. The march, designed to pressure the govern-ment into opening defense industry jobs to blacks, was cancelled when President Roosevelt outlawed discrimination in defense hiring. During World War II, Rustin was imprisoned as a conscientious objector; he was released in 1945. In the years to come he was often back in jail: first for demonstrating for independence for India outside the British Embassy, then for protesting chain gang abuses in North Carolina. In 1955 Rustin joined Martin Luther King's Southern Christian Leadership Conference, and in 1963 he was the SCLC organizer of the March on Washington. In the 1970s and 1980s Rutin was increasingly troubled both by the lack of progess in economic equality for African-Americans and by the rise of violence. When the Watts riots broke out in 1965 Rustin rushed to Los Angeles and urged non-violence before largely hostile crowds of youths. Undeterred, he con-tinued to argue that "black power was born in bitterness and frustration" and that inclusion, not exclusion, would eventually yield the answer to America's problems. In his last years Rustin was open about his homosexuality, which he had long concealed, fearing that, if he were open about his sexuality, his work might be discredited in some circles. In fact, since his death Rustin has been in-creasingly recognized for his lifelong com-mitment to the goals of minorities.

Bayard Rustin speaking in 1963.

SCHMOKE, Kurt Lidell
1949-

In 1987 Schmoke was elected mayor of Baltimore and stated in his inaugural address that he wanted to make Baltimore known as "The City that Reads." Schmoke had earned his A.B. at Yale in 1971, had been a Rhodes Scholar at Oxford University, and had received his J.D. at Harvard in 1976. In 1977 President Carter appointed him to the White House Domestic Policy Staff. He served as an assistant U.S. Attorney in Baltimore from 1972 until he was elected state's attorney in 1982. As an attorney, he was known for his vigorous prosecution of drug-related cases; as a mayor, he has concentrated on

Kurt Schmoke in 1987.

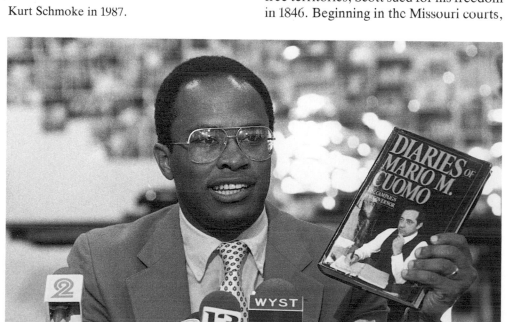

improving Baltimore's schools and economy.

SCHOMBURG, Arthur A.
1874-1938

Born in San Juan, Puerto Rico, Schomburg was an activist for Puerto Rican and Cuban independence from Spain. He came to New York City in 1891 and worked for the Bankers Trust Company (1906-1929). Both incensed and inspired by a former teacher's comment that the Negro people had "no history," Schomburg formed the New York Public Library's division of Negro Literature, History, and Prints in 1925 and served as its curator (1932-1938). His collection became the most comprehensive library of information available on African-Americans. The collection was renamed the Schomburg Collection (1940) and then the Schomburg Center for Research in Black Culture (1973).

SCOTT, Dred
c.1795-1858

The central figure in one of the most famous of all Supreme Court cases, Scott was born in Southampton County, Virginia. He was a slave, and over the years his various owners often took him into non-slave territories, sometimes for protracted periods. Citing this residence in free territories, Scott sued for his freedom in 1846. Beginning in the Missouri courts,

his case made its way to the U.S. Supreme Court, and in 1857 a Democratic majority on the court ruled against him on the grounds that, as a slave, he was merely "property" and could not claim the rights of a U.S. citizen. The court's ruling caused violent political controversy and indirectly contributed to the beginning of the Civil War. Scott himself was freed in 1857 but died of consumption a year and a half later in St. Louis.

Dred Scott (undated engraving).

SEALE, Bobby (Robert G.)
1936-

Bobby Seale was born in Dallas, Texas. He cofounded the Black Panther Party for Self-Defense with Huey Newton in 1966; the organization was originally set up to monitor police who were patrolling Oakland's black community. He was jailed after the riots that broke out during the 1968 Chicago Democratic National Convention, and he was thought to have been connected to the murder of Alex Rackely, a suspected Black Panther informer. In 1969 Seale spoke at a Black Panther meeting of changing tactics from self-defense to socialism. In 1973 he ran for mayor of Oakland and narrowly lost. Having left the Black Panther Party, he has lectured at Philadelphia's Temple University, and written books which include *Seize the Time: The Story of the Black Panther Party and Huey P. Newton, A Lonely Rage*, and a cookbook, *Barbeque with Bobby*, which he sells to benefit various grassroots political organizations.

SHABAZZ, (Hajj Bahiyah) Betty
1936-

First known as the widow of Malcolm X, who was assassinated in 1965, Shabazz is

ABOVE: Black Panther Bobby Seale (center) at a rally in Chicago in 1969.

to run again for the Senate. Whatever the outcome, another strong showing could only help his political future.

SHAW, Bernard
1940-

Shaw's live coverage of the Gulf War in 1990-1991 for the Cable News Network (CNN) brought him to international attention. He first worked as a reporter for the Group W. Westinghouse Broadcasting Company (1966-1971), before going to ABC, where he was Miami bureau chief (1977). He left ABC for CBS's Washington, D.C., bureau. While at CBS he had an exclusive when he broke the story that powerful congressman Wayne Hayes would resign. In both 1988 and 1992 he moderated a presidential debate.

BELOW: New York activist Rev. Al Sharpton holds a press conference in 1990.

herself an activist in social and health issues affecting the African-American community. After earning her nursing degree, she went on to receive an M.A. in public health adminsitration and then a Ph.D. in educational administration. While raising her six children, she has done extensive volunteer work and has served as director of communications and public relations at Medgar Evers College in Brooklyn, New York.

SHARPTON, Al
(Alfred Charles, Jr.)
1954-

Born in Brooklyn, New York, Sharpton is closely associated with New York City. He was founder and president of the National Youth Movement, Inc. from 1971 to 1986, having previously been the New York youth director for the Southern Christian Leadership's Operation Breadbasket. In 1991 he founded the National Action Network. In addition to his social activism, which made him a frequent, often controversial figure in the news in the late 1980s and early 1990s, he serves as pastor at the Washington Temple church of God in Christ. In addition, in 1992 he became the first African-American to run for the Senate from New York. Although his candidacy had not been taken very seriously by the political establishment, he won a surprising 16 percent of the primary vote. In 1994 he announced his intention

SHIRLEY, George Irving
1934-

A tenor and teacher, he was graduated from Wayne State University in 1955, received additional vocal training in Washington and New York, and made his operatic debut as Eisenstein in *Die Fledermaus* at Woodstock, New York, in 1959. Following performances in Europe, he debuted at the Metropolitan Opera in New York in 1961 and sang there until 1973. Other operatic engagements were at Covent Garden, Glyndebourne, Ottawa, San Francisco, Sante Fe, La Scala, and Spoleto. He created the role of Romilayu in Kirchner's *Lily* in 1977. In addition to performing, he has taught in universities.

SHORT, Bobby (Robert Waltrip)
1926-

A classic cafe/supper-club singer, Short has become a sort of a one-man institution, a master at investing old songs with new meanings. Born in Danville, Illinois, he taught himself piano and worked in vaudeville as a child before gravitating to Chicago clubs and radio stations. He eventually established himself as a sophisticated singer-pianist in the best nightclubs of Manhattan, Los Angeles, and Paris. In 1968 he made some highly successful recordings of Cole Porter songs that he performed with Mabel Mercer at Carnegie Hall. Short now alternatives between his regular appearances at Manhattan's Cafe Carlyle and occasional forays into the recording studio and other supper clubs.

SIMONE, Nina
(b. Eunice Kathleen Waymon)
1933-

Famous for her 1959 recording of Gershwin's "I Loves You Porgy," singer Simone took up the cause of civil rights and expatriated herself in angry protest over the treatment of African-Americans in the U.S. Born in Tryon, North Carolina, she studied piano and attended The Juilliard School for a year, but found herself stymied in the pursuit of higher musical studies because, she believed, of her race. From nightclub performing in Atlanta she rose to national prominence; her greatest songs include "To Be Young, Gifted and Black" and "Four Women". Simone toured internationally in the 1960s. In the early 1990s the "high priestess of soul" returned to the United States from France with her autobiography and a new album.

Nina Simone in 1969.

SIMPSON, Carole
1940-

A respected broadcast journalist, Carole Simpson was born in Miami and studied at the universities of Illinois, Michigan, and Iowa. After quickly rising through the ranks of radio and TV in Chicago, in 1974 she moved to Washington, D.C., to report for NBC News. Joining ABC News in 1982, she became a founding member of the Women's Advisory Board at ABC and pressed hard to force ABC News to give women better opportunities. In 1989 she became the first African-American woman to anchor a major network newscast during the week. She also was one of the principals in producing *Black in America*, an ABC documentary on racism. She continued to cover news assignments and gained national recognition and praise for her astute moderating of the 1992 presidential debates.

SIMPSON, O.J. (Orenthal James)
1947-

"The Juice" led the University of Southern California to victories seen on national television, earned the 1968 Heisman Trophy, and went on to a professional career with the Buffalo Bills. With them he rushed for a total of 11,236 yards, including an incredible 2,003 yards in 1973, when he was the league's Most Valuable Player. The Football Hall of Famer (1985) had a successful later career in movies and TV, but his private life was troubled, and in 1994 he was charged with murdering his ex-wife and one of her friends.

Benjamin Singleton (undated photo).

SINGLETON, Benjamin "Pap"
1809-1892

Born in slavery in Nashville, Tennessee, Singleton twice escaped from his owners. He migrated to Detroit, and then to Canada, but he returned to post-Civil War Nashville in 1865. Finding that most of the farmland of Tennessee was still in white hands, he told fellow African-Americans to go to Kansas and later claimed that he

OPPOSITE: Bessie Smith *c.* 1925.
BELOW: Director John Singleton in 1992.

was the "Father of the Exodus" of 1879, when 20,000 African-Americans moved west. He formed the United Colored Links (1881) in Tennessee Town, Topeka, Kansas, and also formed the Chief League (1883) to persuade African-Americans to migrate to the island of Cyprus. He was a cabinetmaker by trade.

SINGLETON, John
1968-

As the first African-American and the youngest person ever nominated for an Oscar as best director, Singleton burst on the Hollywood scene with work that was both commercially successful and socially controversial. He was born in Los Angeles to teenage parents who took turns raising him. A precocious reader, he decided after seeing *Star Wars* that he wanted to make movies. He went on to the University of Southern California and by the time he was graduated from its School of Cinema-Television in 1990 he had already written the screenplay for *Boyz N the Hood*. When the script was bought by Columbia Pictures he demanded that he also be allowed to direct the movie version. Made for a modest $6 million, it became the most profitable movie of 1991 and gained him an Oscar nomination for best screenplay, as well as for best director. The movie caused some controversy because of violence that accompanied a few of the early screenings, but the film is undeniably an authentic and searing vision of the realities faced by many young, urban African-Americans. His next movie *Poetic Justice* (1993), was less successful, but he still has a long career ahead of him.

Robert Smalls *c.* 1870.

SMALLS, Robert
1839-1915

Born in Beaufort, South Carolina, Smalls grew up on the coast and became a sail-maker and pilot. Forced into the Confederate naval service, he took the ship *Planter* out of Charleston (May 13, 1862) and led her to Union waters. He subsequently became a pilot and then a captain (1863) in the Union navy. After the war he served in the South Carolina legislature and then in the U.S. House of Representatives for South Carolina (1875-1879, 1882-1887). He became a major-general in the South Carolina militia and served as the federal collector of the port of Beaufort, South Carolina, from 1897 until two years before his death in 1915.

SMITH, Bessie
1894-1937

By phrasing her vocals closer to the style of the great instrumentalists of the era than to the rural folk-blues from which her material was drawn, "The Empress of Blues" set the tone for all contemporary female blues singers, as well as for subsequent generations of jazz singers. Born in Chattanooga, Tennessee, Smith began her career touring in the minstrel shows of her mentor, vocalist Ma Rainey. Between 1923 and 1927 her recordings with such luminaries as Louis Armstrong and Coleman Hawkins sold in the millions, but a combination of changes in public taste and her hard-living rendered her incandescent success short-lived. She died of injuries sustained in an automobile accident.

STEWART, Ellen
1931-

A theater producer and director, she worked first as a fashion designer in New York (1950-1972). Beginning in 1962, she established her own Greenwich Village coffeehouse, then theater clubs and companies – La Mama, Cafe La Mama, and La Mama ETC (Experimental Theatre Club). They have performed over 1,000 plays by a wide range of avant-garde playwrights, from Arrabal and Artaud to Warhol and Weiss. She hosted many visiting companies, toured successfully in the 1960s and 1970s, and set up branches worldwide. A major influence, her encouragement has inspired many.

STILL, William Grant
1895-1978

Raised in Little Rock, Arkansas, he rose to be called the "Dean of Afro-American Composers." He played violin in the U.S. Army during World War I, worked with W. C. Handy and Paul Whiteman, and played oboe in the *Shuffle Along* orchestra (1921). He attended Oberlin and the New England Conservatory and won Guggenheim and Rosenwald fellowships. Between 1926 and 1970, he wrote more than 35 orchestral works, nine operas, seven chamber pieces, and four ballets. Especially regarded are his *Afro-American Symphony* (1931) and the opera *Troubled Island* (1941).

William Grant Still (left) in 1938.

STOKES, Carl
1927-

Stokes became the first African-American mayor of a major American city when he was elected mayor of Cleveland in 1968. A high school drop-out in 1944, he earned his high school degree in 1947 after serving in the army. After earning his A.B. he earned a law degree at Cleveland-Marshall Law School and entered private practice. He immediately involved himself in civic affairs and did volunteer work for the National Assocaition for the Advancement of Colored People. After his term as mayor he worked as a TV anchor from 1972 to 1980. In 1983 he became a judge for the Cleveland Municipal Court.

SULLIVAN, Leon (Howard)
1922-

A clergyman and businessman, he was educated at Union Theological Seminary and Columbia University (M.A., 1947). He served Zion Baptist Church, Philadelphia, as pastor (1950-1988, afterwards emeritus). He was a founder of Self-Help, the Zion Home (1960), and the Opportunity Industrial Centers of America (1964). He was on the board of the Mellon

Carl B. Stokes in 1989.

Bank and GM Corporation – the first African-American elected to these posts. He was known for formulating the Sullivan Principles (1977), voluntary guidelines for U.S. companies to promote an end to apartheid in South Africa. By 1985 over 150 companies had adopted them.

Rev. Leon Sullivan in 1987.

TANNER, Henry Ossawa
1859-1937

The son of a bishop in the African Methodist Episcopalian Church, Tanner disappointed his father by pursuing a career as a painter. When his father was transfered from Pittsburgh to Philadelphia in 1880 Tanner began his studies at the Philadelphia Academy of Fine Arts with Thomas Eakins, now recognized as one of America's greatest painters. Eakins befriended Tanner and helped him to get his first commissions to paint genre scenes and landscapes. In 1891 several wealthy patrons banded together to send Tanner to France, where he studied with Paul Laurens and Benjamin Constant, painted landscapes in Brittany, and began to paint religious scenes, which were to become one of his favorite subjects. In the late 1890s his patron, Rodman Wanamaker of Philadelphia, sent Tanner to the Holy Land, where he continued to paint religious motifs. Tanner continued to live in Paris, returning only briefly to the United States from 1902 to 1904, at which time Eakins painted his former pupil's portrait (which now hangs in the Hyde Collection, Glens Falls, New York). In 1908 Tanner had his first one-man show in the United States, and the next year he became the first African-American to be elected to the National Academy of Design. Some of his best known paintings are "The Banjo Lesson," "Daniel in the Lion's Den," and "The Resurrection of Lazarus".

TATUM, Art (Arthur)
1909-1956

A piano virtuoso whose mastery inspired and intimidated his colleagues, Tatum's dazzling technique and imaginative harmonic approach profoundly influenced his contemporaries and the evolution of

modern jazz. Born nearly blind into a musical family in Toledo, Ohio, Tatum studied piano formally but chose jazz over classical music and had his own radio show in Toledo by the time he was 18. After establishing his reputation in New York City in 1932, he worked primarily as a solo artist for the remainder of his career, recording prolifically and performing in public and in private for many celebrities.

TAYLOR, Billy (William, Jr.)
1921-

Unique in linking jazz education and entertainment to national audiences, master painist Taylor was born into a musical family in Greenville, North Caro-

Nearly-blind piano virtuoso Art Tatum, as he looked in 1934.

lina. He was raised mainly in Washington, D.C. He studied the classics and worked in New York City with players as diverse as Ben Webster, Artie Shaw, Charlie Parker, Dizzy Gillespie, and Miles Davis. Convinced that jazz could be taught, his involvement in promoting jazz education has included the creation of New York's Jazzmobile (1965); his service on the National Council for the Arts and on the board of the American Society for Composers, Authors, and Publishers; and his celebrated broadcasts on public radio and TV. He leads his own outstanding trios and holds a doctorate in music.

Mary Terrell *c.* 1884.

TERRELL, Mary Church
1863-1954

A life-long activist for women's rights and civil rights, Terrell grew up among the black elite of Memphis, Tennessee. After her graduation from Oberlin College in 1884 Terrell moved to Europe to escape racism at home. In 1896 she returned to the United States and founded the National Association of Colored Women, an important force for childcare, schools for domestic sciences, and equal rights. She became more radical as she aged: in the 1950s, cane in hand, she successfully led the fight to desegregrate Washington's public restaurants. (On June 8, 1953, the U.S. Supreme Court ruled Washington's segregated restaurants unconstitutional.) Born in the year of the Emancipation Proclamation, Terrell died two months after *Brown v. Board of Education* outlawed school segregation.

THOMAS, Clarence
1948-

When, in 1991, Thomas took his seat on the U.S. Supreme Court, he became only the second African-American to do so (Thurgood Marshall having been the first). Born into a poor but highly motivated family, Thomas attributed much of his success to the lessons he received from the Catholic nuns at the parochial school he attended. After graduation from Holy Cross College (1971) and the Yale Law School (1974), Thomas held staff positions under John Danforth, first when Danforth was attorney general of Missouri and then when he moved to Washington as a Senator. He began to emerge as one of a small circle of African-Americans who spoke as both conservative and Republicans, and he was named to chair the Equal Employment Opportunity Commission in 1982, a post he held under both presidents Ronald Reagan and George Bush; in this office Thomas generally opposed such liberal policies as affirmative action quotas. President Bush appointed him to the federal court of appeals for the district of Washington, D.C., (1990-1991) and then nominated him for the U.S. Supreme Court in 1991. During Thomas's confirmation process Anita Hill, an African-American professor of law at the University of Oklahoma, testified that Thomas had subjected her to sexual harassment when she worked with him at the EEOC; after highly publicized hearings, Thomas's nomination was confirmed by the U.S. Senate by the margin of 52-48. During his first years on the court Thomas proved to be somewhat reticent as a questioner in public court sessions, but he did not shirk from taking decisive positions in his strong written opinions.

TILL, Emmett Louis
1941-1955

A Chicago resident vacationing with relatives in Mississippi in August 1955, he allegedly "wolfwhistled" at a married white woman and asked her for a date. Male relatives of the woman shot him in the head and threw him into the Tallahatchie River. His murder and pictures of his body outraged African-Americans and Northern white liberals. Those accused were acquitted on September 23, 1955, prompting demonstrations in many cities. The death of this 14-year-old remained a symbol of the evil of racial bigotry. It was the subject of two well-known books: Huie's *Wolf Whistle* (1959) and Whitfield's *A Death in the Delta* (1988).

TOUSSAINT, Pierre
1766-1853

Praised by many Catholic church historians as the most outstanding black Catholic in New York's history, Toussaint was born in Saint Mark, Haiti, and brought to New York by his master in

Justice Clarence Thomas in 1991.

1787. Considered the most fashionable coiffeur in the city, he supported his owner's widow and was freed in 1797. A devout Catholic, he gave generously to others, and is best known for his financial support of a white Catholic orphanage and for giving the first subscription to build the St. Vincent DePaul's Church.

TRAYLOR, Bill
1854-1947

A folk artist, he was born in slavery near Benton, Alabama, and worked on a plantation near Selma until his early eighties. He then moved to Montgomery and at the age of 87 started painting. His bold strokes, in mixed media, resembled primitive cave art; published reproductions include "Blue Dog with Figures", "Dancing Man, Woman, and Dog", "Drinker with Hat and Bottle", "Fighting Dogs", "Mule with Red Border", and "Seated Cat". His paintings number over a thousand. "Discovered" in the 1980s, his work has been exhibited worldwide.

TROTTER, William Monroe
1872-1934

A journalist who vigorously opposed discrimination during the early twentieth century, Trotter employed methods notably non-violent protest – that would be used in the twentieth century. Born in Ohio, but raised in Boston, he was an honors student at Harvard University. He founded the *Guardian* (1901) and worked with W.E.B. Du Bois in founding the Niagara Movement (1905). Regarding the NAACP as too moderate, he formed the National Equal Rights League. He went to the Paris Peace Conference (1919) and tried to persuade the delegates to outlaw racial discrimination.

TRUTH, Sojourner (b. Isabella)
?1797-1883

A leading abolitionist and possibly the most famous of all African-American women's rights activists, she was born in Ulster County, New York. Her parents were slaves, and she too was enslaved from 1810 to 1827. Freed when New York abolished slavery in 1827, she was helped by the Van Wagener family, whose name she took. Having lost children to slavery, she successfully sued to get her son back and in 1829 moved to New York City with

TOP: Emmett Till in 1955.
LEFT: William Trotter (undated photo).

this son and a daughter. She became involved with religious mysticism and in 1843 changed her name to Sojourner Truth and moved to a Utopian community in Northampton, Massachusetts. Though illiterate, she was endowed with great natural eloquence and a commanding personal presence, and she soon became one of the nation's most sought-after speakers for the causes of abolition and women's rights. Her "Ain't I a Woman?" address to the Second National Women's Suffrage Convention in 1852 is still quoted. Though she lived in Washington during the Civil War, she eventually settled in Battle Creek, Michigan.

TUBMAN, Harriet
(b. Araminta Ross)
?1821-1913

Often called the "Moses of her People," Tubman was the best-known African-American woman abolitionist. Born into slavery in Maryland, Tubman was considered slow as a child and was repeatedly punished by her master. When she was about 13 her master threw a rock which hit her in the head and caused her periodic black-outs for the rest of her life. Throughout her teens and early twenties, she worked as a fieldhand, but in 1849 she and two of her brothers escaped and headed north on the Underground Rail-

Heroines Sojourner Truth (opposite) and Harriet Tubman (below).

road, for which she soon began to work. She made repeated trips back to the South to assist others to escape and is credited with leading as many as 300 Maryland slaves to freedom over the next decade. When the Fugitive Slave Act was passed in 1850, Tubman urged the fugitives to head for safety in Canada; most did. She herself remained in the United States, although segregationists offered a $40,000 reward for her capture. In 1859 she helped John Brown plan his famous raid on Harper's Ferry, Virginia; ill-health prevented her from accompanying Brown on the raid – and saved her from his fate. Throughout the Civil War she assisted the Union Army as a spy, repeatedly undertaking dangerous missions and encouraging slaves to enlist in the Grand Army of the Republic. In addition to this hazardous war work, she worked as a nurse and cook for the troops. When the war was over Tubman turned her energies to trying to ease the lot of freedmen, especially the elderly. She raised funds for a home in upstate New York for indigent elderly African-Americans, assisted by some of her prominent abolitionist friends such as Senator William Seward. In addition, the proceeds from Sara Bradford's biography, *Harriet Tubman: the Moses of her People* (1869), went for this project. Astonishingly, Tubman accomplished all this despite the fact that she could neither read nor write.

TURNER, Nat
1800-1831

Born in Southampton County, Virginia, Turner was a field hand in the cultivation of both cotton and tobacco. His father was a successful run-away slave, and Turner

Tina Turner (with Mick Jagger) in 1985.

himself ran away in 1821, but he returned after one month, explaining that his religious convictions had persuaded him to do so. Around 1828 he became convinced that visions had instructed him to lead the struggle of enslaved African-Americans to free themselves from their oppressors, and he began to lay plans for a major rebellion of the slaves in his area. Various astronomical signs in 1831 convinced Turner that the time to revolt had arrived. Starting during the early morning hours of August 22, Turner and 60-80 African-American slaves launched a reign of terror in Virginia, killing between 57 and 65 whites, starting with the Travis family, Turner's masters. State militias responded to the situation, and by August 24 Turner's revolt had been suppressed. Turner escaped and hid in a cave, but he was caught on October 31, tried and found guilty on November 5, and hanged on November 11, 1831. Sixteen of his fellow rebels were also executed. The event was later fictionalized in William Styron's *The Confessions of Nat Turner* (1967).

TURNER, Tina
(b. Anna Mae Bullock)
1938-

Turner first became a star as one-half of the Ike and Tina Turner Revue, but she went on to become a superstar on her own. She has remained at the forefront of soul/pop evolution, fusing old-fashioned rhythm-and-blues singing with the strongest elements of rock. Born in Nutbush, Tennessee, she began singing with Ike in St. Louis in 1956 and then became

Cicely Tyson in a 1978 TV film.

his featured vocalist and wife. When their marriage broke up in 1975 Tina, with the support of Mick Jagger and the Rolling Stones, triumphantly established her solo career with the release of her album *Private Dancer* in 1983. Known for her raw stage performance and powerful voice, she has remained incandescent on stage into the 1990s. Her autobiography, *I, Tina* (1985), was made into the movie *What's Love Got to Do With It* (1993).

TYSON, Cicely
1942-

One of the most respected American actresses, Tyson was born in New York City to poor Caribbean immigrants. As a young woman she worked as a secretary and model and studied at New York University. She began acting in film and on stage in the early 1960s and helped to found the Dance Theatre of Harlem with Arthur Mitchell. One of her strongest stage roles was in the off-Broadway production of *The Blacks* (1971). She has found great success in films and on television, where she won an Emmy for her role in the television movie *The Autobiography of Miss Jane Pittman* (1974). She was nominated for an Academy Award for her role in *Sounder* (1972), and in 1989 she returned to television in the special *The Women of Brewster Place.*

VAN PEEBLES, Mario
1957-

The son of writer-director Melvin Van Peebles, he was born in Mexico City and spent his childhood moving about with his peripatetic father, along the way mastering Spanish and French. He had a minor role in his father's controversial movie *Sweet Sweetback's Baadasssss Song* (1971). He was graduated from Columbia with an A.B. in economics and held a variety of jobs, including fashion modeling and Off-Broadway work, before acting in such movies as *Rappin'* (1985) and

Heartbreak Ridge (1986). He also appeared on TV in the play *Children of the Night* (1985), on the series *L.A. Law*, and as the private-eye title character in *Sonny Spoon* (1988). By 1989 he was directing some episodes for TV series, and in 1991 he made his big breakthrough when he directed the movie *New Jack City*, controversial for its portrayal of the violence in the black drug world. In 1993 he directed and acted in his second movie, *Posse*, which deals with African-Americans on the Western frontier.

VAN PEEBLES, Melvin
1932-

A talented director, writer, and composer who has been called "the godfather of African-American moviemakers," Van Peebles was born in Chicago and served in the Air Force after his graduation from Ohio Wesleyan. He drifted for several years – working in San Francisco, studying and acting in Holland – before settling in Paris, where he sang and danced on the streets to support himself while writing novels. With a French government subsidy, he made a movie from his own script, *Story of a Three Day Pass*, which gained

Mario Van Peebles in *Posse*, in 1993.

him favorable notice at San Francisco's International Film Festival in 1967. This led to his being hired by Columbia Pictures to direct his own satiric comedy *Watermelon Man* (1970), starring Godfrey Cambridge. Working as an independent, he then made *Sweet Sweetback's Baadasssss Song* (1971). With its defiant violence, sexuality, and radicalism, the movie gained him instant notoriety and considerable financial returns, but it did not lead to many offers from Hollywood. He turned to Broadway with *Ain't Supposed to Die a Natural Death* (1971) and *Don't Play Us Cheap* (1972), both fairly successful with African-American audiences. He has continued to work at various movie and video projects, including the movie *Identity Crisis* (1990).

VAUGHAN, Sarah Lois
1924-1990

Internationally-acclaimed singer "Sassy" Sarah Vaughan combined operatic range and power with blues sensibilities and bebop rhythms: the result was both a celebrated jazz career and great popular success. Born in Newark, New Jersey, she studied piano and began singing in church. After winning an Apollo Theatre singing contest, she came to prominence with the Earl Hines Band (1944-1955) and recorded with Dizzy Gillespie and other modern jazz greats, as well as in lush, commerical, orchestral settings, alternating between jazz and mainstream popular music. She returned to small-group recording in the 1980s with such masters as Count Basie, Oscar Peterson, and Dizzy Gillespie.

VESEY, Denmark
?1767-1822

Vesey's birthplace is unknown; he was brought to Charleston, South Carolina, by his master, Captain Joseph Vesey, in 1783. He won a $1,500 lottery in 1799, bought his freedom, and became a master carpenter. Incensed that his wives and children were still enslaved, and inspired by the war of liberation in Haiti, Vesey planned an uprising of the field hands in and around Charleston in 1822. Betrayed by household slaves, Vesey was captured on June 22, 1822. He cross-examined the witnesses against him and defended himself ably at his trial, but he was convicted (June 28) and hanged on July 2, 1822. Thirty-three other persons were likewise hanged as conspirators.

Sarah Vaughan (undated photo).

registered voters in Georgia, worked for the Head Start program in Mississippi, and worked with the welfare department in New York City. Her early poetry and fiction drew on both her family's history and her own work and travels and already revealed her special concern for the African-American woman's experience. She gained a broader public with her novel *The Color Purple* (1982), which won her the Pulitzer Prize and was made into a successful movie starring Oprah Winfrey and Danny Glover. Two subsequent novels, *The Temple of My Familiar* (1990) and *Possessing the Secret of Joy* (1992) involve some of the characters introduced in *The Color Purple*.

WALKER, Fleet (Moses Fleetwood)
1856-1924
WALKER, Welday
(Weldon Wilberforce)
1860-1937

The first African-Americans to play major league baseball, the college-educated (Oberlin College and the University of

Michigan) brothers Fleet and Welday Walker were members of the 1884 Toledo American Association club. After that season Fleet continued to play ball, but Welday returned to Oberlin College to complete work for his degree. In 1887 Fleet teamed with pitcher George Stovey in the International League to form the first black battery in organized baseball. Stovey won 35 games – still the league record. Fleet had to deal with racial incidents, such as the time Cap Anson, the Chicago White Stockings manager, threatened to pull his club from the field if Walker played. But the Stovey-Walker battery remained in great demand for exhibition games. Fleet later teamed with another African-American pitcher, Robert Higgins, to lead the Syracuse Stars in their 1888 pennant-winning season. Fleet's brother, Welday, became a leader in an early civil rights movement. He wrote *Our Home Colony* and published a newspaper, *The Equator*. Welday was a confidant of Marcus Garvey and saw his ideas incorporated into the Back-to-Africa movement of the 1920s.

WALKER, Alice Malsenior
1944-

A prominent novelist and poet, Walker was born in Eatonton, Georgia, and attended both Spelman College and Sarah Lawrence, where she received her A.B. in 1965. Before settling in San Francisco she

Alice Walker *c.* 1983.

Maggie Walker (undated photo).

WALKER, Maggie Lena
1867-1934

A social activist, Walker was born in Richmond, Virginia. She taught school until she married in 1886 and then joined an African-American fraternal and insurance cooperative called the Independent Order at St. Luke. She became the order's executive secretary-treasurer in 1899 and in 1903 founded the St. Luke Penny Savings Bank in Richmond, making her the first female bank president in the United States. By 1929 her bank had become quite large and had bought out several other banks. She spent much of her life in a wheelchair after an accident in 1907, but she never ceased her activities, especially promoting economic opportunities for African-Americans.

WALKER, Sarah Breedlove
(Madame C.J. Walker)
1876-1919

One of the first American women to become a self-made millionaire, Walker was born in Delta, Louisiana, and was orphaned at the age of six. Widowed when she was 20, she moved to St. Louis, Missouri. She invented a method for straightening African-Americans' hair (1905), using her special preparations and heated combs. She promoted her method and de-

Madame C.J. Walker *c.* 1910.

veloped a business that flourished in Pittsburgh, Denver, and Indianapolis, where she built a large factory in 1910. Her company, Madame C. J. Walker Laboratories, manufactured cosmetics and trained sales beauticians who took her process throughout the United States and to the Caribbean. Intent upon teaching black women how to be successful in business, Walker (who, after 1913, lived in New York) organized clubs and conventions for her representatives and was active in philanthropy. She left one-third of her large estate to her daughter and the rest of the money to a variety of philanthropic causes.

OPPOSITE: Jazz pianist Fats Waller.

WALLER, Fats (Thomas Wright)
1904-1943

Irrepressible singer, prolific composer, and consummate entertainer, Waller was a virtuoso jazz pianist whose stride style directly influenced Count Basie, Duke Ellington, and Art Tatum. Born in New York City, he began playing organ in Harlem's Abyssinian Baptist Church. After "Squeeze Me" (1923), his first hit, he composed such landmarks as "Ain't Misbehavin'," "Honeysuckle Rose," and "The Jitterbug Waltz" with collaborators Andy Razaf, Irving Mills, and Billy Rose. He also composed the popular musicals *Keep Shufflin'* (1928) and *Hot Chocolates* (1929). A popular performer throughout Manhattan in the 1920s, his career was hampered by alcoholism and overeating, but at his peak Waller was a commercial recording success and star of stage and screen second in public recognition only to Louis Armstrong.

WARD, Douglas Turner
(a.k.a. Douglas Turner)
1930-

Actor, playwright, and director, he combined these roles with unusual success. As an actor, chiefly in New York, he had over 30 roles (1957-1990) and directed over 30 plays (1968-1990). He won Obie awards for writing and performing in *Happy Ending* (1966), *Day of Absence* (1966), and *The Reckoning* (1970). With Robert Hooks, he co-founded the Negro Ensemble Company in 1968. Its notable successes include Lonnie Elder III's *Ceremonies in Dark Old Men* and Charles Fuller's *A Soldier's Play*. His focus is on using satire to express contemporary themes, especially those relating to African-American survival.

WARFIELD, William
1920-

A baritone soloist, he was graduated from the Eastman School of Music in 1946. His career began with a recital at New York Town Hall in 1950. Known for his leading role in New York and Vienna productions of *Porgy and Bess*, he also performed on Broadway in *Showboat, Call Me Mister*, and *Let My People Go*. His repertoire included Mozart's *Requiem* (1956), Handel's *Messiah*, and many operatic arias. A University of Illinois professor since 1974, he became president of the National Association of Negro Musicians in 1984. His wife from 1952 to 1972 was soprano Leontyne Price.

WASHINGTON, Booker Taliaferro
1856-1915

Born into slavery, Washington was the most prominent spokesperson for African-Americans after the death of the fiery Frederick Douglass (1895). Much more conciliatory than Douglass, Washington sought – but never demanded – social betterment for African-Americans through economic progress. His enslaved mother was a cook on a Virginia plantation, and his father was a local white (whose identity he never knew); as a boy, he picked Washington as his last name. After emancipation his mother and stepfather moved to West Virginia, where Washington worked in the coal mines, but he attended school whenever possible. In his autobiography, *Up From Slavery* (1901), Washington said that what he learned about character, cleanliness, and hard work while working as a manservant in the home of General Lewis Ruffner was an experience that was "As valuable to me as any education I have ever gotten anyplace." In 1871 Washington returned to Virginia and enrolled in the Hampton Institute, a school for African-Americans founded by General Samuel C. Armstrong, a missionary's son who had commanded black soldiers during the Civil War. Washington would later describe Armstrong as the "noblest, rarest, human being" he ever met. After being graduated from Hampton in 1875 Washington first taught in West Virginia and then studied at the Wayland Seminary in Washington, D.C., (1878-9) before returning to teach at Hampton. In 1881 he left Hampton to begin the single most important undertaking of his life: founding the Tuskegee Normal School (later the Tuskegee Institute) in Alabama. Washington, his small staff, and their students worked as carpenters to build Tuskegee. In its first year of operation Tuskegee had 37 students and a faculty of three; when Washington died in 1915, Tuskegee had 1,500 students, a faculty of 180 (including the distinguished scientist

Booker T. Washington (front, left) and the Tuskegee faculty *c.* 1885.

George Washington Carver), and an endowment of $2,000,000. A good deal of Tuskegee's success came from Washington's tireless fundraising, much of it among wealthy white Americans such as Andrew Carnegie. Perhaps inevitably, some African-Americans criticized Washington for what they saw as his overly-deferential attitude to his white benefactors and for his position that university education was basically irrelevant for blacks, who should concentrate on vocational training. This, along with his acceptance of segregation, increasingly led W.E.B. Du Bois and other leaders to speak out against Washington's leadership. This was especially the case after 1895, when Washington delivered the speech Du Bois called "the Atlanta Compromise." That conciliatory speech, along with his silence during the Brownsville, Texas, affair of 1906, when black soldiers were discharged from the army on unproven charges of rioting, diminished Washington's influence – as did the fact that he did not participate with Du Bois and others in founding the National Asso-

Denzel Washington, with the Oscar he won for his role in the 1989 film *Glory*.

ciation for the Advancement of Colored People in 1909. In October 1915 Washington collapsed while delivering a speech in New York City and was hospitalized. He asked to be returned home to die. He was taken back to Tuskegee on November 13, 1915, and died the next day at his home on the campus of his beloved institute.

WASHINGTON, Denzel
1954-

Perhaps currently the most successful African-American actor, Washington was born in Mount Vernon, New York, and received his A. B. in journalism from Fordham University. He studied at the American Conservatory Theater in San Francisco and acted with the New York Shakespeare Festival and the Manhattan Theatre Club before beginning a film career in the early 1980s. He won an Academy Award for his role in *Glory* (1989) and has gained considerable critical acclaim in the Spike Lee films *Mo' Better Blues* and *Malcolm X*. Washington has made movies appealing to all audiences, ranging from the off-beat *Mississippi Masala* to such mainstream hits as *The Pelican Brief*.

Singer Dinah Washington (undated photo).

WASHINGTON, Dinah
(b. Ruth Jones)
1924-1963

An original stylist whose synthesis of gospel and blues made her a favorite of jazz musicians and a major influence on soul and rock, Washington's passionate vocalizing mirrored her short, turbulent life. Born in Tuscaloosa, Alabama, and raised in Chicago, she played piano and sang with the Sara Martin Singers and was influenced by Bessie Smith and Billie Holiday. Featured with the Lionel Hampton band primarily as a blues singer (1943-1946), she went on to pursue a commercial career as a pop stylist, yet she also continued to make important jazz recordings until her death from abuse of alcohol and amphetamines.

WASHINGTON, Harold
1922-1987

The first African-American mayor of Chicago (1984-1987), he was born in that city and served with U.S. forces in World War II before beginning in his career as Chicago's assistant city prosecutor (1953-1958). He went on to serve in the Illinois legislature (1966-1976), the state senate (1976-1980), and the U.S. House of Representatives (Dem., 1981-1983). He was active in Americans for Democratic Action and received the Outstanding Legislator's Award of the Southern Christian Leaderhsip Conference. He won a second term as Chicago's mayor in 1987 but died before he could begin it.

ABOVE: Ethel Waters with Eddie Anderson.
RIGHT: Mayor Harold Washington in 1986.

WATERS, Ethel
1900-1977

Actress and singer, she is remembered for her "laughter through tears" performance as Berenice in *A Member of the Wedding* (1950 play, 1955 film). The first woman to sing "St. Louis Blues" (1913), she first appeared on Broadway in *Africana* (1927), then in Lew Leslie's *Blackbirds* (1930). Irving Berlin heard "Stormy Weather" and invited Waters to play in *As Thousands Cheer* (1933). In *Mamaba's Daughters* (1939) she was the first African-American actress to star in a Broadway play. Her films include *Cairo* (1942) and *Pinky* (1949). In 1957 she joined the Billy Graham Crusade.

WATERS, Muddy
(b. McKinley Morganfield)
1915-1983

One of America's great country blues singers and primary shaper of modern Chicago-style blues, Muddy Waters was born and raised a sharecropper in Clarkes-

dale, Mississippi. He moved to Chicago after having been recorded by folklorist Alan Lomax (1941-1942) and established himself and Chess Records with his hit "Rolling Stone" (1950). In the 1950s his six-piece unit pioneered the electric Chicago blues sound and profoundly influenced the British rock scene. A central figure in the folk-blues revival of the mid-1960s, his songs became widely recorded by rock groups. He toured with such headliners as the Rolling Stones and Eric Clapton, won several Grammies in the 1970s, and was inducted into the Rock 'n' Roll Hall of Fame in 1987.

WATTLETON, Faye
1943-

In 1978 Wattleton became the first African-American, the first woman, and, at 25, the youngest person to be elected president of the Planned Parenthood Federation of America. Her interest in reproductive rights began when she was a young nurse in Ohio and intensified when she received a M.S. in maternal and infant health care from the Columbia University Medical School in 1967. Her many honors include the Humanist of the Year Award for 1986, the same award once given to birth control pioneer Margaret Sanger. After serving as president of PPFA from 1978 to 1992 she resigned to host a television talk show.

Faye Wattleton, President of the Planned Parenthood Federation of America, in 1990.

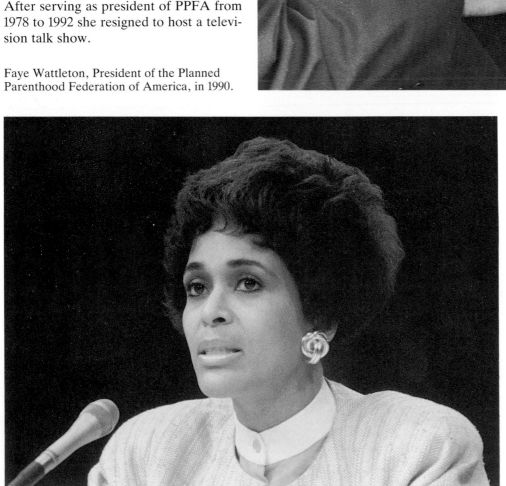

Famed classical pianist André Watts. He gave his first recital when he was nine.

WATTS, André
1946-

Born in Nuremberg, Germany, the son of an African-American soldier and a Hungarian mother, he became a brilliant pianist. With the Philadelphia Orchestra, he played Haydn at the age of nine and César Franck at the age of 14; at 16 he played Liszt on TV with Leonard Bernstein's New York Philharmonic. He debuted with the London Symphony and then with the Amsterdam Concertgebouw in 1966. In 1967 he toured Europe with the Los Angeles Philharmonic. His was the first recital nationally telecast live (from Lincoln Center in 1976). A favorite at international political ceremonies, he received an honorary doctorate from Yale in 1973, the Lincoln Center Medallion in 1974, and the Avery Fisher Prize in 1988.

ABOVE: Robert Weaver, flanked by Jacob Javits and Robert Kennedy, in 1966.

WEAVER, Robert Clifton
1907-

Weaver's success in government and academia seemed to offer hope to African-Americans during decades when few were given the chance in such circles. Born in Washington, D.C., he earned his B.S., M.A., and Ph.D. degrees at Harvard, and, while serving as an adviser to the Department of the Interior, he became a member of President Franklin Roosevelt's informal "Black Cabinet". He became a housing commissioner and the rent administrator for the state of New York (1954-1959) and then a Federal Housing Agency administrator (1961-1966). He co-authored *The Dilemma of Urban America* (1965). As President Lyndon Johnson's secretary of the Department of Housing and Urban Development (1966-1969), he was the first African-American cabinet member. He went on to serve as the president of Bernard Baruch College in New York City (1969-1978).

WELLS-BARNETT, Ida Bell
1862-1931

This civil rights advocate was born in slavery in Holly Springs, Mississippi. After emancipation she attended Rust College and was fired in 1891 from her teaching post in Memphis, Tennessee, due to her outspoken criticism of segregation in the schools. She became editor and

part-owner of a Memphis newspaper, for which she wrote anti-lynching articles. She moved to the Northeast when her writing provoked threats and continued as a strong anti-lynching activist. She was secretary of the National Afro-American Council from 1898 to 1902 and one of the founders of the National Association for the Advancement of Colored People (NAACP) (1910).

WEST, Cornel
1953-

One of the most prominent African-American educators of this day, West was born in Sacramento, California. He re-

ABOVE LEFT: Ida Wells-Barnett (undated).
ABOVE: Cornel West in 1988.

ceived his undergraduate education at Harvard and then went on to Union Theological Seminary. He became a highly respected writer and lecturer, espousing a philosophy he calls "prophetic pragmatism," addressing concerns of racial oppression, violence, sexism, and homophobia through the life of the mind. Among his books are *The American Evasion of Philosophy* (1985) and *Race Matters* (1993). He became the director of the African-American studies department at Princeton University in 1988, and left to join the Harvard faculty in 1993.

WHARTON, Clifton Reginald, Jr.
1926-

The son of one of the first African-American career diplomats, Wharton became the first African-American president of a major American university in 1970 when he became president of Michigan State University. In 1977 he left Michigan to become chancellor of the State University of New York. The recipient of a University of Chicago Ph.D. in economics (1958), Wharton has taught economics and served as an advisor to the U.S. Department of State and AID on East Asia and the Pacific.

WHEATLEY, Phillis
?1753-1784

The first African-American woman to have her poetry published, Wheatley was born in Africa and sold in slavery in 1761 to the Wheatley family in Boston. She was educated with the Wheatley children and began writing poetry as a young girl. In 1778 the Wheatleys sent her to London with their son, where she published her first volume of poetry *Poems on Various Subjects, Relgious and Moral*. She was freed on her return to Boston and married and had children. She continued to write and in 1784 published a collection called *Memoirs and Poems of Phillis Wheatley*. Although her poetry adheres to conventions not in fashion today, she served as a powerful model for earlier generations in establishing that it was only lack of education that kept African-Americans from achieving.

Phillis Wheatley (undated portrait).

Josh White in the 1940s.

WHITE, Bill (William DeKova)
1934-

In 1956 White hit a home run for the New York Giants in his first major league at-bat. After that he never looked back. His accomplishments on the field include seven Gold Glove Awards and selection for the All-Star team five times. After his playing days (always in the National League), he had a long, successful career as a Yankees broadcaster and as an articulate "straight man" to Phil Rizzuto's off-beat humor. In 1989 White became one of the first African-Americans to attain a position at the top level of league management when he became the president of the National League.

WHITE, Josh (Joshua Daniel)
1915-1969

A charming and urbane troubadour who was equally accomplished in blues and folk music, White's easy mastery of various musical forms prefigured the work of a whole generation of African-American performers. Born in Greenville, South Carolina, he learned his trade on the streets and began recording, on the guitar, at the age of 13. In the 1930s he recorded blues and gospel tunes such as "There's a Man Goin' Around Taking Names" (1933). A favorite of President Franklin Delano Roosevelt, he performed at the White House with his Josh White Singers. White sang in New York City musicals during the 1940s and 1950s and was an important part of a folk scene that included Leadbelly, Woody Guthrie, and Paul Robeson.

WIDEMAN, John Edgar
1941-

In 1993 Wideman received a MacArthur Foundation "genius" grant that freed him from his teaching responsibilities at the University of Massachusetts at Amherst and allowed him to concentrate on his writing. Ever since his first novel, *A Glance Away* (1967), Wideman has written mainly about many of the issues confronting contemporary African-Americans, especially urban dwellers. In addition, he has written *Brothers and Keepers* (1984), an autobiographical account of the very different path taken by his brother, who is serving a life term in prison. (Sadly, Wideman's own son, Jake, at the age of 18 confessed to two murders.) In addition to the MacArthur award, Wideman's many honors include twice winning the P.E.N./Faulkner Award for fiction: in 1984 for *Sent for You Yesterday* and in 1990 for *Philadelphia Fire*.

WILDER, L. (Lawrence) Douglas
1931-

When he became the governor of Virginia in 1990, the first African-American to be popularly elected governor of any state, the majority of his support came from white voters. He had been awarded the Bronze Star for heroism during the Korean War (1952), had received his law degree from Howard University (1959), and had practiced law in Richmond for a decade. He had served Virginia as the first African-American state senator (1969-1985) and as lieutenant governor (1985-1989). He has won many awards, and his remarkable successes spawned several books, among them *When Hell Froze Over* (1988) and *Claiming the Dream* (1990).

Gov. Douglas Wilder (center) in 1990.

Roy Wilkins (right) in 1955.

WILKINS, Roy
1910-1981

One of the most influential civil rights activists and a steady voice for non-violence, Wilkins served as executive director of the National Association for the Advancement of Colored People from 1955 to 1977. At the time of his death he was the last survivor of the prominent civil rights leaders of the 1950s and 1960s, having outlived Martin Luther King, Jr., Whitney Young, Malcolm X, and A. Philip Randolph. Born in Saint Louis, Missouri, Wilkins was raised by an aunt and uncle in Saint Paul, Minnesota, where he grew up in a mixed neighborhood. He attended the University of Minnesota, and while in college, he showed a flair for journalism, serving as night editor of the campus newspaper, the *Minnesota Daily*, and editing a black weekly, the *Saint Paul Appeal*. After graduation in 1923 he went to work on a black weekly, the *Kansas City Call*; Wilkins later said that it was in Kansas City that he first experienced real discrimination. After leaving the *Call* in 1931 he went to work for the NAACP, which was to be his most important life work. When asked what he did for a living, Wilkins often replied, "I work for Negroes." He never became comfortable with the term "blacks," and had no patience with black separatism or nationalism. From 1934 to 1949 he served as editor of *Crisis*, the magazine founded by W.E.B. Du Bois, but he was best known for his work for equal rights and economic opportunity during his long term as executive secretary at the NAACP. In 1964 he won the Spingarn Medal, the highest annual award given by the NAACP. His other honors included awards from virtually every American civil rights organization, including B'nai Brith, the Japanese-American Citizens' League, and the Unitarian Fellowship for Social Justice. Often regarded as old-fashioned by young leaders, Wilkins was nonetheless praised by Jesse Jackson, who said in 1972 that blacks needed both the "vitality of the Panthers and the wisdom of Wilkins." When he died, President Ronald Reagan ordered American flags on all government buildings to be flown at half mast.

WILLIAMS, Bert (Egbert Austin)
?1874-1922

A stage actor and songwriter, he was considered by some to be the greatest African-American vaudevillian. Born in the Bahamas, he settled in the U.S. and played in minstrel shows. In 1895 he worked up an act with comedian George Walker in which Williams played a downtrodden dupe; shuffling along, he delivered lines that hid a surprise punch. Their four Broadway shows included *The Gold Bug* (1896) and *Bandana Land* (1908). After Walker's death, Williams appeared in the *Ziegfield Follies* (1910-1919) and challenged some stereotypes in his songs "Nobody" and "That's a-Plenty". In 1906 he founded an African-American actors' society.

WILLIAMS, Billy Dee
1937-

This popular and versatile actor was born in New York City, grew up in Harlem, and was a child actor on stage. He studied both at the National Academy of Fine Arts and Design and at Sidney Poitier's Actor's Workshop in Harlem. He made his adult debut in the Broadway play *The Cool World* in 1961 and began his movie career with *The Last Angry Man* in 1959. He became a successful leading man, playing opposite Diana Ross in the 1970s in the films *Lady Sings the Blues* and *Mahogany*, and in the 1980s he made memorable appearances in *The Empire Strikes Back*

RIGHT: Daniel Hale Williams (undated).
BELOW: Billy Dee Williams (right) in 1992.

and *Return of the Jedi*. He has frequently been seen on television in such series as *The Jeffersons, Mod Squad*, and *Dynasty*. When he is not busy acting, he is a devoted painter.

WILLIAMS, Daniel Hale
1858-1931

The most prominent African-American in medicine for many years, Williams was born in Hollidaysburg, Pennsylvania. He worked as a barber before he was graduated from Chicago Medical College in 1883. He organized Provident Hospital in Chicago in 1891. He performed the first successful surgical closure of a wound to the heart and the pericardium in 1893. He was surgeon-in-chief at Freemen's Hospital in Washington, D.C., (1893-1898) and in 1899 became a professor of clinical surgery at Meharry Medical College in Nashville, Tennessee. He was also a charter member of the American College of Surgeons.

WILLIAMS, John Alfred
1925-

A prolific writer, Williams's first novel, *The Angry Ones*, was published in 1960; by the end of the decade, he had more than ten books in print (some under the name "J. Dennis Gregory"). One of the best-known, *The Man Who Cried I Am* (1967), was a thinly-veiled account of the life of writer Richard Wright. In 1970 Williams wrote *The King God Didn't Save*, a book about Dr. Martin Luther King, Jr. Although Williams insisted that his intention had been to write an impartial account of King's life and work, some complained that his tone was overly hostile. In addition to writing, Williams has worked as a publisher, journalist (he was a correspondent in Africa for *Newsweek* and in Europe for *Ebony* in the 1960s), and teacher. He is currently on the faculty at Rutgers University at Newark, New Jersey.

WILLIAMS, Mary Lou
(b. Mary Elfrieda Scruggs)
1910-1981

Mary Lou Williams's accomplishments go far beyond her label as the first great woman instrumentalist in jazz. Born in Atlanta, Georgia, and raised in Pittsburgh, Pennsylvania, she taught herself piano by listening to Jelly Roll Morton, Earl Hines, and Fats Waller. After moving with saxophonist husband John Williams to Kansas City, she played piano and was chief arranger for the prominent Andy Kirk band (1929-1942). In New York she led her own groups; arranged for Louis Armstrong, Earl Hines, Benny Goodman, and Duke Ellington; and assimilated the new bebop. In 1946 her "Zodiac Suite" was performed in Carnegie Hall by the New York Philharmonic Orchestra. After working in Europe during most of the 1950s she converted to Catholicism and devoted herself to the Church. "Mary Lou's Mass," (1969), one of her several sacred works, was commissioned by the Vatican and choreographed by Alvin Ailey. She returned to performing in the 1970s to promote jazz, recorded duos with avant-garde pianist Cecil Taylor (1977), and was artist-in-residence at Duke University from 1977 until the year of her death, 1981.

Playwright August Wilson (above) and jazz instrumentalist Mary Lou Williams (left).

WILSON, August
1945-

Despite never finishing high school, Wilson holds the distinction of having twice won the Pulitzer Prize, for plays depicting the African-American experience: *Fences* (1987) and *The Piano Lesson* (1990). Like his contemporary African-American playwright, Charles Fuller, Wilson has set out to write a cycle of plays on the African-American experience. While Fuller has concentrated on the nineteenth century, Wilson has focused on the twentieth century. Wilson's first play, *Ma Rainey's Black Bottom*, set in the 1920s, won the New York Drama Critics Circle Award for 1984-1985. Next came *Fences*, set between the 1930s and 1950s. *Joe Turner's Come and Gone*, set in 1911 and focusing on black migration to the North, was voted the best new play of 1988 by the New York Drama Critics Circle. While many of Wilson's plays have opened in New Haven, Connecticut, all have moved on to long New York runs and to countless productions elsewhere. He is also founder of the Black Horizons Theater Company.

ABOVE: Teddy Wilson *c*. 1950.

WILSON, Teddy (Theodore Shaw)
1912-1986

The first black musician to work with a prominent white band in the U.S., pianist Wilson is equally celebrated for leading numerous all-star recordings in the 1930s, and especially for his selection, arrangement, and brilliant accompaniment of some of Billie Holiday's most memorable performances (1935-1939). Born in Austin, Texas, and raised in Alabama, where his father was English department head at Tuskegee Institute, Wilson's formal music studies resulted in the disciplined, cleanly articulated right-hand swing style that became his hallmark. His early work with Benny Goodman (1936) was termed "chamber jazz." He led units of various sizes in the 1940s, worked on the staff of CBS in the 1950s, and taught at The Juilliard School from 1945 to 1952 and periodically thereafter.

WINFREY, Oprah (Gail)
1954-

One of America's most popular TV talk-show hosts and entertainers, Winfrey not only bested veteran Phil Donahue in ratings within three months of going on the air in 1984, she also won an Academy Award nomination for her first film appearance, in *The Color Purple* (1985). Born in Kosciusko, Mississippi, at the age of four she went to live with her maternal grandmother when her parents separated. When she was six she was moved north to Milwaukee to join her mother, an unfortunate decision: Winfrey has revealed that she was subjected to both physical and sexual abuse between the ages of nine and 12. She had better luck when she was 12 and was sent to join her father and his family in Nashville, Tennessee. Her father, a barber, was a strict disciplinarian in matters of education, and Winfrey's resultant success in high school won her a full scholarship to Tennessee State University, where she was crowned Miss Black Nashville and Miss Tennessee during her freshman year. She received her A.B. in 1976, but while still an undergraduate she had worked on WJZ-TV, the local ABC affiliate, and in 1977 she began to appear on "Good Morning, America." After moving to Chicago in 1984, and successfully challenging Donahue, she won

BELOW: Oprah Winfrey in 1993.

her own program, "The Oprah Winfrey Show," in which she continues to appear. In 1988 she won the International Radio and Television Society's Broadcaster of the Year Award, the youngest person ever to do so. She has also formed her own production company, which produces movies and television specials such as "There Are No Children Here," set in Chicago and in which she starred, in 1993.

WONDER, Stevie (b. Steveland Judkins)
1950-

A child prodigy and adult superstar who became a children's and civil rights advocate, Wonder set precedents by gaining complete artistic control over his work and negotiating a $13-million recording contract in 1976 (the largest to that date). Born in Saginaw, Michigan, and blinded soon after birth, Wonder began playing the harmonica, signed with Motown Records in 1960, and had his first million-selling hit in 1963. Following numerous classic Motown rhythm-and-blues-style hits, in the 1970s he added electronic keyboard accompaniment to his soaring voice and created a highly innovative and suc-

Stevie Wonder with his 1985 Oscar.

cessful blend of socially conscious rock-and-soul mixed with sentimental ballads. He was inducted into the Rock 'n' Roll Hall of Fame in 1989.

WOODS, Granville T.
1865-1910

This inventor, known as the "Black Edison," was born in Columbus, Ohio. After a sketchy early education he went to work as a railroad fireman and engineer. Though he moved about a great deal for several years, at some point he seems to have studied electrical technology. By 1884 he had settled in Cincinnati, Ohio, the same year that he took out the first of some 60 patents – for an improved steam boiler furnace. Thereafter he devoted himself to electrical inventions, including a telephone transmitter (1884), the overhead grooved wheel for trolley cars (1886), the multiplex telegraph (1887), a circuit-breaker (1900), and an improved system for electric trains (1901). By 1890 he had moved to New york City. He had earned large sums of money from the sale of his patents, yet he died in poverty, apparently because of huge legal fees. In his day, he was widely celebrated for having contributed so many inventions that became a part of everyday life.

WOODSON, Carter G.
1875-1950

The oldest of nine children, Woodson had to drop out of school to work to help support his family. Despite this, he went on to earn his A.B. and M.A. from the University of Chicago (1908) and his Ph.D. from Harvard (1912). Often referred to as the "father of African-American studies," Woodson hoped that a greater understanding of African-American history and culture would improve race relations. Along with several others, he founded the Association for the Study of Negro Life and History in 1915, *The Journal of Negro History* (1916), the black-owned Associated Publishers press (1921), the *Negro History Bulletin* (1937), and Negro History Week (1926). He published more than 20 books and countless articles, both popular and scholarly.

WRIGHT, Richard Nathaniel
1908-1960

The son of a sharecropper, Wright became the best-known African-American novelist of the 1940s and 1950s, a role model and inspiration for a whole generation of African-American writers. Wright's best-known works were *Native Son* (1940), a Book-of-the-Month-Club selection later produced as a film by Orson Welles, and the heavily autobiographical *Black Boy* (1945), again a Book-of-the-Month Club selection and a best-seller. Wright got his start as a writer in 1938 as a member of the Federal Writers' Project for the Works Progress Administration in Illinois. The WPA published Wright's first book, *Uncle Tom's Children*, four novellas drawing on his youth in Mississippi. The book won immediate acclaim, winning Wright both an award for the best piece of fiction published by the WPA and a Guggenheim Fellowship. Wright moved to New York City, where he worked as an editor on the communist newspaper the *Daily Worker* and continued to write fiction. The result was first *Native Son*, set in a Chicago ghetto, and then *Black Boy*. Despite the acclaim he received, Wright was increasingly disillusioned with American society, and he moved first to Mexico (1940-1946) and then to Paris, where he was soon at the center of a group of young African-American writers that included James Baldwin. Today's critics tend to value Baldwin's work above Wright's, but Baldwin himself often said that if he had never read Richard Wright he might never have become a writer.

YOUNG, Andrew Jackson, Jr.
1932-

A major figure in American public life for several decades, he was born in New Orleans and was graduated from Howard University (1951) and the Hartford Theological Seminary. Ordained in 1955 as a minister in the United Church of Christ, he served at several churches in Alabama and Georgia, and from 1957 to 1961 he was associate director of the National Council of Churches' department of youth work. He had meanwhile joined the Southern Christian Leadership Conference (SCLC), the civil rights organization led

ABOVE RIGHT: Mayor Coleman Young, 1990.
BELOW: Mayor Andrew Young, 1988.

by Martin Luther King, Jr., and Young became its executive director in 1964. Young was one of King's most trusted aides and was himself jailed on two occasions for his role in civil rights demonstrations. In 1971 Young became executive vice president of SCLC. In 1972 he was one of the first two blacks to be elected to Congress from the South since the nineteenth century when he won a seat in the U.S. House of Representatives as a Democrat from Georgia. He was both forceful and effective in Congress until 1977, when President Jimmy Carter named him the U.S. ambassador to the United Nations. He earned respect in this role but was forced to resign when it was revealed that he had met secretly with members of the Palestinian Liberation Organization to try to advance the peace process with Israel. He re-entered public life as mayor of Atlanta, Georgia, (1981-

1989) and thereafter continued to speak out forcefully on issues that he saw as relevant to African-Americans.

YOUNG, Coleman Alexander
1918-

The first African-American mayor of Detroit, Young was also that city's longest-serving mayor (1974-1993). As a young man working in the auto industry, he was an organizer for the Congress of Industrial Workers. After serving as a USAAF bombardier in World War II, he became director of organization for the Wayne County AFL/CIO. His political career advanced rapidly, from delegate to the Michigan constitutional convention (1961) to state senator (1964-1973) and mayor. His principal goals as mayor were to improve Detroit's flagging economy, ease racial tensions, and combat crime.

YOUNG, Whitney M., Jr.
1922-1971

A life-long worker for social reform and improved race relations, Young was perhaps best known as executive director of the Urban League, a post he held from 1961 until his untimely death by drowning while on a visit to Africa. Dedicated to communication and cooperation, Young came in for his share of criticism from younger and more militant African-Americans. He wrote several books, including *To Be Equal* (1964) and *Beyond Racism* (1969), and lectured widely both in America and abroad. In 1969 President Lyndon Johnson gave him the Medal of Freedom, the country's highest civilian award.

Whitney Young (center) in a 1962 meeting with President John F. Kennedy.

Acknowledgments

The publisher would like to thank David Eldred, who designed this book, and Sara Dunphy, who did the picture research.

Picture Credits

American Red Cross, Washington, DC: 49 (bottom).
AP/Wide World Photo: pages 7 (bottom), 10 (bottom), 48 (top).
The Bettmann Archive: pages 7 (top), 11 (top), 12, 13 (bottom), 16 (bottom left), 17, 21 (bottom), 22, 27 (top), 28 (bottom right), 31, 33 (top left), 34 (bottom), 35, 36 (top), 39 (bottom right), 45 (bottom left), 47, 50 (both), 51, 67 (top), 70 (top left), 71, 72 (both), 73 (top), 74, 92 (bottom), 94 (bottom), 104 (both), 107 (top), 111 (bottom), 112 (both), 118 (bottom), 119 (left), 122 (bottom), 125 (top right), 131 (top), 135, 137, 140, 143, 146, 148 (top), 149 (top), 150 (top), 152 (both), 154 (top), 155 (bottom), 156 (top).
Bettmann/Hulton: pages 15 (top left).
Bettmann/Springer Film Archive: page 76.
Brompton Picture Library: pages 43 (top), 142 (bottom).
Denver Public Library, CO, Western History Department: page 18 (top).
Courtesy of Hagley Museum and Library, Wilmington, DE: page 134 (top right).
Harvard Medical Area News Office, Boston, MA, photo by Barbara Steiner: page 116 (bottom).
Harvard University Archives, Cambridge, MA: page 139 (bottom).
Harvard University News Office,

Cambridge, MA: pages 21 (top), 60 (bottom right).
Langston Hughes Memorial Library, Lincoln University, PA: page 57 (top).
Hulton Deutsch Collection Ltd.: page 105 (top).
The Kansas State Historical Society, Topeka, KS: page 134 (top left).
Dwayne Labaacus: page 101 (top).
Library of Congress: page 141 (bottom).
Louisiana State Museum, New Orleans, LA: page 114 (bottom).
Courtesy of the Lynn Historical Society, Lynn, MA: page 100 (bottom center, right).
Museum of the City of New York, The Theater Collection: page 8.
National Baseball Library, Cooperstown, NY: pages 58 (top), 61 (top), 97 (bottom).
New Bedford Whaling Museum, New Bedford, MA: page 39 (bottom left).
Oberlin College Archives, Oberlin, OH: pages 93 (bottom left), 138 (top left).
Princeton University, Princeton, NJ, photo by Robert Matthews: page 151 (center right).
Reuters/Bettmann Newsphotos: pages 10 (top), 11 (bottom), 24 (both), 39 (top), 42, 44, 52 (top), 59 (top), 62 (bottom), 63 (bottom), 69, 75, 79, 80 (bottom right), 82 (bottom), 85, 90 (both), 91 (bottom), 94 (top), 110 (top), 111 (top), 117, 129 (top), 134 (bottom), 138 (bottom), 148 (bottom), 154 (bottom), 156 (bottom).
Roman Catholic Diocese of Portland, ME: page 70 (top right).
Roosevelt University Archives, Chicago, IL: page 48 (bottom).
Schomburg Center for Research in Black Culture, New York Public Library, New York, NY: pages 29 (bottom), 38

(center), 62 (top).
UPI/Bettmann Newsphotos: pages 6 (both), 9, 13 (top), 14, 16 (center), 18 (bottom left), 19, 20, 23 (both), 25 (both), 26 (both), 27 (bottom), 28 (bottom left), 29 (top), 30 (all three), 32, 33 (right), 34 (top), 36 (bottom), 37 (both), 38 (left), 40 (both), 41 (both), 43 (bottom), 45 (right), 46 (both), 49 (top), 52 (bottom), 53, 54 (both), 55 (both), 56, 57 (bottom), 58 (bottom), 59 (bottom), 60 (bottom left), 61 (bottom), 63 (top), 64, 65 (both), 66 (both), 67 (bottom), 68, 70 (center), 73 (bottom), 77, 78, 80 (top left), 81, 82 (top), 83, 86, 87 (both), 88 (both), 89, 91 (top), 92 (top), 96, 97 (top), 98, 99, 101 (bottom), 102 (both), 103 (both), 105 (bottom), 106 (bottom), 107 (bottom), 108 (both), 109 (both), 110 (bottom), 113 (both), 114 (top), 115, 116 (top), 118 (top), 119 (right), 120, 121 (both), 122 (top), 123, 124, 125 (left), 126, 127, 128, 129 (bottom), 130, 131 (bottom), 132 (both), 133, 136 (all three), 139 (top), 141 (top), 142 (top), 144, 149 (bottom), 150 (bottom), 151 (top, center), 153 (both), 155 (top), 157, 158-59 (all three).
US Department of the Interior, National Park Service, Edison National Historic Site, West Orange, NJ: page 93 (center).
Wadsworth Atheneum, Hartford, CT: Gift of The Palm Society African American Reading Group: page 15 (bottom right); Amistad Foundation: pages 84, 147.
Maggie L. Walker National Historic Site, Richmond, VA: page 145 (left).
Westchester County Historical Society Picture Collection: page 145 (right).
The Western Reserve Historical Society, Cleveland, OH: pages 33 (bottom center), 106 (top).